FOUNDATIONS

APPEARANCES 2

(A MATT & OLLIE ROMANCE)

T. H. FOREST

Other books by T.H. Forest

Adult
Twinkies & Beefcake
Appearances (A Matt & Ollie Romance)

Young Adult
Kelly's Folly

For my cousin Tom Holdorf,
I promise, I'm still listening

AUTHOR'S NOTE

CONTENTS

PART TWO

BUD

PART THREE

WEED

PART ONE

SEED

1

London Calling

2016

MATT PULLED HIS RANGE ROVER over to the curb among the crowd of cars at Logan Airport's international terminal and looked at Ollie. Drinking in every perfect feature (the curve of his ear, the spot on his cheek where his dimple hid, the Mediterranean Sea in his eyes) as though it were the last time he would be seeing him. He itched to run his fingers through the soft waves of Ollie's neatly styled blonde hair, though he had done so only ten minutes prior.

"It's only for six days, and I'll be home in time for our Christmas together on Boxing Day," Ollie said in his crisp British accent, his dimple winking as he smiled and shook his head. "Don't look so desperate. It hurts my heart."

Matt grinned and ran his hand over the stubble on his jaw to keep from touching Ollie. "I'm really going to miss looking at you." He scanned his eyes over Ollie's muscular but trim body. "I'm going to miss your laugh, your body, your mess." He dodged the back of Ollie's hand with a laugh. "Seriously, I'll have so much free time not picking up after you it will only make the week go slower."

"I'm not messy. You're pathologically neat," Ollie scoffed. "And I'm sure you'll use the time to dream up new rules and regulations for towels and toiletries." Ollie jerked with a yelp as Matt jabbed the tickle spot in his side.

"Not that you'd follow them anyway." Matt quirked his brow. "Tell your parents hello for me. I hope they like the presents."

"I will, and Cassie too, I'm sure she'll have a million questions for me about you as usual: 'how's your hot boss? Is he looking for a British girlfriend? Did you tell him I'm single?'" Ollie asked in a sing-song voice.

Matt laughed and shook his head. "Tell her I have my hands full with the Brits, I'm seriously overworked with the one I have."

"*You're* the high-maintenance one, Lieutenant," Ollie scoffed indignantly. "But I love you anyway."

"I love you too," Matt said in a soft voice before getting out of the car and helping Ollie with his luggage. He shook Ollie's hand firmly. "See you in a week."

"Bye," Ollie said and disappeared into the terminal.

Matt watched for a moment, mindful of the people around him, wishing that he could allow himself to admire his boyfriend openly.

Ollie breezed through security and knew it was as much his appearance as it was his pre-check status. Matt had taught him early on that wearing a suit (which had taken a little getting used to compared to the loose, casual clothing he had preferred) afforded him respect and garnered him all the extras that made commercial travel bearable. He far preferred traveling on the SharkFinn Gulfstream, but Matt was using it for domestic travel the following day. So, with a small sigh, he wheeled his suitcase beside him as he made his way to the first-class lounge.

He grabbed a water from the lounge fridge and found a chair in a quiet corner to work. He swiped into his phone and smiled as his assistant answered on the first ring.

"Your hotel is confirmed, and the company you were waiting to hear back from called to say their offices are closed for the holiday, but they want meet you while you're there," Kerry said. "I've scheduled a morning meeting, but they wanted to speak with you first. I emailed you the number."

"Wonderful. Thank you, Kerry."

Ollie dialed the number and spoke to the director of sales in rapid and flawless French. He could hear the surprise in the man's voice (clearly not expecting fluency from someone in America), and he happily confirmed the meeting.

"Oliver?" a woman's hesitant voice interrupted when he ended the call.

Ollie looked up and saw a trim, blonde woman with brown eyes and an oval face holding a glass of wine in one hand and her rolling suitcase in the other.

Ollie closed his laptop and stood, trying to place her familiar face. "Yes?"

"Heather, hi." She smiled and held her hand out. "We met a couple of years ago, on your first trip to Boston. We sat across the aisle from each other."

"Oh, right." Ollie returned the smile. "Hi, nice to see you again." He shook her hand as he remembered how she flirted and gave him her business card in hopes of hearing from him.

"I wasn't sure if it was you. The suit and the French threw me." She laughed and looked at him with appreciative eyes. "You look amazing."

"Thank you. You're looking well, yourself."

Heather looked down at her jeans and sneakers and chuckled self-deprecatingly. "Thanks. Were you in town for business?"

Ollie gestured to the seat next to him and waited for her to sit before taking his seat. "I live here now, in Boston. I'm just going home for the holiday."

Heather raised her eyebrows and made a surprised sound. "Wow. That's great. You working at a law firm?" she asked. "You're a lawyer, right?"

"Yes, but actually I'm general counsel for SharkFinn. It's a cybersecurity company, though we've branched out into other technologies."

"I've heard of it. I think my company uses your software." She smiled. "When did you start? You're awfully young to be GC. That's impressive."

"The summer of 2015. Actually, the friend I was coming to visit when you and I met is the CEO and founder, Matthew Dion." He titled his head and waited for the inevitable name recognition. "I guess I rose through the ranks because I'm friends with the owner."

"Well, you certainly have friends in high places." She chuckled. "But that can't be the only reason for your rapid ascent. From what I remember, you were doing a dual degree at Oxford; an MBA and what else?"

Ollie gave her a humble smile. "An LLM. You still doing global marketing?"

They bantered back and forth until Ollie looked at the Submariner Rolex on his wrist (a Christmas gift from Matt their first year together).

"I assume you're flying into Heathrow? Our plane is boarding soon." He put his laptop in the monogrammed, leather folio case Matt had given him that same Christmas and zipped it closed as he stood and pocketed his phone.

Ollie saw Heather sweep her gaze over him from the corner of his eye and straightened his coat.

"You look even more like that actor Charlie Hunnam," Heather remarked as she put her purple Patagonia coat back on. "I went back and watched his older stuff after we met. What was the show he on where your friend thought you looked like him?"

"*Queer as Folk*," Ollie answered as they walked out of the lounge. "And it was my flatmate who said that."

"He watched that show?" Heather raised her eyebrows.

"He's gay," Ollie answered. "He made me watch the first episode. He loved that show." Ollie chuckled. Henry had been his flatmate and his boyfriend. "I liked that you thought I looked like someone from a California biker gang, rather than a gay teenager, when we met."

Heather laughed as she walked with him to the gate. "Well, you definitely don't look like a gay teenager. In fact, I'd say you look a lot like he did in *Pacific Rim*."

"I've not heard of that one. Did he play a gay character in that too?"

Heather chuckled and gripped Ollie's bicep briefly. "No, it's an action movie, sci-fi; my ex loved it. It was okay, but the best part was when Charlie was shirtless," she said and waggled her eyebrows, giving Ollie's chest the side-eye. Ollie laughed and wondered how many glasses of wine Heather had had.

They went their separate ways in first-class, as Ollie took his seat on the opposite side of the plane. He got out his laptop after take-off and began prepping for his new meeting, using the notes that Kerry sent him. He was engrossed in his research, sipping his club soda, getting into what Matt called his Ollie-Off-World mode, when he felt someone touch his shoulder. He looked up and saw Heather standing in the aisle.

"Mind if I join you?"

Ollie waffled between not wanting to be rude, and not wanting to be trapped. "Sure, for one drink. I have a meeting to prep for." He put his laptop on the empty seat next to him and stood with a roll of his shoulders. "Let's go to the bar." He gestured for her to lead the way to the small bar area at the front of the cabin.

She ordered a Pinot Grigio, and he ordered a pint.

"Cheers." She clinked her glass to his and sat facing him from the corner of the bar.

"*Slainte.*"

"You have a meeting in London?" she asked after taking a sip.

"No, Paris the day after tomorrow. Two meetings actually."

"Ah, thus the French." She nodded. "How do you speak it so well?"

"My uncle married a French woman, and they live in France, as do my three cousins. One is like a brother to me and whenever we're together we only speak French. Our families would spend August in France, and often holidays as well, either in London or Paris," Ollie answered taking a swallow of beer.

"Wow, that sounds amazing. I summered in Ohio, and sometimes went to see my grandparents in Kansas." She laughed and sipped her wine. "Will you see your cousin when you're there?"

"No. Sadly, Guy's skiing for the holiday." Ollie looked at her over his glass with a smile. "You're having Christmas in Geneva and New Year's in London; I'd say you've come a long way from the flyover states."

"Ohio isn't a flyover state," she replied defensively.

"It is to me, sorry." He grinned to soften the dig. "We've done business in Cincinnati, but not me personally."

"Where do you travel, aside from France?"

"Overseas a bit. Canada, New York, the south, the west coast, which is why Ohio is a flyover state for me."

Heather titled her head. "So, you travel a lot, you work hard. We're two peas in a pod." She smiled. "Do you live in Boston or on the other side of the river?"

"Back Bay. How about you?"

"Oh, we're neighbors. I'm on Beacon Hill. A tiny apartment, but I love my neighborhood. I'm surprised I've never bumped into you out and about. But then again, we both travel a lot. . . ." She chuckled. "We should have dinner when we're both back."

Ollie finished his beer. "I'm in a relationship. Sorry."

"Of course you are. Is it serious?"

"Yes, quite."

Heather made a disappointed sound. "What does she do for work?"

Ollie ignored the assumption. Even if he weren't dating Matt (who didn't want anyone to know about them) he wouldn't correct her. He wasn't in the closet like Matt was, but he didn't know her well enough to share his sexuality with her; so, he thought of Naomi, his *beard*, when he responded.

"She's an interior designer. Has her own company."

"How long you been together?"

"Two years. The same woman who introduced me to my boss, introduced me to her, they were roommates in college." Ollie put his glass down and stood. "I'm sorry, but I really need to get back to work. It was nice to bump into you again."

Heather stood and gave Ollie a tight hug. "Please call me if you ever break up." She grinned and gave him her business card.

2

Home Alone

MATT THREW HIMSELF into work and working out while Ollie was gone, keeping his strict schedule of long runs and long swims, a habit he formed first at the U.S. Naval Academy and then with the Navy SEALs. He ran every morning and swam every day after work at the L.A. Sports Club in Boston, and then stayed up late working, unable to sleep soundly without Ollie beside him. He traveled to Atlanta and Charlotte for two days of meetings before returning home to the townhouse on Marlborough Street, which felt cold and empty without Ollie's warm body and infectious laugh.

The one bright spot was that Finn, his best friend for nearly two decades, was in for the holidays from Baltimore and joining him as his date for a charity event. They had grown up around the corner from each other, and, despite the three-year age difference that usually prevented closeness in youth, had instantly bonded. Matt trusted her like no one else. She was the only one he ever opened up to, telling her (in a moment of weakness and teenage confusion) that he thought he was attracted to men.

Finn was the one who introduced him to Ollie, a fellow grad student with her at Oxford. Matt had been living a lie for nearly a decade, happily he thought, until he found himself instantly attracted to Ollie. It took him months to finally allow himself to admit it, to act on his feelings, but when he did, it was indescribable bliss. It was like one of those cheesy romances his sisters always had hidden in their rooms, and Matt couldn't believe his luck.

He was just imagining Ollie's smooth naked ass, and the heady taste of it on his tongue when he was interrupted by the sound of a key in the door.

"Chuckleberry Finn," he exclaimed as she let herself in, calling her by the nickname he gave her when she was in middle school.

"Hi, babe!" She put her suitcase and long garment bag down to hug and kiss him. Her honey blonde hair was up in a French twist, with loose tendrils curled around her heart-shaped face.

"You're fucking gorgeous."

"Thank you," she said as she preened jokingly.

"How are things at Hopkins? How's Jayne?"

"Work is great, and Jayne is great and huge. She's staying with my dad tonight, tormenting him and poor Kodi with her puppy energy. She'd stolen Kodi's bone and dog bed by the time I left."

Matt laughed. "Classes are good? You have students?"

Finn swatted his arm. "Of course I have students, they love my classes. I'm a fun professor."

"I don't doubt that. I bet you're the most popular professor on campus, particularly with the boys," he teased as he picked up her bags. "I just didn't think the students of Johns Hopkins would be all that interested in learning a language no one even knows how to pronounce."

"I'm only teaching undergraduate electives right now. My most popular class, *Myths and Monsters in Mesopotamia*, is basically making those fantastic ancient stories more interesting to this generation. In fact, I'm so popular, the department wants me to pick up some more *recent* history. So, I'm working on the curriculum and syllabus for one on the Crusades. I think I'm gonna call it, *Christianity and the Crusades: God, Demons, and War.*"

Matt made an appreciative sound. "I'd take that class." He led Finn to the elevator. "You know anything about the Crusades? Doesn't seem nearly ancient enough for your taste. I mean they spoke English, and used a normal alphabet."

Finn swatted his arm again. "Yes, I know about the Crusades. Though I am teaching myself Arabic so I can read about the wars from both perspectives."

"Of course you are." Matt shook his head with wonder. "You trying to get your language count into the triple digits?"

"Maybe," she replied in a dramatic voice and followed him out of the elevator.

He put her bag on the bench at the foot of the bed in the large guest room overlooking Marlborough Street, and hung her garment bag on the back of the closet door. "See you in a bit," he said with a smile and closed the bedroom door behind him.

Matt and Finn stayed at the event for the minimum amount of time, posing for the society photographers that glommed on to Finn the minute they recognized her. Matt rested his hand low on her hip where it fit naturally and schmoozed with his top-brass at the two tables he bought, before skipping out for fried chicken at their favorite Boston restaurant.

"What stupid magazines are we gonna end up in? And do people read those anyway?" Matt asked as he took a large bite of his chicken.

Finn leaned over her plate, careful not to drip grease on her Gucci dress as she bit into the crispy wing. "*Town & Country*, probably the *Globe*," she replied around her small mouthful. "I'll be ragged on for wearing a dress from 2014, and everyone will drool over you. There'll be the usual speculation of our relationship, which we will continue to ignore and tease, and then something else shiny will come along and we'll be forgotten again."

Matt shook his head and picked up another piece of chicken, cleaning the meat from the bone before sucking the grease off his fingers. His phone buzzed and he smiled when he saw "princess" on his screen.

"It's just not the same without Naomi and Ollie. One home in California, the other home across the pond," Finn said around her chicken wing, likely guessing from Matt's big smile that it was Ollie who'd texted him. "We should go away! The four of us."

Matt mulled the idea over in his head as he chewed. "How would that work? Two hotel rooms? You and Naomi sneaking back and forth."

"No, you ding dong." Finn threw a tiny wing bone at him, laughing as it bounced off his shoulder and onto the table.

Matt looked at the bone and then at the crowded restaurant around them. "How much did you have to drink?"

Finn giggled. "Not nearly enough, but the look on your face. . . ." She wrinkled her nose and wiped her eye. "As I was going to say, we can rent a villa in the Caribbean. Three bedrooms, or four, or two and Naomi and I share. We can get limited maid service, a chef and staff that come when scheduled, and we don't give a shit about what they think." She put her hand over Matt's. "You can relax and swim and be your usual god-like self, and Ollie will love being away with you. He's used to being affectionate, and holds back a lot with you every day at work and in public. A vacation away from prying eyes would be the perfect opportunity to give him what he needs while indulging the secrecy you need, and Naomi and I will be there to ensure everyone has a blast."

Matt studied Finn as though she were a unicorn, because in so many ways, like Ollie, she was. He nodded slowly and then more emphatically as he envisioned being away with Ollie, with Naomi and Finn as their cover.

"Let's do it, after SharkFinn's year-end. But don't say anything to Ollie. I want it to be a surprise."

3

Over the Hills
and Far Away

OLLIE SPENT THE FIRST TWO DAYS in London catching up with his parents, who knew about his relationship with Matt, and his sister, Cassie, who didn't. He had to work into the night on US time and stay in near constant contact with Matt, and Sharkfinn's VPs, but he didn't mind, despite Matt's strictly professional emails, because their text exchanges and phone calls more than made up for it.

On his third day in Europe, Ollie headed to Paris. The first meeting was with a current client, where he planned to negotiate an upgrade, and the second was with a new potential client. He left both meetings with proposals to review and spent the night at the same hotel on the Seine where he and Matt had stayed their first time in Paris. He smiled, remembering that passionate night and then looked at his Rolex.

He pulled out his phone and swiped in as he adjusted his half-hard cock in his pants. "Hello, gorgeous. Guess where I am," he asked, looking out the window at the river before drawing the curtains.

"Are you still in Paris?" Matt responded with a smile and a warm feeling in his belly at the sound of Ollie's smooth accent and deep voice. "I know that tone, Mr. Turner. Are you having naughty thoughts?"

"I'm in our hotel, feels like almost the same room. It's triggering the most fantastic memories," Ollie replied in a husky voice.

"Well, it's three in the afternoon here, Ollie, and I'm at work," Matt said pointedly and looked out his glass office wall at his assistant, Stacey, sitting behind her desk.

"So, go to the bathroom," Ollie whispered, and Matt heard the rustle of clothing. "I'm undoing my pants right now. Just the zipper, but next comes the button."

Matt closed his eyes as he felt himself stir, Ollie's accent smoothing the edges of his words in that sensuous way he loved. "Ollie, I have a sales meeting in ten minutes."

"You'll be quick, imagining my soft tongue swirling around the tip of your glorious cock. How I push your foreskin back and tease that sensitive bit at the tip before taking you deep and cupping your balls."

It sounded as though Ollie was sucking on something and Matt's dick swelled behind his zipper at the thought of Ollie sucking on his fingers as though it were his cock.

"I've got my hand in my pants. I'm so hard for you." Ollie sighed ardently. "Shall I take them off, or come in my underwear? Make a mess like I can't help myself. What about my shirt? On, but unbuttoned? Off? I could leave my tie on; I know how you love that. Remember that time when you held onto it and fucked me from behind? I swear I nearly passed out when I came."

Matt groaned; the erotic image of that particular encounter burned onto the inside of his lids. "Now I can't get out of my chair. Stacey is sitting out there; she'll turn her head when I stand up." He looked up at the ceiling with a grimace as he trailed his fingers over the outline of his hard dick. "We need new office space, with solid walls and a couch for me to fuck you on," he added, his erection straining urgently against his zipper at that added thought. He shrugged on his suit coat and stood. Stacey turned her head to look as predicted. Matt angled his body and covered himself with his coat as he strode quickly into his private bathroom and stood in the shower stall.

"Okay, Ollie. Take off all your clothes," he commanded as he unzipped his pants and pushed them down in the front. "And get on the bed. I want you on your knees, just like you were when I was there with you. *Behind you.*" He spat in his hand and stroked himself, closing his eyes at the memory.

Ollie moaned and Matt heard the sound of clothing coming off. "Okay, I'm in position. My nipples are so hard and so sensitive, and I'm covered in goosebumps at the thought of you behind me, your lips on my neck. My cock is dripping at the memory of you with your fingers inside me, you whispering Italian in my ear."

Ollie let out a low moan that sent a jolt straight to Matt's dick.

"Oh god, Ollie. I want you to twist those perfect rosebuds of yours one at a time, and then I want you to wet those long fingers of yours," Matt breathed looking down at himself and ran his hand over the outside of his shirt, feeling his own nipples harden.

Ollie moaned lightly as he presumably did as he was told. "I wish you were here to brush your stubble around my nipples, between my thighs, between my ass cheeks. My fingernails are no substitute."

Matt heard the wet sound of Ollie sucking on his fingers again and increased the speed of his stroke with another moan. He paused to spit again in his palm and resumed stroking himself with the image of Ollie naked on a hotel bed across the ocean.

"Where are you, Lieutenant? Do you have your magnificent cock out?"

Matt chuckled low in his throat. "I'm in the shower. And yes, it is rock hard for you, and desperate to be inside that beautiful mouth of yours." He moaned at the thought. "You on your knees, under my desk, or maybe in our bed, me fucking your mouth. Deep inside that beautiful throat of yours. Get those fingers in your ass now, Ollie, don't be gentle."

The was a pause as Ollie shifted and Matt wondered if Ollie was reaching behind and sticking his ass out or if he was angling his hips up and slipping them in behind his balls.

"Christ, Lieutenant." Ollie's voice came back, but from further away, like he was on speaker. "I wish your cock were in my mouth, gagging me, making me tear up and struggle for breath. The sounds you're making now, the sounds you make when you fuck my throat, make me want to come," Ollie whispered urgently. "Do you want me to come?"

"Not yet, but you won't have to wait long," Matt gritted out, mindful of his voice echoing in the stall walls. "You get those fingers in? How many knuckles?"

"I'm all the way in, and it feels so good, but my fingers are not your fingers, my hand is not your hand. It's cold without your furnace of a body behind me. I miss the way your chest hair tickles my back." He moaned again. "Or when you're fucking me, staring down at me with those intense eyes of yours. Ahhh, the way the moon pendant on your necklace sways back and forth over my face as you pound in and out of me."

Matt groaned as he pictured the image Ollie was describing for him. "Are you still on your knees?" he asked breathlessly and looked down at his dick. The tip was so dark it was nearly purple and glistened with pre-cum.

"Yes," Ollie gasped.

"Roll onto your back. We're both going to imagine me coming on your fucking spectacular and smooth chest. You're going to aim for your six pack and those dusty rose nipples of yours, while I'm gonna aim for your balls first, and then my trident pendant hanging from the chain around your neck."

He closed his eyes picturing it, the sound of Ollie's stuttered breathing panting in his ear.

"Okay. I'm on my back, but I'm afraid I can't hold it any longer. Oh, Matt, I'm—" He gasped and then moaned through his orgasm.

"Oh, god," Matt groaned and nearly dropped his phone as he came at the sound of Ollie's moaning. He slowed his hand as he watched his load paint the floor of the shower. "Jesus Christ, Ollie."

He heard Ollie's labored breathing through the phone and wished he could feel his strong heartbeat against his own pounding one.

"Christ, I'm covered. I feel like you did come all over me." Ollie chuckled. "Definitely got some on my necklace."

Matt groaned with pleasure at the visual and checked his watch, seeing he had less than two minutes before his meeting.

"I am going to come all over you the minute you get home. I love you. I gotta get cleaned up."

"I love you too. I can't wait to see you in three days."

* * *

On his return to London, Ollie made plans to meet his best mates at a pub in Chelsea. He dressed in jeans, a navy cashmere V-neck sweater, and his favorite pair of trainers, the ones he never wore around Matt for all his teasing. He pulled on the black Burberry pea coat that Matt had given him for his birthday and checked his hair in the mirror before leaving.

"Bye, Mum. Leave the light on for me. I may be late."

"Have fun," she called from the sitting room. "Say hello to the boys for me."

His friends, dressed in jeans and hoodies, greeted him raucously and ribbed him for arriving late.

"On brand," Sahil remarked, his dark eyes flashing as he raised his pint glass in salute.

"What the fuck are you wearing, Captain America?" Ivan shook his head as Ollie pulled out the chair next to him after hugging them all. "You look like a catalog model, and just as stuck up."

Ollie laughed along with them, his heart full and not at all upset about the teasing. This group of friends were among his closest, two of whom, Ivan and George, he had known since their first year at Eton, and Sahil, who they met during undergrad at Oxford.

They barely waited for him to get comfortable before peppering him with questions about America.

"What have you been up to otherwise, Ollie?" George asked and sipped his beer. "You met a bloke yet?"

"Yes, but he's allergic to idiots, so you'll never meet him," Ollie replied. "And, check out my girlfriend," he said with a grin and pulled out his phone.

The guys groaned over Naomi's blonde, willowy beauty as Ollie swept through the pictures.

"She looks like Gwynny Paltrow. Have you turned hetero, Ollie?" Ivan teased, his pale blue eyes twinkling. "You want to come out carousing with us?"

"Yes, I have, and I'm coming for your bird, Ivan. She'll leave you for me in heartbeat." He raised his eyebrows. "She tells me every time I see her."

Ivan roared with laughter. "You fucking wish." He held up his empty glass. "Get us another round, Mr. Moneybags."

"Your father is a literal Lord, shut up," Ollie laughed and flagged the server over. "What are you having then, Ivan, a wine cooler?" The guys laughed as he ordered another round and gave the waitress his black American Express to open a tab.

"Oh, big money," George called from across the table. "We should order some Cristal."

"Your palate couldn't tell the difference between Cristal and a Tesco sparkling wine," Ollie teased with a laugh.

"Fair enough. I don't drink sparkling wine anyway," George countered. "Does your boyfriend make you drink it out of his shoe?"

"No, but your father really likes it when I spray it all over him," Ollie retorted with a grin. They clinked glasses and continued teasing each other, ordering another round when Ollie got up to use the restroom.

"There are no hook-ups in the bathroom in this pub, Ol, just to warn you," George said with a wink.

"Fuck you, George. Your father's waiting for me at home anyway," Ollie laughed and walked away.

On his way back from the bathroom Ollie heard someone with a Geordie accent call his name. He turned to see Andy, the college boyfriend he and the guys called Andy-the-Asshole, sitting with a group of men at a table against the wall of the pub. Andy stood to greet him with a hug, his tall, lean body foreign in Ollie's arms.

"Hello, Andy." Ollie returned the hug reservedly. "You're back here then."

Ollie looked him over. Andy was dark haired like Matt, but with brown eyes, and an angular face, a face he couldn't believe he once craved looking at. He was dressed in jeans and a button-down shirt with the top two buttons undone, exposing his chest hair. He was handsome to be sure, but nothing close to Matt.

"Yeah. I was only in Boston for the summer, waiting tables. Wasn't able to find a job or a visa to stay any longer," he replied with chagrin. "It was great to see you at your company party. I'm guessing you didn't put in a good word for me with your boss after all," he added with a sharp-edged grin.

"He was in a foul mood, it was a tricky time," Ollie replied, not wanting the reminder of Matt's jealousy over Andy hitting on him at said party.

"You back here as well?" Andy asked speculatively.

"No. Just home for Christmas." Ollie looked at his friends who were chatting and oblivious to his whereabouts.

"How'd you get that gig anyway?"

"My boss's girlfriend is one of my closest friends."

"Well, I'm hoping to come back this summer. I fucking love Boston. Maybe you can get me a job now, hm? Friends getting friends jobs and all," Andy suggested, raising his eyebrows.

Ollie made a non-committal sound and shrugged.

No fucking way.

"You're looking gorgeous, Ollie. Nice bloody watch." He nodded at Ollie's wrist. "You must be making the big bucks."

"I do alright. You should've studied law instead of English," he joked good-naturedly and stepped back, hoping to end the conversation.

Andy made a speculative sound. "Maybe I'll write a story about you, Ollie." He swept his gaze over Ollie's body. "Or you could just get me a job. I've taken other classes; I could do anything at your company. Let me send you my CV. I'm working here for a publishing firm, but I'd much rather be in America. I'd much rather be with you," he added in a low voice. "I've thought about you *a lot* since I saw you last summer. You were my favorite; that tongue. Why did we break up?"

"You fucking cheated on me. A lot," Ollie scoffed. "You're so full of shit. Christ, do you believe the things you say?"

Andy shrugged sheepishly, though to Ollie it seemed fake. "I was daft, Ol. Give me another chance. I would love to fuck you again. You know you loved it," he said with a cocky grin that was more his style. "I can still hear your moans," he added cryptically.

Ollie wrinkled his nose. "No, thanks. I've got someone, and he fucks me a thousand times better."

"Is that right? I thought you said you weren't gay anymore." Andy made a dramatic face.

"I said that so you would shut up about it around my coworkers." Ollie frowned. "They still don't know, and it's no one's business. You should keep that in mind. People appreciate discretion." He looked over his shoulder. "Nice talking with you, Andy. Happy Christmas." He turned to leave.

"Ollie, I mean it. Give me your email. I want to send you my CV," Andy said firmly. "I want to work in Boston. Get me a visa."

"I don't have anything to do with HR at my company. No one listens to me," Ollie lied.

"Fuck you, Ollie. You're bloody General Counsel." Andy's eyed flashed. "Oh yeah, I Googled you. You're second in command at that 'little' half billion-dollar company of yours. You fucking swan over HR. The only one bigger than you is that hot boss of yours. I'd fuck him in a heartbeat if he were gay. He's so hot I'd even let him fuck me. I wonder what he would think if he knew you were gay." He raised his eyebrows meaningfully.

Ollie slid his glance away to hide his ire and then reached into his pocket. "Fine, here's my card. Send me your resume. I'll see what I can do, but no promises. We're not hiring at the moment."

Andy took the card with a happy smile and pulled Ollie into his arms. He kissed Ollie's neck and breathed in through his nose. "Christ, you smell as expensive as you look. I can't wait to fuck you again."

"In your dreams, Andy." Ollie pushed away, fighting the urge to wipe Andy's kiss from his neck and rejoined his friends.

"Who the hell was that?" Ivan asked as he returned to the table. "Were you looking for love tonight, Ollie?"

"Fuck you, Ivan, I told you, I have a boyfriend." Ollie shook his head and drank half his beer in one swallow. "That wanker was Andy-the-Asshole. You remember him?"

Sahil and George turned their heads to look at Andy again. "Oh fuck!" George exclaimed. "I knew he looked familiar. He's a right fucking tosser."

"God, he was a knob." Ivan agreed. "What did you see in him?"

Ollie pulled a face. "Christ, I was eighteen. What the hell did I know? You dated some *very* questionable women during your time, the three of you." Ollie swept his eyes and finger around the table. "Fuck off."

They all laughed and shook their heads.

"You're not wrong, Ol. Some *very* questionable women," Sahil said and raised his glass with a wink.

4

Bring it on Home

OLLIE WOKE WITH a not-insignificant hangover on Christmas Eve from staying out and drinking until the wee hours. He and the guys left the pub in Chelsea as soon as they finished their round—to get away from Andy—and stayed at the next pub until closing. He hazily remembered the ride home in the taxi, and then crashing naked into bed, before waking up with fuzzy teeth.

His mother, a slim blonde with a wide smile and twinkling eyes, was impossibly cheerful and demanding for the state Ollie was in, but somehow, he made it through the day. He decided after lunch to check for an earlier flight back to Boston and found one for Christmas day. He was missing Matt (and home), so happily paid to change his booking.

"How did your meetings in Paris go?" Ollie's father David asked as they were cleaning up the wrapping paper, his face an older, more solemn version of Ollie's. "Any chance you'll need to go back?"

"They went really well, and yes, I'm certain I will be hearing from them again. Why?"

"Well, it's been ages since you've been to see Uncle Llyod and Aunt Clare. I spoke with them last night and they're hoping we could have a reunion in Lyon this summer. So if you had something lined up in July, or miraculously August, we could try to schedule it around your work. And if Matt was traveling with you, he'd be welcome too," David added for Cassie's benefit. "They have plenty of room but worst-case scenario you'd have to share one of the twin-bed rooms with Guy, or maybe with Matt if neither of you would mind. It all depends on whether Sophia brings her babies, and what rooms are being renovated."

Ollie looked away, appreciating his father's willingness to lie on his behalf in front of Cassie, but wishing he didn't have to. Cassie couldn't detect the subtext of their father's disappointment, but Ollie could. He tightened his jaw and pushed the judgment aside. Matt's love was worth the subterfuge, and Ollie didn't care if no one understood.

Ollie shifted his thoughts to Lyon and how much he loved spending August there with his cousin Guy; the memories of the two of them spending their youthful days swimming in the nearby river, fooling around with the local girls (Guy more than Ollie), and riding their bikes all over the countryside.

"You're right. It's been since before graduation actually." Ollie nodded. "I'll let you know; and as far as Matt is concerned, if either company I've been negotiating with wants to meet with him then I'll invite him to the chateau."

"Wonderful," David replied with a genuine smile. A smile that made Ollie's insides warm.

"Genny and I have been plotting and scheming our summer," Cassie chimed in. "I'm just planning around my trip to Boston with Mum and Dad," she added with a grin.

Ollie rolled his eyes and hoped to put off his sister's visit for as long as possible.

Matt was not going be happy about that.

Ollie's parents were disappointed but understanding when he told them about his flight change after dinner and insisted on driving him to

Heathrow in the morning. His father helped him get his luggage from the trunk and gave him a tight hug.

"I would like to spend Christmas day with Matt. Someday, I'd really like to spend it with *all* of you," he added with a wry smile.

His father nodded. "I get it. Your mother and I had to spend our first few holidays apart, before we married."

"Oh, Dad. Matt and I are never getting married, if that's what you're insinuating, and you know *all* the reasons why. We had our commitment ceremony; that'll be all." He kissed them both and tamped down the disappointment his words caused him. "I will see you for Easter, and when you come to the beach this summer."

"Never say never, Oliver," David said with a hug.

"I can't wait," Ollie's mother said with a big smile. "I love Cape Cod. Oh, and Ollie, as you heard from her, Cass has been making quite a bit of noise about coming with us, especially if Matt sends his plane, like he has offered." She patted Ollie's cheek. "Just something to think about and prepare for. I don't think you can put her off any longer."

"Okay, Mum. Thanks for the heads up. I love you both." He swung his carry-on bag over his shoulder and wheeled his suitcase into the terminal, determined not to let the renewed worry of Cass coming to America ruin his pending reunion with Matt.

Ollie arrived at the empty townhouse, travel weary and looking forward to relaxing after a long hot shower, knowing that Matt was still in Wellesley celebrating with his family. He hoped Matt wasn't going to spend the night at Bill's with Finn like he had last year. He hadn't called to let Matt know of his change of plans, and his body tingled with the expectation of their surprise reunion.

He turned on the Christmas lights Matt had strung around the living space and the ones on the tree, then took a long, hot, *thorough* shower. He toweled off and put on lounge pants and one of Matt's US Navy t-shirts before going downstairs to sit by the tree with herbal tea and a book. He closed his eyes happily thirty minutes later, when he heard the soft whir of the elevator coming up from the ground floor.

The doors opened and Matt strode out, looking to his right toward the tree, his eyes lighting on Ollie. He dropped the bags of gifts in his hands and grinned as he opened his arms.

"Bloody hell," he said, mimicking Ollie's accent. "It's a Christmas miracle! Get the fuck over here," he commanded happily and gestured with his head.

Ollie stood with a broad grin and crossed the room. He wrapped his arms around Matt and let out a small gasp when Matt lifted him off the ground as if he weighed nothing. He tilted his chin up for a kiss and sighed when his lips met Matt's firm mouth. Matt tasted of mulled cider and sweet dessert.

"Christ, Lieutenant. I couldn't stay away another day," he murmured against Matt's lips.

Matt ran his hands over Ollie's back, gripping his bottom tightly, and hugged Ollie close to his body. "I am so fucking happy to see you, gorgeous. Merry Christmas." He swept his tongue slowly through Ollie's mouth and then kissed a path along Ollie's smooth jaw, pausing to place a kiss on the hidden dimple in Ollie's cheek before continuing to his ear. He took a deep breath through his nose. "Someone's all freshly showered and delicious smelling. I believe I promised to do something to you when you got home. . . ." His eyes were dark with lust as he held Ollie's gaze and stroked him over the front of his thin cotton pants. "And I really need to follow through on that promise, or my word is worth shit." He led him to the fireplace. "Get the blanket off the couch, and take off your clothes," he said over his shoulder as he turned the gas fireplace on and began stripping off his suit. "You're going to make me come all over your beautiful body."

Ollie's dimple appeared as he shivered in anticipation and did as he was told. After spreading the blanket on the floor along with two pillows from the couch and a small bottle of lube from the wooden box on the side table he helped Matt out of the rest of his clothes. Ollie kissed all the spots on Matt's body that he missed so desperately, starting with his Adam's apple, moving to the trident tattoo over Matt's heart, and ending up on his knees with his tongue in Matt's bellybutton.

Matt's fingers dove into the waves of Ollie's hair and gripped tightly. He wrapped his other hand around the base of his cock. "Open up. I got something to feed you."

The corner of Ollie's lips turned up and then he opened wide as he met Matt's eyes. Ollie stuck out his tongue and felt Matt's smooth hardness glide along the surface, like velvet covered steel. Matt exhaled a moan once he was buried in Ollie's throat, his knuckles brushing Ollie's lips as he paused for a moment and then rocked his hips.

Ollie's eyelids fluttered closed at the salty, musky taste of Matt in his mouth, a flavor and scent that shot bolts of desire straight to his cock. He closed his lips around Matt's girth and sucked, rolling his tongue around and over the head of his cock as Matt thrust in and out. Matt buried his fingers in Ollie's hair again and then pulled away.

"My turn. Lie back." Matt followed Ollie to the floor, buried his nose in Ollie's trim bush and breathed in. "God, I love the way you smell."

Matt nuzzled the spot between Ollie's balls and his thigh before running his tongue up the side of Ollie's cock and over the tip. He slid Ollie's foreskin back and ran his tongue around the underside of the head. Ollie closed his eyes on a moan and pressed back into the pillows.

"Christ, that feels so good," Ollie groaned as Matt took him deep, his lips stretching around the shaft of Ollie's cock.

"Lift up," Matt commanded and slid a pillow under Ollie's hips.

Matt teased with his tongue and then his fingers as he dipped his head lower and spread Ollie's thighs wide. Ollie felt Matt's tongue flatten over his taint and then circle his hole. Ollie pressed his heels into the floor and arched into Matt's mouth with another groan.

"Mmm, you taste like Christmas," Matt breathed and then nipped Ollie's ass cheek. "I love the bum balm you use."

Matt licked him again, his tongue swirling and probing as he worked Ollie open. Ollie heard Matt murmuring to himself in Italian as he eased a second finger inside. He lifted his head to see Matt propped on his elbows and stretched out on floor between his legs, his naked body long and hard. Ollie ran his eyes over the perfect curve of Matt's muscular ass and watched the muscles flex in his cheeks as Matt humped the blanket slowly.

Ollie brought his eyes back to Matt's face and found him staring up at him.

"Like the view, huh?" Matt smirked and looked at the drip of pre-cum stretching between the tip of Ollie's cock and his goody trail.

"Your body is a masterpiece, and I really want it on mine," Ollie replied with a flutter in his stomach.

Matt wiped his mouth on his bicep, pushed himself to his knees and crawled up to hover over Ollie as though he was doing a plank. Ollie trailed one hand up Matt's side and gripped his heavy cock with his other as Matt kissed him. Ollie pulled Matt closer until his cock lined up alongside his own and breathed a sigh into Matt's mouth. Matt lowered himself with a groan and rolled his hips. His cock was smooth and rock hard in Ollie's hand as Ollie stroked Matt's foreskin up and down over the wide mushroom head.

Ollie flexed and shuddered lightly with desire from the pulse of pre-cum in his palm and he raised his knees to squeeze Matt's sides in silent invitation. Being with Matt, having his strong warm body against his own, more than made up for their time apart but Ollie was feeling impatient and hoped that Matt wasn't going to tease him like he did the last time he'd returned from a business trip. He felt Matt smile against his lips as he swirled his tongue around Ollie's.

"I see someone still hasn't learned patience," Matt teased. "Do you need another lesson?"

"You can edge me next time," Ollie countered and slid up, so Matt's cock was between his legs. "I promise."

Ollie smiled to himself when Matt reached for the lube and popped the top. He knew Matt was as eager for immediate gratification as Ollie was. Matt's fingers, cold with lube, were back inside him in a flash, nearly taking his breath with pleasure. His cock followed a moment after, and Ollie moaned with the burn.

God, there is nothing like it, Ollie thought as everything went right in his brain.

"Shit, you're so tight. So perfect. Remind me why I ever let you leave my bed?" Matt moaned and surged slowly forward until his hips were flush with Ollie's ass.

"Because you'd starve. Mmmm," Ollie moaned as Matt began moving slowly inside him.

Matt reached down and cupped Ollie's ass as he picked up the pace; his other hand remained flat on the blanket next to Ollie's shoulder. Ollie studied Matt's handsome face as Matt concentrated on the sight of himself easing in and out of Ollie's body. For someone so secretive Matt sure loved being a voyeur. Ollie thought of the large mirror opposite their bed upstairs and the one at their beach bouse and wished there was a floor-level one in the living room so he could watch as well. Matt in motion, any kind of motion but especially when he was fucking Ollie senseless, was a sight to behold.

Matt caught Ollie's gaze and lowered himself to capture Ollie's mouth in a breathtaking kiss. He panted into Ollie's mouth as his tongue teased Ollie's. For endless moments there was nothing but the sound of panting and grunting and wild, sloppy kisses as Matt and his cock continued to unravel Ollie until he was a dizzy mess. Ollie always lost track of time and often location when Matt was working his magic on him. He became aware only when Matt pulled out, leaving him whimpering at the sudden emptiness. Matt easily manhandled him onto his stomach, Ollie's body as loose as a rag doll's, and slipped back inside with a guttural groan.

Matt slipped an arm under Ollie's abdomen and hoisted him a few inches off the ground. Ollie spread his knees wide and kept his shoulders on the blanket at Matt's insistence. With one hand between Ollie's shoulder blades and the other on Ollie's hip Matt began hammering into him. Ollie felt his eyes roll back and his mouth go slack as Matt's cock slid over and over that swollen bundle of nerves that lit Ollie up.

"Oh, god. Right there. . . . Don't stop," Ollie pleaded. His voice sounded desperate and winded to his own ears, but he couldn't care less, all he wanted was that sweet release that was building in his groin.

"Fuuuck, Ollie. Your ass. . . . The view," Matt gritted out between breaths. "You have no idea how beautiful you are. Touch yourself. I'm close, and I want you to come on my dick."

Ollie grabbed his weeping cock without hesitation and began stroking in sync with Matt's thrusts, managing about four good tugs before crying out as he tipped over the edge. He was dimly aware of Matt emitting a string of Italian before his hips stuttered and he came deep inside Ollie.

Matt collapsed against Ollie's back and peppered his neck, ear, and shoulders with kisses as he caught his breath.

"I love you. Christ, that was amazing," Matt whispered.

Ollie turned his head to meet Matt's lips in an awkward kiss that felt like heaven. "I love you. You fuck like a god. I'm not sure I can walk. Better just bring me another blanket and I'll sleep here."

Matt chuckled, the rumble of it vibrating through Ollie's back, and rolled onto the blanket next to Ollie. "You're far too much of a princess to sleep on a floor. I mean, have you ever?"

Ollie scoffed indignantly and rolled onto his side. "I am not a princess."

Ollie watched the smile nearly split Matt's face. "Who demands coffee in bed every morning?"

"You started that, not me."

"Who returned four sets of sheets before settling on the ones that cost more than most people make in a month?"

"Thread count and type are very important, Lieutenant. Those other sheets lied."

"Who gets his hair done on Newbury Street instead of going to a barber like a normal man? And pays a fortune for that too, mind you."

"Pedro is an artist, and you love my hair. It's what drew you to me."

Ollie shrieked when Matt reached out and poked his tickle spot. "Stop! I can't breathe."

Matt poked him again and then laughed. "I could go on, the list is quite long, but it's just distracting from the fact that you haven't answered the question."

Ollie looked away. He knew which question Matt meant, but he wasn't going to admit anything to Matt. "Get me a towel. Your little minions are dripping out of my ass."

Matt pushed himself to his feet with a grin. "Spread your legs, I wanna see."

Ollie lifted his leg with ease and held it against his shoulder.

Thank you, yoga.

Matt sighed with a hum as he pressed a finger into Ollie's ass, stuffing his cum back inside. "What a beautiful fucking view."

Ollie ran his eyes over Matt's muscular backside as he crossed the room to the kitchen and disappeared from view. Ollie heard the water and then Matt reappeared a moment later wiping his cock with a damp kitchen towel. Matt knelt and cleaned Ollie gently with the other end of the towel and then rose to his feet with his hand out.

"On your feet. I wanna get this blanket to the washing machine."

Ollie wanted cuddles but he guessed that wasn't in the cards. He knew Matt had already moved on to the next task in his head and probably planned to work for the rest of the night. Ollie stood and put on his lounge pants as Matt put on his underwear and gathered up the things from the floor. Ollie followed him onto the elevator and waited as they traveled to the fifth floor.

"You'll never believe who I bumped into on the plane to London," Ollie said as he followed Matt down the hall.

"Who?" Matt asked as he put his clothes along with the blanket and Ollie's shirt in the laundry room and then continued into their suite.

"That Heather chick, from my first trip here to see you; do you remember her?" Ollie pulled a fresh shirt out of a drawer in their large closet and put it on as he watched Matt hang up his suit.

"Oh, wow," Matt replied and raised his eyebrows. "Did you recognize her or she you?"

"She came up to me in the lounge, and then hit on me on the plane. Told me I looked like Charlie Hunnam in some movie called *Pacific Rim*. She assured me it wasn't a film about gay sex." Ollie grinned. "Honestly sounds like a San Francisco euphemism. 'I gave him the Pacific rim last night,'" Ollie said in an American accent.

Matt laughed as he pulled on a pair of grey sweats and a US Navy t-shirt. "I'll give you the *Atlantic* rim again later," he said and smacked Ollie's ass as he left the room.

"Oh no, Lieutenant," Ollie called after him. "I call that *The Italian Job*." Ollie smiled at Matt's laughter echoing in the hallway.

5

New Year, New You?

OLLIE WOKE SLOWLY, jet lag and sexual satisfaction making his body languid and slow moving. He looked at Matt's side of the bed.

"Morning, sleeping beauty. Happy Boxing Day." Matt glanced down at him from his side eye.

Ollie ran his eyes over Matt's length. His hair was damp, and his skin smelled freshly showered and delicious. He was wearing blue Tom Ford trunks and had his laptop open. Ollie leaned into Matt's body and breathed deeply through his nose, smiling contentedly before turning to his side table for the coffee Matt had left him. It was just shy of hot, and Ollie took several swallows. He looked at his watch.

"I hope I wasn't expected to report to work. It's well past nine, so I'm already late. And I'm horny." Ollie pushed the covers down, his erection springing up eagerly. "Which means it'll be at least an hour before I can get my head straight, and focus." He shrugged with a sexy smile. "Maybe two." He quirked his eyebrow. "Besides, it's a holiday back home, and I've a religious exemption for it I believe."

Matt's eyes locked on Ollie's erection. He closed his laptop and put it on the side table.

"Boxing Day is not a religious holiday." Matt shook his head with a low laugh. "But I'm willing to give you a religious *experience* and call it even." Matt licked his lip and leaned over to kiss Ollie's nipple.

Matt closed the shower door behind him as he joined Ollie, kissing his shoulder as he pushed Ollie out of the stream of water. "Pass me the soap. I'll do your back."

Ollie handed Matt the bar of soap and nudged his way back under the water. "You've already had your shower."

Matt grinned and lathered the washcloth. "Tell me about your visit with your *bros*. Did you say anything about us?"

Ollie closed his eyes as Matt washed his shoulders and then worked his way down his back. "It was great, as always. They razzed me about my love life. I told them you're an investment banker. . . ."

Matt made a sound of approval.

"Who does drag," Ollie added, grinning to himself. He wished he could see the expression on Matt's face but didn't dare turn his head.

Matt's hands stilled. "Drag?"

Ollie made a playful sound of agreement, biting his lip to keep from laughing. "Told them your drag name was *Annie Port-In-A-Storm*, and that you do a brunch on the weekends at Carrie Nation. Also, that we're waiting to hear back from *Ru Paul's Drag Race* about your audition tape." Ollie tried to pull away as Matt gripped his hips and dug his fingers into Ollie's tickle spots. "No, no, stop! I can't breathe!" Ollie gasped and writhed. "I didn't tell them your real name."

Matt stopped tickling him. "You made me a drag queen though. Are you serious?"

"A *successful* drag queen," Ollie clarified shrilly as he inched to the shower door. "I told them you were a headliner at the brunch, and that your signature song is *In the Navy*, by The Village People."

Matt scoffed loudly as he twisted the washcloth and snapped it against Ollie's bottom.

"Ouch!" Ollie shrieked as he jumped out of the shower and grabbed his towel.

"Oliver!" Matt shouted. "Get back in here."

"No way," Ollie laughed from the doorway.

"You still have soap on you, and you haven't washed your hair."

"You seem angry, and I know the perils of being around an angry queen." Ollie shuddered dramatically. "I knew several back in Oxford."

"Oliver." Matt opened the door and gave him a quelling look, trying to hide his amusement but not succeeding. "Get back in here, or I'll spank you."

Ollie snickered. "You say that like it's a punishment."

Matt shook his head with a grin. "Just get back in here. The soap suds are drying on your skin and I won't be able to get through the day knowing you'll be itchy."

Ollie put his towel down and approached the shower apprehensively, yelping as Matt grabbed his wrist and pulled him in with a kiss.

"My dad brought up going to Lyon this summer," Ollie said as he toweled off for the second time, watching Matt leave the bathroom. "I haven't been in two years, and he suggested maybe we go when we're there for work." Ollie waited for a response from the bedroom. "Matt?"

Matt reappeared in the doorway. "I'm thinking. Who would be there?"

"Well, it depends on when we go and who can make it at that time. But my aunt and uncle for sure, my parents, Cassie, probably Guy. Not sure about Sophia, she's married and has twin babies, but Guy's other sister Genevieve is a year younger than Cass, so will probably be there, especially if Cass is."

Matt chewed his lip and looked at the frosted window as he rubbed the towel over his head.

"The place is massive. It's a chateau on acres and acres of land; there's a vineyard, and an apricot orchard. It's from the sixteenth century or something and in a constant state of renovation. Dad mentioned we could share one of the rooms with twin beds." Ollie smiled. "Or I could just sneak into your room."

Matt chuckled and walked away, leaving Ollie frowning at the empty doorway. He left his towel on the counter and followed Matt into the dressing room.

"You don't want to meet my family?" Ollie asked quietly as he pulled on his underwear.

Matt straightened from putting on his socks. "I never said that. I just don't think I'll be able to get away, and I'm not sure I'd want to be away with you and have to pretend for days on end. We've only ever been to the Cape with your parents, and they know about us so it's fine."

"Speaking of the beach, Cassie wants to come this summer," Ollie said as he ran his hands through his wet hair.

"Jesus Christ." Matt scowled. "She's not staying at our house; she's way too nosey," Matt said firmly. "I'll ask Chuck."

"Matt she's young. She's not a super spy." Ollie frowned. "And she's my sister. She wouldn't say anything."

"I told you; she can never know. Not now, not for eternity." Matt pulled on his shirt and left the bedroom. "I want breakfast," he called from the hallway.

Ollie twisted his mouth slightly at the command. "There's cereal," he called back, and continued dressing.

Matt was sitting at the kitchen island reading the *Boston Globe* with a mug of coffee. There were eggs, a bag of spinach, shredded cheese, a container of mushrooms, and a pound of bacon on the counter next to the stove and the oven was on. Ollie rolled his eyes and grabbed his phone, calling up his playlist (the one with the pop music Matt always complained about but secretly sang along to) and started making breakfast. One Direction blared through the speakers and Ollie bopped as he made breakfast. He put the bacon in the oven, whisked four eggs and found a loaf of sliced sourdough in the freezer. He put four pieces in the toaster oven and grabbed the tub of farmstand butter from the fridge when he put the bread away.

"I don't know what I love more: watching you shake your ass to this awful music as you make me food, or eating the food you make me," Matt said with a grin.

Ollie looked at him over his shoulder and smiled, finding it difficult to stay irritated at Matt. "You're a walking stomach. I'm guessing it's really the latter." He seasoned the eggs with salt and pepper and a bit of dried dill, continuing to move with the music. "You going swimming later?" Ollie asked as he began sautéing the spinach and mushrooms with a pinch of red pepper flakes.

"Yeah, after I talk to Fred about expanding our engineering department," Matt answered as he finished his coffee. "I need to know real-time budget numbers and where we can expand. I'm looking at adding offices in Silicon Valley, Ireland, and, depending on what we hear from the companies you met with, in France. I'm thinking of setting up an office there to begin my European takeover," he added with a grin.

"Does this mean even more travel for you?" Ollie poured the eggs into the pan with the vegetables.

"For a few months anyway. I'll leave the VPs to handle the hiring and training of their departments. I'll probably send Barbara to oversee the establishment of the Human Resources satellites. The first location should be fully functioning within six months."

Ollie plated the omelet with most of the bacon and three buttered slices of toast and put the heaping plate down in front of Matt, along with a fork and napkin and turned back to the stove.

"Is there juice?" Matt asked expectantly.

"Did you buy any while I was gone?" Ollie countered.

Matt shook his head with a sigh and shoveled a large forkful of eggs into his mouth, followed by two slices of bacon and a bite of toast.

Ollie snickered. "You are a caveman." He turned and filled a glass with water from the fridge dispenser and put it in front of Matt.

Matt grabbed Ollie's wrist and pulled him to his side. "You love it," he said and kissed Ollie with gusto.

"I do. I really do."

Matt slapped Ollie's ass when he turned away to make himself eggs. "Thanks for breakfast; it's delicious as always."

* * *

Matt and Ollie strode into Finn's New Year's Eve party at her dad's house in Wellesley. Matt finally convinced Ollie that it would be fun, and necessary to do after their last time there. They were both in jeans, Matt wearing a white shirt with blue detail on the inside of the cuff, which he had folded back, and Ollie in a grey cashmere sweater.

Matt looked down at his leather loafers, and then at Ollie's feet. "I can't believe you wore sneakers." He shook his head. "What are you twelve?"

Ollie straightened with indignation. "These are Duke + fucking Dexter Ritchie trainers."

Matt rolled his eyes. "There you go, speaking that foreign language again. What the hell did you just say to me?"

"Did you just roll your eyes at me, Lieutenant?"

Matt gave Ollie the side-eye. "Did you just question your commanding officer?"

Ollie smirked and rolled his eyes.

Matt widened his eyes and opened his mouth in mock disbelief. "Oh, you will be dropping to your knees and giving me twenty in the tool room later," he threatened before turning to greet the people shouting his name exuberantly.

Ollie was pleased to hear his name called just as enthusiastically and saw some familiar faces from the fateful party two years prior. He shook hands and kissed cheeks as he followed Matt deeper into the house. He beamed widely when he saw Naomi, dressed in a sparkly halter-top pantsuit that hugged her lean curves, talking to someone with their back to him. Her light blonde hair was loose around her shoulders, and her clear blue eyes shined as she squealed with happiness when she saw Ollie. Ollie enveloped her willowy frame against his body and kissed her on the lips.

"Christ, I've missed you, and *cor*, love the shag bangs. You look like a model," Ollie praised.

"Jesus, Ollie, that accent." Naomi smiled seductively for the audience around them. "Every freaking time."

He kissed her again and kept his arm around her waist to really sell the role Matt set them up in. "All my friends back home are in love with you. I showed them pictures from the last charity dinner. If they were here and saw you now, I wouldn't be able to relax all night," he said with a grin as Matt handed Ollie a beer. "*Slainte.*" Ollie raised his beer to Matt.

"I only have eyes for you, Ollie. But are any of them cute?" she whispered and hugged him to her side with a grin.

Finn joined them, with a gleeful shout. She was dressed in a sequined cocktail dress that hugged her slim curves and tucked herself into Ollie's designated spot under Matt's arm. Ollie tightened Naomi to his side with a pointed look at Matt which went unnoticed, and then shook off his futile disappointment, focusing instead on the happy vibe around him.

He and Matt stayed close to each other most of the night, before peeling off discreetly just before midnight to meet in Finn's father's tool room in the garage, as they had the last time.

Matt pulled a piece of cardboard from the recycling bin before closing the door behind him and looked at Ollie. "I know this is hard for you, and please remember I'm only doing it for appearances." He held Ollie's gaze before kissing him deeply. "I know how jealously you guard your spot under my arm," he added with his sexy grin as he dropped the cardboard on the floor in front of him. "Please know that spot is yours, and yours alone. As is the one in front of me. On your knees. I want a hundred licks," he commanded, his eyes smoky with lust.

Ollie's heart soared with Matt's words, and he pressed himself against Matt with a low chuckle and kissed him deeply. He unzipped Matt's jeans and slipped his hand in before slowly lowering to his knees. "Here's to a fabulous twenty-seventeen," Ollie said against Matt's bellybutton.

—

6

—

Caribbean Queen

"WHERE ARE YOU TAKING ME, LIEUTENANT?" Ollie asked Matt's broad back as he stuffed his hands in his coat pockets against the chill and took in the icy-looking harbor between the buildings as they walked.

Matt stopped and opened the door of a tall glass building at the harbor's edge and waited for Ollie to walk through. "You'll see."

They rode the elevator to the top floor and Ollie raised his eyebrows appreciatively at the large, open space that was abuzz with construction workers. "What is this?"

"SharkFinn's new office space."

"This is ours?" Ollie looked around in wonder.

"Yup. I got this floor and the two below. Naomi's working on the design, naturally, and down here, is where we'll be." He led Ollie through a glass door into a large foyer outside two giant offices. "Here's where Stacey and Kerry will sit, and that's my office." He pointed to the corner one. "And this one's yours."

Ollie looked through the gutted space to the windows overlooking the harbor. "Bloody hell. This is amazing!"

Matt opened a door in the wall and peered in. "They've combined the two half bathrooms that were here into one so I can have a shower, and that door goes to my office." He pointed at the black door on the opposite wall, "and Naomi's had this doorway put in, which will be glass." He walked a few steps and pointed at an opening near the windows. "That way you and I can communicate without having to go out and around. It'll be the only glass in either office aside from the windows." He swept his hand at view.

"All of those will be solid?" Ollie gestured to the exposed studs they walked through. "And the doors looking out?"

Matt nodded. "Yes. I hate working in a fishbowl. I don't want anyone to be able to see in. We'll both have sofas, and I'll have a conference table that seats eight."

"I thought you were kidding about the sofa. You can't possibly think we'll be having sex here?" Ollie shook his head in disbelief.

"It's for conversation, Ollie. Some meetings need less formality. I put one in your office too because I know how much sleep you need, and thought you could have a nap at work on the days that I intend to keep you up late." Matt winked. "And I fully intend to fuck you at least once on both couches," he added with a shrug. "There will be sturdy locks on these doors."

Ollie grinned as his stomach fluttered happily. "You're crazy, but I love you."

* * *

Matt scheduled the office move for early March, when he, Ollie, Naomi, and Finn would be in in the Caribbean for Finn's spring break from university. He left it to the division heads to oversee the moving of their departments before he returned, with Stacey as point person for the movers and space organization.

Matt rented a large villa on the ocean for four nights, with a chef and staff for meals, and a catamaran to take them out among the islands.

They flew to Baltimore in the Gulfstream to get Finn, before continuing on to Tortola and the Bitter End.

"Cheers!" They clinked glasses after Grace, the flight attendant Matt had hired on a trial run and then kept because she was perfect, served their margaritas and Matt's beer.

"You don't like margaritas?" Naomi asked Matt after they all sipped their drinks.

"Tequila and I aren't friends."

"I know what you mean." Naomi grinned and looked at Finn. "It took me a long time to stand even the smell of it after drinking way too much on spring break sophomore year in college."

"Oh, god, I remember that trip." Finn shook her head with a wince. "You fell down that giant marble staircase at the hotel. Not that you remembered doing it at the time, but every picture of you from the trip shows that thigh length bruise."

"I'm so lucky I didn't break anything or split my head open."

"Ouch. Sounds awful." Ollie winced.

"I never did anything like that." Matt shook his head. "No, I don't drink it because it makes me angry."

"Oh. Well, then *definitely* no tequila for you. We are going to have a happy, fantastic vacation. I feel it in my bones." Naomi raised her glass and blew a kiss to Ollie.

Naomi was right, they had an amazing five days, swimming, sunning, and exploring the islands on a private boat. Ollie was especially delighted that most of the vacation was spent nearly naked and he was able to eye-fuck Matt whenever he wanted. And Matt did plenty eye-fucking of his own, giving Ollie a lust-filled expression on more than one occasion when his gaze lingered on the white, crescent-shaped scar on Ollie's shoulder. Ollie's blood turned hot, and his face flushed each time, to Matt's delight.

Ollie took advantage of every bit of privacy they were afforded, and there were lots of opportunities. Matt was ever vigilant and concerned about anyone finding out, even there, where no one knew them. On trips to town or to the Soggy Dollar, Finn was tucked in Ollie's spot, and Naomi was glued to Ollie's side. There were plenty of same sex couples around them, but Matt wouldn't relent.

What kept Ollie happy, and his heart full, was how Matt touched the moon pendant from their commitment ceremony at the base of his throat whenever he sensed Ollie watching Finn with envy, or when he got quiet at dinner.

"You know Chuck is my closest friend, and it means nothing to me when I touch or kiss her," Matt whispered as he trailed his fingertips over Ollie's naked body in bed later.

Ollie watched the gauzy curtains billow out to the balcony with the night breeze, and then back in with the sound of the ocean. "I know."

"And I don't need to touch you in public for you to know that I love you, and will forever. You are my moon, and I am your ocean to control. I would do anything for you." He trailed open mouthed kisses over Ollie's shoulder and across his collar bone.

Well, not anything, obviously, Ollie thought before stifling the petulant voice.

"I know." He turned his head to look at Matt. "I love you. I just can't help but feel selfish sometimes." He leaned into Matt's kiss. "Now, please pull the screen down." Ollie pointed toward the balcony. "I don't want another lizard in my hair."

Matt snorted as he pulled back. "The lizard was on the ceiling, in the corner and nowhere near you."

Ollie came up on one elbow and swept his hair off his brow indignantly. "It was headed right for me, if I hadn't shouted it *would've* been in my hair."

"You mean, screamed," Matt corrected. "Luckily, we don't have any neighbors here. I'm certain someone would've called the police to report a woman being murdered."

Ollie dropped his mouth open. "I do not scream like a woman!"

"You're right, babe." Matt patted Ollie's thigh. "It was more like a teenage girl."

Ollie gasped and made to roll off the bed. "That's it. I'm going to sleep with Naomi."

Matt grabbed him around the waist with a laugh and pulled him back. "I didn't say you could leave."

"I didn't ask your permission," Ollie retorted haughtily as he playfully struggled to get away.

Matt gripped Ollie's wrists in one hand and forced them over his head as he rolled on top of him. "You know what happens when you don't ask permission, Oliver." Matt raised his eyebrows and waggled the fingers of his free hand.

"NO!" Ollie began writhing in earnest, trying to buck Matt off to no avail. "No, stop. I can't breathe!"

Matt furrowed his brow. "I haven't even started tickling you. Give me a minute." He dug his fingers into Ollie's tickle spots and was rewarded with Ollie's infectious laughter.

"Stop!" Ollie laughed. "I can't—I'm gonna pee!"

Matt stopped with a big smile as Ollie caught his breath. "Maybe I want you to pee on me." He quirked his eyebrow.

What?

"What? You're joking." Ollie stared up at him.

Matt relaxed but kept his grip on Ollie. "Of course I am, Oliver." He paused and then resumed tickling. "I would be the one doing the peeing."

Ollie groaned through his laughter and doubled his efforts to get away, managing to free a hand from Matt's strong grip. "You're a disgusting, depraved, sadist and I can't believe I'm stuck with you."

"Come on, Ollie. Clearly, you're not that disgusted." He pulled back and looked meaningfully at Ollie's half-hard dick.

"The idea of you peeing on me is not what's turning me on," Ollie scoffed. "It's that you're so bloody hot when you're being sadistic. All those muscles." Ollie swept his free hand up and down in front of Matt's chest. "I can't believe it, but I blame you for making me like it."

"Oh yeah?" Matt asked huskily and straightened Ollie beneath him. He covered his body with his and kissed him deeply with a sigh.

Ollie felt his body come alive as Matt's cock hardened against his. He closed his eyes as Matt trailed kisses down his chest and over his nipples. He was close to forgetting everything except the feeling of Matt's hands and mouth on him, but then his eyes opened and scanned the ceiling for movement.

"The screen, Lieutenant," he whispered.

Matt dropped his forehead to Ollie's stomach as his body sagged. "Yes, princess."

* * *

"My dad told me you guys are taking his polo ponies out," Finn said to Ollie as Grace served them bottled water and juice and then went back to the galley and closed the door.

Ollie glanced at Matt. "Yes. He said he's got an indoor ring somewhere or something and we're just going to chase each other around with our polo sticks." Ollie grinned.

"You play polo?" Naomi asked, her voice trailing up with interest. "Jesus Christ, what can't you do, and will you please stop being so fucking hot?" She laughed. "It's not fair."

Ollie laughed humbly.

"But seriously, you gonna start playing polo?" Finn asked Ollie. "Please go easy on my dad. I'm worried he has a bit of a recklessness about him since my mom died," she said, a sad look flitting across her features.

"I'll watch out for him. I promise, Chuck," Ollie replied with a soft smile. "That being said, I can't wait to get back on a horse. I gave it up for football and school, and was fine about that, until your father told me there's a decent polo presence here in the Boston area, and the bug bit me again." He looked over at Matt. "If I don't break my head open practicing, would you come watch a match?"

Matt held his gaze. "Sure," he replied and looked at Finn and Naomi. "I'd need a date, but something tells me that wouldn't be hard to find."

"I'll come to every match or game or whatever they're called. I promise," Naomi offered enthusiastically.

"Okay." He looked again at Matt. "If you mean it, I will pour my heart into it."

Matt held his gaze, and Ollie thought he saw something behind his eyes. "I mean it."

7

Mile High

MATT AND OLLIE returned to Boston and their new office space. Stacey and Kerry had set up their offices as planned, making sure everything was where it should be according to Naomi's diagrams and Matt's specifications.

Stacey had been working for Matt and SharkFinn since the beginning and knew everything: from how he liked his office organized to how he wanted his days scheduled, to how he took his oatmeal. He rewarded her accordingly, knowing that he put her through the ringer at times, especially when he and Ollie were separated, and he had been a miserable brute to work for.

Kerry had come on board after Ollie's first promotion, but before he was made general counsel, and had been hand-picked and trained by Stacey. She was undeniably Stacey's protegee, and as dedicated to supporting Ollie as Stacey was to Matt. They were both discreet, professional, and utterly indispensable.

"How was the trip?" Stacey asked as Matt came through the door.

"Fantastic, Stacey. Thanks for booking everything. We're gonna want to go again next year, but a different island. I'll tell Finn to email you when she decides the particulars." Matt walked past her desk without stopping, anxious to survey his new office and get caught up with work.

Ollie appeared ten minutes later and stopped to get his messages from Kerry.

"You got a great tan, Oliver." Kerry admired politely.

"Thank you, Kerry. I had to be careful with my British skin, unlike Mr. Italian." He nodded at Matt's door with a smile and continued into his office, pleased to be able to shut the door and not be seen.

* * *

"Let's see your parents for Easter," Matt said over dinner later that week. "I have a meeting to schedule in London, and can make it for the Friday before."

"I'll call them in the morning to confirm. They were already expecting us," Ollie answered, wondering how Matt could've forgotten the discussion they'd had. "Will you need me in the meeting? Just wondering how many suits I should pack."

"You should never travel with less than three, Ollie. I taught you that. One to wear on the plane and two in the bag." He finished his fish taco and wiped his mouth. "And yes, I want you in the meeting."

"Great. Is this a new company, or follow-up?" Ollie asked as he took a small bite. He smiled to himself knowing Matt would pack his bag for him, and that Matt loved deferring to him when contracts were being negotiated.

"One is with that company I was wining and dining when you and I were first dating. I'm giving them a great deal on upgrading, simply because of the happy memories I have of being in Oxford with you while negotiating." Matt grinned. "And the other is one someone Krish brought to my attention," Matt said, referring to SharkFinn's chief technology officer. "I was also thinking we didn't get a chance to renew our Mile-High Club memberships on our trip to the Caribbean, and I know how much you hate falling behind in dues." He leaned over and kissed Ollie with a smile.

"Well, now you definitely have my and little Oliver's attention." Ollie grinned and sat back as Matt cleared the dishes. "In the meantime, you can show the both of us what it is you had in mind for the flight." He looked down at the front of his pants and back up at Matt's face with a grin.

* * *

They boarded the Gulfstream and made their way to the back cabin to drop their luggage. Matt smiled, noting that the double bed and one of the couches mid-cabin had been made up for sleeping, as requested. He winked at Ollie as he put a small bag down on the bed, and went back to the main cabin for take-off.

"Hello, Mr. Dion, Mr. Turner," Grace greeted them in her Irish lilt with a smile. "Nice to see you again so soon."

"Hello, Grace. Good to see you again as well." Matt looked at his watch. "We'll only need you a couple of times on the flight. I'll buzz for you like last time. We've got a lot of prep for our meetings in London."

Grace nodded. "What can I get you to drink?"

"I'd like a martini, and he'll have a pint." He looked at Ollie. "How does eight o'clock sound for dinner?"

"Sounds great," Ollie agreed.

Grace looked at the cockpit door and then at her watch. "We should be cleared for take-off in about five minutes. I'll be back with the drinks in a flash."

Matt looked at Ollie when Grace shut the galley door. "That gives us an hour." He made a thoughtful sound as his stomach flipped with the anticipation of burying himself deep inside Ollie's ass. "What will we do to pass the time?"

Ollie looked at Matt's lap and licked his lips. "I, for one, can't wait to get to work."

They took their drinks into the back once they reached altitude and Matt pushed the door button, watching the automatic door slide out and up from inside the partition. He turned to look at Ollie, who was already undressing, with a smile.

"Oh, someone's eager to have me inside him." Matt put down his drink and kissed the sensitive spot behind Ollie's ear before kissing Ollie's waiting mouth.

"Yes, Matt. I've been fantasizing about this since you mentioned the trip. I can't wait to renew my club membership," he murmured against Matt's lips as he undid the buttons on Matt's shirt.

"Well, good. I've got your paperwork right here." Matt gripped Ollie's wrist and put his hand over his crotch, moaning when Ollie tightened his grip around his hard dick.

"I love paperwork," Ollie whispered. "This big, thick stack will take at least an hour to finish off." He stroked Matt before undoing the button and zipper of his pants and lowering to his knees. "I'll need to take a look at the fine print." He nuzzled into Matt's trimmed bush and breathed deeply through his nose and sighed. "So bloody fine."

Matt stepped out of his pants with a chuckle and sucked in a sharp breath as Ollie gripped the base of his dick and swirled his tongue around the tip before taking Matt as deep as he could. He looked up and held Matt's gaze intently as he began bobbing and sucking. His mouth was warm and wet and made for his dick.

"God, you're so beautiful on your knees with my dick in your mouth," Matt panted. He dropped a hand to Ollie's head and gripped his hair, forcing himself deeper. "I want in your throat, baby."

Ollie opened wider and took Matt nearly to the root, his throat bulging with the invasion. Matt groaned and thrust until Ollie gagged around him, driving him to the edge. Matt withdrew and exhaled the breath he'd been holding, his orgasm aching in his balls at being denied. Ollie's gag reflex was as remarkable as his tongue, but Matt wanted to be buried deep inside Ollie's hot ass when he came.

Matt ran his hands through Ollie's hair as he coaxed him off his knees. He kissed him deeply, tasting the saltiness of himself on Ollie's tongue with a moan. Ollie's nipples pebbled under Matt's fingers and he couldn't resist a taste, a nibble, before continuing with his mission.

Matt reached into the side pocket of his overnight bag for a condom and the lube as he watched Ollie sway with desire, his perfect, uncut erection straining away from his body as if in search of Matt.

"On your back. Knees to your chest," Matt ordered softly and knelt on the bed. He pulled Ollie's socks off and kissed the big toe of each foot. "So sexy," he complimented as he stared down at him. "Eager Ollie is beautiful." He trailed a fingertip down the back of Ollie's thigh to his ass. "But Begging Ollie is my favorite." He raised his eyebrows expectantly.

Ollie's eyes were dark, and his lips were puffy. "I want you to fuck me with your tongue, and then with your magnificent cock, *please*, Lieutenant."

Ollie leaned forward and ran his hand from Matt's shoulder to his nipple, and pinched. Matt gripped Ollie's wrist and held his hand in place with a moan as Ollie rolled the nipple between his thumb and forefinger.

"You'll get the tongue, but I'm gonna want more begging for this." He gripped his erection before lowering himself between Ollie's spread thighs.

Ollie smelled of mint and cloves and tasted like heaven. Matt gripped Ollie's ass cheeks in his hands and dove in, alternating between flat strokes and spearing with his tongue as Ollie moaned and writhed. He bit Ollie's cheeks lightly, one after the other, smiling at Ollie's squeaks of protest and then licked a long swath from the top of Ollie's crease to his balls.

Matt gave Ollie's pucker an open-mouthed kiss and then pulled back to admire the beautiful pink star. There was nothing like it in the world. The mere sight of Ollie's asshole, never mind the taste, roused the inner beast in him. It took every ounce of restraint to not plunge himself inside with a roar.

"Please . . . more. Fuck that feels so good . . . *s'il te plait*," Ollie begged and dropped his knees open when Matt added his fingers.

Matt wanted to lay flat and hump the bed like he did at home but didn't want to make a mess of the sheets. He pulled away and glanced at the air purifier, there to minimize the smell of sex, and then down at the condom in his hand, to minimize the mess. He tore open the condom with his teeth and rolled it on as he stared down at Ollie's blissed out expression.

"I want to look out the window," Ollie said and rolled over.

Matt wanted to smack Ollie's beautiful ass but didn't want to risk the sharp sound carrying.

"Okay. On your hands and knees," Matt breathed and squeezed Ollie's ass cheeks again, pleased at the sight of his reddened fingerprints in Ollie's white flesh. "I don't mind standing."

Matt eased slowly into Ollie and closed his eyes with a moan, letting his other senses take over. The smell and taste of Ollie was on his skin, in his mouth, and the warm heat of his tight sheath sent shivers down his spine. He looked over Ollie's head at the clouds he was watching and moved his hips in slow circles. Ollie let out a soft moan and pressed back.

"God. You're so tight, and you feel so good. What is it about you?" Matt ran his hand down Ollie's smooth muscular back and gripped his hips, increasing his pace at Ollie's insistence.

Ollie purred under his touch and clenched around Matt's dick. "Christ, Lieutenant; it's you who feels so good," Ollie breathed.

"Get up. I want to feel your skin against mine."

Ollie pushed himself up and Matt hugged him tightly, Matt's chest hairs tickling his back. He rested his head against Matt's shoulder behind him as Matt kissed his ear with a small moan.

"Touch me," Ollie whispered.

Matt shook his head once and ran his hands over Ollie's chest, feeling Ollie's nipples harden under his probing fingertips. He teasingly touched Ollie everywhere but where he knew Ollie wanted him to. "You can't come on these sheets, babe."

Ollie groaned and turned his head to bite Matt's neck gently.

Matt slowed his pace, tormenting Ollie as he watched his dick disappear between Ollie's cheeks in long, slow strokes. He raised his eyes to the flushed skin of Ollie's neck and captured the warmth there with his lips. Ollie reached up behind him and ran his hands through Matt's hair grasping the back of Matt's neck briefly before running them down his own body.

Matt gripped his wrists before he could touch himself. "No, Ollie," Matt chided. "I know you want to, but I told you, you have to wait," he whispered and increased his pace. "I'm so close. Can you feel how hard I am? How hard you make me? Do you want me to come?"

"Yes, Matt," Ollie answered urgently. "I wish you were bare. I want to feel your cum inside me."

Matt groaned loudly against Ollie's neck as he filled the condom, happy that the sound of the engines hid his voice. He held Ollie close against him, his heart thudding against Ollie's back, before pulling away and disposing of the condom in the zip-top baggie he brought with him.

"Turn around," Matt commanded and knelt on the floor next to the bed, his knees weak from his orgasm.

He took Ollie's smooth and perfectly sized dick in his mouth, his tongue coming alive at the salty sweet taste of Ollie's pre-cum. He looked up at Ollie and saw his eyes focused (or rather, unfocused) on the window behind Matt's head as his balls drew up tight under Matt's hand.

"Oh, god, I'm gonna come," Ollie cried, and tightened his fingers in Matt's short hair as he met Matt's eye. He pumped his hips as his mouth went slack with pleasure and his eyes rolled back into his head.

Yes, that's my favorite expression, Matt thought as Ollie's dick swelled and he came in thick spurts on Matt's tongue.

Ollie pulled on lounge pants as he came out of the small but well-appointed bathroom at the back of the plane. He ran his eyes over Matt in his grey sweatpants and zip hoodie over a US Navy t-shirt.

"God, you look so sexy, and so obviously satisfied. I hope Grace doesn't notice."

Matt grinned. "So do you, but we do have *actual* work to do, which will erase all this in five minutes." He waved his hand around his face and then opened the door to the main cabin. He set up his computer at the table that had been folded down between the wide, plush seats and dove into work, while Ollie sat down across the aisle at another table with his laptop. They both looked up ten minutes later as the galley door opened, and Grace came out to set up the dinner table.

"Can I get you another drink, or would you like wine?" she asked, not blinking an eye at their change of apparel. They always switched for long flights, and would put their suits back on for landing.

"I'll have wine," Matt said, and looked at Ollie expectantly.

"I'll have wine as well. Thank you."

They ate and then disappeared into the bedroom again. Matt fell asleep curled around Ollie. He woke an hour later and was temporarily disoriented before slipping out of bed, getting dressed, and moving to the couch that was set up in the next compartment. Ollie didn't even stir in his sleep as Matt left.

8

Amendments

THEY SPENT THREE NIGHTS in a two-bedroom suite at the Four Seasons in Mayfair where Matt swam for an hour every morning after his run while Ollie slept. Matt took Ollie to dinner at a tapas place in Soho their first night in town to go over their busy schedule.

"Our meeting with the current client is in the morning and shouldn't take too long. Then we can have a quick lunch and get across town to the next meeting before dinner. Saturday will be for any follow-up." Matt took a large bite of shrimp risotto and chewed. "Then we'll fly out Sunday night after Easter with your folks."

"Is there a back-up plan if the morning meeting runs over, or if either client wants us to come back on Monday?"

"Oliver, that's a dumb question." Matt shook his head.

"Right, OODA loop. Sorry." Ollie grinned, knowing how Matt planned for every contingency using his Naval training: Observe, Orient, Decide, and Act. Ollie took a small bite of his roasted vegetables and scanned his eyes over Matt. "You're so sexy when you're laying out plans in that gravelly officer voice of yours."

Matt grinned as he looked around at the crowded restaurant. "And you're so sexy when I'm laying you out," he said quietly as he leaned into the table for his glass of water.

Matt kissed Ollie goodbye Easter morning. "I'll see you in an hour or so."

"I love you." Ollie returned the kiss, left the hotel room with his suitcase, and headed to his parents' house in Kensington.

Ollie's parents greeted Matt happily when he arrived with a large bouquet of tulips and a bottle of Ollie's father's favorite scotch. David and Maggie were a handsome couple, and while Ollie looked very much like his father, there was evidence of Maggie in the shape of Ollie's eyes and the slope of his perfect nose.

"Matt." Ollie's mother smiled and kissed him, taking the flowers. "You're looking well. So glad you could join us again."

"Yes, Matt. Wonderful to see you," David said as he shook Matt's hand firmly and thanked him for the bottle. "Ollie's been telling us all kinds of wonderful things about work and how well your company is doing. Congratulations."

"Thank you, sir. It's due in large part to Ollie. He's been a gift," Matt said with a smile, genuinely happy to see them. Ollie appeared in the kitchen doorway followed by Cassie as Maggie disappeared with the flowers.

"Hello, Matt. Long time no see," Ollie feigned as Cassie pushed past him to hug Matt tightly.

"Hi, Matt!" she exclaimed with a bright smile and kissed both his cheeks, just missing his mouth.

Matt glanced at Ollie with a grin, amused as always at Cassie's not-so-subtle advances.

"Hello, Cassie," he said with a smile. "Looking forward to life in the real world after you graduate this summer?"

"Yes, and I have a job lined up, but I'd much rather be working and living in Boston with you. I mean, for you," she corrected with a flirty face.

Matt laughed with a wink and thought, *never*.

"No way, Cass." Ollie shook his head. "I would red flag your application."

After dinner David invited Matt into his study for scotch, as had become their habit.

"*Slainte.*" David raised his glass once they were seated on the couch.

"Cheers, sir," Matt said with a smile and pondered his opening. It was a conversation they needed to have. Matt needed David to trust him again.

"Haven't seen you since your ceremony. It's good to lay eyes on you again."

"Yes, sir, I feel the same." Matt looked down at his glass as he swirled the liquid lightly. "We never got a chance to speak or clear the air last year." He looked up at David, who returned his gaze with a bewildered expression that quickly changed to one of realization.

David nodded slowly and looked around the room before bringing his eyes back to Matt. "You're so private. It makes it hard for me to speak about my doubts and concerns. I've always been very open with my children, Ollie in particular. My parents weren't with me or my brother, but Maggie's were with her, and I learned a lot as a parent and wanted to do better for my children." He took a sip of scotch and let it sit on his tongue as Matt waited patiently. "I know conversations like this make you tremendously uncomfortable, just like they did for my father, but it is not my intention at all to make you uncomfortable. Maggie and I really like you. Truly. You make Oliver so happy.

"That being said, I was worried about you last year. You hurt my son. I'm not sure you realize just how much. I had never seen him like that. Maggie and I were extremely concerned for his well-being, so my worry about you was arguably justified," David said adamantly. "Your commitment ceremony was astonishing. Quite a surprise, and I know what it took for you to be open like that. So, I apologize for having doubted you. I see how much you love him."

Matt took a deep breath and exhaled, studying David's face as he measured his words carefully. "I loved my dad, but I wish I had father like you." He looked down and released the tension in his hands. "I knew from the minute that I met you, I could be honest and speak freely. That was and is a scary thing for me.

"Ollie is a treasure, and hurting him weighs heavily on me," Matt went on as he held David's gaze. "I have made it up to him, tenfold. I love him. That I disappointed you has weighed on me as well. Naturally you're protective of him. But he's mine to protect now, and I will do so with my life. You have nothing to worry about anymore, I promise." Matt finished his scotch in one swallow.

David sat back and nodded slowly. "I'm so glad to hear that, Matthew. It's hard as a parent. You never truly stop worrying." He paused and a mischievous look passed across his features. "I knew you must really love him if you committed yourself to him despite knowing what a slob he is," David said with a grin.

Matt threw his head back and laughed, flooded with relief. "Honestly, how can one person make such a mess?" He grinned as Ollie appeared in the doorway.

"What's so funny?"

David looked at Matt with a laugh.

"Nothing." Matt smiled, rising partway off the couch.

"Join us, Ollie." His father gestured to the bar. "I wonder if you boys have had a chance to talk about Lyon this summer," David said changing the subject. "Uncle Lloyd keeps asking."

Ollie poured a little more scotch for Matt and David before sitting down in the club chair with a glance at Matt. "I'm not sure this summer is going to work for us both, but I will be there. I have a meeting lined up for the third week in July. Would that work for everyone?" Ollie asked.

David looked at Matt briefly. "I'll let Lloyd know, that sounds wonderful, though we will miss you, Matt. I understand."

Matt took a sip of scotch and brushed imaginary lint off his pants as he worried about disappointing David again so soon.

9

Riders on the Storm

OLLIE MET FINN'S FATHER, Bill, a tall athletic man with salt and pepper hair, a square jaw, and bright blue eyes at his barn in Dover. Ollie was in his new polo gear: white pants, riding boots, knee guards, gloves, and layers of tops, knowing from their last riding session he'd need to shed jackets and shirts as he began to sweat in the cool air. He carried his new helmet under his arm and shook Bill's hand tightly.

"Wonderful to see you again, Ollie," Bill said with a broad smile. He was dressed similarly, with tall, expensive-looking but worn polo boots, knee guards, and a zip-up fleece jacket. "How'd you feel after our last ride?"

"Sore from head to toe." Ollie grinned. "How about you?"

"I'm still popping pain pills." Bill shook his head with a smile. "But it was worth it. I forgot how much I love to ride, and you are quite good," he said appreciatively. "Your dad was right. I can't wait to see you actually play."

Ollie smiled, pleased at the compliment. "You're quite good yourself for having not played in what, five years?"

"It hasn't been quite that long, I used to sneak it." Bill grinned. "Diana worried so much." He twisted his mouth sadly and blew out a breath. "Anyway, let's go."

Xander, Bill's groom, had saddled their horses and he held the reins as they buckled their helmets. Ollie passed Bill a mallet and pulled himself onto the beautiful chestnut thoroughbred, waiting for Bill to mount his grey and then rode into the large indoor ring making a beeline for the arena polo ball with the sound of Bill's horse gaining on him.

An hour and a half (and three horses each) later, Ollie wiped the sweat from his brow after removing his helmet and slid off the horse in the stable. He passed the reins to Xander with a tired smile, then helped with removing the saddle and brushing down the sweaty horse while Bill did the same with his.

"That was even better than last time," Ollie said, breathing with exertion as he brushed the horse, his muscles flexing with the motion.

"Agreed. You got me a few times there." Bill nodded. "I'll get four more players from the Sentry Club for next time and we'll play an arena game before braving the open fields."

"Sounds perfect. My boss is traveling to the west coast the week after next, so I can meet you any afternoon except Saturday, because of football," Ollie replied with a glance at Xander.

Bill stopped brushing and Ollie felt his eyes on him. Bill looked at Xander. "Can you grab our jackets and things in the ring? Thanks." He waited until the young man left. "What's going on, Ollie? Matt was away last time we played, and today. You sneaking?"

Ollie stopped and turned. "No," he replied less than convincingly, and then sighed under Bill scrutiny. "Matt's on board with us playing; I just get the sense he doesn't *love* the idea as much as he does with us playing squash or tennis. I wanted to ease him in. Once he comes to watch, if he ever does, then I'll feel better about it."

"Why doesn't he feel good about it now?"

Ollie looked away. Matt had been very angry about Ollie discussing their relationship with Ollie's father, he wasn't sure how much to share with Bill. "I think it's hard for Matt to escape his childhood and feeling like he couldn't afford things, particularly growing up working-class in a town like Wellesley. You have to admit, polo isn't for the poor. It isn't even for the middle class." Ollie pulled a face. "He was bothered initially when he found out I played, and I don't want to rub it in his face. You know I love him more than life. Please don't tell him I said anything," Ollie added with a wince. "He's very private and gets upset if I talk about us to *anyone*. I only said something to you because you've known him so long."

Bill wiped his forehead on his still impressive bicep and made a thoughtful sound. "I won't say a word. I love him like a son; you know that. We'll just have to get him to join us." He smiled. "He'd look pretty remarkable on a horse."

"He would that," Ollie agreed with a light laugh. "Thank you, Bill."

"Let's hit the showers and head to lunch."

* * *

Ollie picked up Matt at Hanscom Field in his Audi S5 and switched to the passenger seat.

"I missed you," Ollie said studying Matt's handsome profile as Matt got behind the wheel and adjusted the seat for his longer legs. Matt had shadows under his eyes and a dusting of stubble on his jaw. "How was the trip?"

"Hot. I don't know how anyone can live in Arizona. I left Bryan's favorite sales guy in charge of the meeting in Phoenix and only joined for dinner on one of the nights. I flew to Scottsdale for a round of golf with another company CEO and then was dragged to Vegas on his jet."

"I'd take a little sunshine and heat right now." He gestured to the rain outside. "Though I know what you mean about the desert. It is a wonder anyone ever settled there."

"Seriously," Matt agreed and merged onto the Mass Pike.

"Did what happen in Vegas, stay in Vegas, Lieutenant?" Ollie asked pointedly, wondering at Matt's evasive mood.

"Of course. Business is business. It has nothing to do with you."

"I know. I'm the same when I travel for work," Ollie said offhandedly, hoping for a rise out of Matt with that cryptic reply.

Matt turned his head sharply to frown at Ollie, before looking back to the road.

"You had better be kidding, Oliver."

"What's good for the goose is good for the gander." Ollie shrugged, irritated that his suspicions were confirmed by Matt's jealous response.

"Ollie, everything I do or say in the presence of other CEOs is done for appearances only. I never touch any of the women they have around, and I never do anything except flirt. You know that," Matt said firmly.

"Same with me, so why did you get so upset?" Ollie studied his profile. "Something more happen this time?"

Matt shrugged. "I got a lap dance, but don't worry; I didn't get hard. I wouldn't care if you got a lap dance either, you can have those 'til the cows come home. But if you flirt with or touch another man, and I find out, I will lose my shit," Matt said in a threatening voice.

Ollie scoffed. "I would never, Lieutenant. That's absurd and insulting for so many reasons."

"I know," Matt said apologetically, putting his hand on Ollie's thigh. "I guess I've just been away too long and seen too much debauchery."

"I don't doubt that." He looked at Matt's lap. "Maybe when we get home, I'll give you a *proper* lap dance. She was clearly an amateur."

Matt chuckled low in his throat. "That could've been it, or it could have simply been, like in every other instance, she just wasn't you," Matt said sweetly as he exited the Pike onto Storrow Drive.

"It is so good to be home," Matt said as he put his bags down just inside the door. He took Ollie in his arms and hugged him tightly, savoring their first contact in a week.

Ollie pulled back for a kiss. "I'm so glad you're home," he said against Matt's lips, and followed him up to the laundry room, where Matt left his suitcase of dirty laundry outside the door.

Matt stopped in the hallway and sniffed. "You've been spending quite a bit of time in the barn, haven't you?"

"Why do you ask?"

"Well, it's either that or you've got a horse living here." Matt wrinkled his nose and looked around teasingly.

"I didn't have time to do laundry before you came home."

Matt snorted. "You don't *ever* do laundry, Ollie."

Ollie shrugged nonchalantly and walked away with a smirk. Matt was the neat freak and did laundry better than Ollie ever could or would.

"Am I going to have to get a separate washing machine? I don't want my clothes smelling like *Mister Ed*."

"Who?" Ollie stopped and looked back at him with a furrowed brow.

"*Mister Ed.* A show from the sixties about a talking horse. You never heard of him?"

Ollie rolled his eyes. "The *sixties*, Lieutenant? You're not serious; we've been through this," he scoffed. "How bloody old are you?" He made to walk to the bedroom but Matt lunged forward and dug his fingers into Ollie's tickle spots.

Ollie shrieked. "Stop! Stop! I can't breathe," he laughed and struggled to get away. "You're not old! I'm sure it's a beloved show watched by many. . . ." he trailed off as Matt stopped tickling him and then kissed his neck before letting Ollie go.

Ollie smiled mischievously. "Patients in nursing homes," he finished, skipping out of Matt's reach and dashing through the bedroom door.

Matt tackled him onto the bed, his approach as silent and swift as a tiger. Ollie was laughing so hard that he really couldn't breathe as Matt tickled him mercilessly, his body pinning Ollie to the bed as he squirmed to get away. Matt's fingers slowed in response to Ollie's laughing and writhing under him. He kissed Ollie's neck again with his firm lips.

"Not so old that I can't subdue you." He moved his fingers to the waistband of Ollie's sweatpants and pulled them down, spanking him once sharply. "That's for the eyeroll."

Ollie flinched and cried out as his dick twitched with pleasure.

Matt spanked him again. "That's for the nursing home comment." He spanked him a third time. "And that's for being so fucking sexy I couldn't help myself."

Ollie ass tingled, and he knew it was red by the way Matt was gazing hungrily at it. Matt moved down Ollie's body and stood to peel off his sweatpants, admiring the straps of Ollie's jockstrap before peeling those off and biting him gently on each cheek.

"This fucking gorgeous ass," he murmured and swept his tongue up Ollie's crease.

Matt took his time, sweeping teasingly with the tip of his tongue around Ollie's hole as he squeezed Ollie's cheeks tightly. He slipped his hands under Ollie's hips and lifted his ass higher, giving him full access to Ollie's taint. Ollie moaned and pressed back, urging Matt to stop teasing.

"So greedy for my tongue, you are," Matt chided and nipped Ollie's left cheek with his teeth. "Patience, or I'll edge you all night."

Ollie groaned. He hated when Matt did that, though the orgasm was always mind-blowing. Matt continued what he was doing when Ollie stilled, the flat of his tongue warm on his taint. Soon he was lapping at Ollie's hole, apparently forgetting that he wanted to tease Ollie. Ollie fought to remain still, especially with the sounds of pleasure Matt was making and the way he was humping the side of the bed as he buried his face in Ollie's ass.

Ollie whimpered when Matt straightened to take off his suit. He rolled onto his back and sat up to help Matt disrobe, returning Matt's smug smile with a small grin. Matt wiped his face on his shirt before tossing it on the upholstered bench at the foot of their massive bed. He rolled his head back as Ollie licked his nipples, biting them until they pebbled into hard nubs before moving lower and nuzzling his face in the soft hair of Matt's goody trail.

"I missed you and your gorgeous body. Christ, these washboard abs," Ollie breathed, unzipping Matt's suit pants. "I can't wait to have all your skin on mine." Ollie felt Matt's eyes on him as he pulled Matt's cock out of his boxer briefs and swirled his tongue around the damp tip. "I missed you especially, you magnificent thing."

"*Prendilo en bocca,*" Matt commanded in his gravelly voice.

Ollie knew that order, more for the delivery than the words, and savored the salty, delicious flavor of Matt's pre-cum and cock before doing as he was told. He opened his mouth wider to accommodate Matt's girth and command. He loved the feeling of Matt's hardness in his mouth, in his throat. The way the prominent vein that disrupted the smoothness of the front of Matt's cock pulsed enticingly under his tongue as he sucked. Ollie fisted the extra length he couldn't fit in his mouth, and jacked slowly in sync with his sucking.

Matt carded his fingers in Ollie's hair and gripped tightly as he pressed himself deeper. His rhythm became insistent, his thrusts increasing in pace as Ollie hollowed his cheeks and sucked with his tongue in the way he knew Matt loved. The vein throbbed under his ministrations and Ollie moved his hand, knowing Matt was close.

Ollie let Matt fuck his throat, his eyes watering as he fought his gag reflex and breathed in short gasps when he was able. Matt pulled Ollie off suddenly, with a groan. Ollie drew in a shaky breath as he wiped his chin and eyes while Matt eyed his bedside table.

"Where's the lube?" he asked in a voice wrecked with passion.

"My side table drawer," Ollie replied and looked up at Matt with a quirked eyebrow. "The cleaners were here and I hid it, though they think I'm the neat freak, and you're the slob." He laughed about his immaculate condo on the first floor which they had cleaned every week though Ollie never used it. "A pervy slob with a bottle of lube in every room."

Matt laughed and retrieved the bottle. "In that case, I have a reputation to uphold. Roll over, Ollie, so I can do all kinds of pervy things to you." He smacked Ollie's ass again when he complied and spread his thighs.

Matt climbed onto the bed and ran his cock between Ollie's ass cheeks, planting a kiss on the back of Ollie's neck before pulling away. Ollie watched over his shoulder as Matt popped the lid of the bottle and coated his fingers carefully. Matt ran his other hand up the back of

Ollie's thigh, over the mound of his ass, and up his side before planting his fist on the bed next to Ollie's bicep.

Matt slipped a single finger between Ollie's spread legs and circled his hole, his breath warm in Ollie's ear as he hovered over him, his body heat radiating against Ollie's back. Ollie closed his eyes and focused on the tip of Matt's large finger. It tapped once, then twice in sync with the kisses Matt dropped on Ollie's neck before adding pressure.

Matt moaned low as his finger sunk into Ollie's softened hole. "God, you're so tight and hot. I can't wait to bury myself inside this portal to heaven." He kissed Ollie's open mouth, stealing the moan from his lips.

Ollie felt a second finger and pressed back, seeking to adjust the angle.

"I know what you want," Matt murmured and paused briefly.

Ollie bit back a sound of frustration and watched Matt look down at what his fingers were doing and felt a third join in the mix. The moon pendant on Matt's chain glinted as it swung in the low light while Matt stretched him and then withdrew his fingers. He swept them over his cock and then guided himself inside Ollie's hole with a contented sigh.

Oh, it's a light lube day apparently, Ollie thought as he closed his eyes and bore down to accommodate Matt. He exhaled a drawn-out moan through the burn and felt his cock twitch. Everything about Matt just felt right, and Ollie was past questioning whether or not he should like it when Matt wanted things his way.

"God, that feels good," Ollie breathed. "Your cock. The way you fuck me—" Ollie gasped as Matt drove deeper into him.

"It feels amazing. You feel amazing," Matt interrupted and then said something in Italian Ollie didn't understand, but had heard a billion times before.

Matt paused once his thighs were flush with Ollie's bottom before pulling out almost all the way and driving back in. He moved his hand from the bed to the back of Ollie's neck as he shifted his angle, the fat head of his cock skimming repeatedly over Ollie's prostate in a way that made his entire body tingle. Ollie slipped his hand between the mattress and his body and gripped the wet tip of his cock to stave off the orgasm that was threatening too soon.

"Stop that," Matt grunted.

"Believe me, I'm not," Ollie panted. "Christ, you're lighting me up. I'm trying to keep from coming."

Matt made a pleased sound and gripped Ollie's ass cheek in his free hand, pulling him open so he could watch his dick disappear into Ollie's hole. "I wish you could see how well you take me. It's perfection."

Ollie craned his neck under Matt's grip and thought the view looked pretty damn good from his angle, and what Matt was doing felt even better. Matt gripped his ass tightly before releasing and slapping it with a sharp sound.

"Roll over." Matt pulled out and sat back on his haunches.

Ollie complied and ran his eyes over Matt's sweaty chest. Matt's cock was almost purple and so hard it looked like bone. Ollie's own cock throbbed at the view, drawing Matt's gaze. Matt grinned and ran the tip of his finger over Ollie's slit to collect the drip of pre-cum and then sucked it into his mouth, humming at the taste.

"Look at you leaking for me." Matt picked up the lube and added a small dollop to his hand. He swiped a bit on Ollie's cock before adding the rest to his own; enough to stave off the burn of friction, but not enough to make it truly slippery.

Ollie tucked a pillow under his ass and ran a finger up his crease as he watched Matt. He bit his lip when Matt came forward with a growl and guided his cock inside Ollie in one swift thrust. He grabbed Ollie's thighs and pulled him flush against his groin. Ollie's legs flopped over Matt's forearms as Matt drove into him with abandon.

"You fucking tease," Matt panted. "This what you wanted?"

"Yes," Ollie replied breathlessly, his moans coming out in staccato as Matt fucked him into the mattress.

Matt leaned over Ollie, bending him nearly in half, as he ran his tongue along the necklace around Ollie's throat. "So fucking sexy. You want me to fill your ass, or cover you in my cum?"

"Oh fuck," Ollie cried. "Just like that, Matt. Oh god, fill my ass. I'm gonna come."

The first splatters of his orgasm hit his chin as Matt pounded his prostate, milking every drop out of him before following suit. He heard Matt cry out and felt his cock jolt inside him as he slowed his thrusts into sharp jerky movements.

Matt pressed his forehead to Ollie's as he caught his breath. "So. Fucking. Perfect. I love you."

"I love you too," Ollie replied and opened his mouth to Matt's tongue.

"I want to spend weekends on the Cape now that the weather is warming up," Matt said over dinner later. "And then starting in July, we can stay for weeklong stretches. We can leave your car there to use and take the ferry," he added. "Starting this weekend."

"Sounds good for most of this month, but summer is polo season," Ollie answered warily.

"What?" Matt frowned. "What does that mean?"

"It means there's a match every Sunday at two, starting the last weekend in May," Ollie replied, taking a bite of his chicken shawarma. "Not to mention the club games mid-week, and tournaments."

Matt looked at his plate and nodded slowly. "So . . . you're not coming to the Cape at all? I'm going to be by myself on the weekends?" he asked with a look of annoyance.

"That's not what I said. It just means I leave on Sunday morning, and I will be back to the beach at night or meet you in town." He put his fork down as the knot in his belly tightened. "Please come watch a match. If you hate it, I'll stop. I won't be able to enjoy it if you're grumpy."

"What I hate, Ollie, is the thought of being alone at the beach. If you're only gone Sundays, that's fine." He popped two pieces of chicken into his mouth and a forkful of rice, his cheek bulging with the large bite. "I'll come to the first match. Is Bill playing or watching?"

"Bill is quite good," Ollie said with a smile that barely contained his relief. "He's playing. He's a really great number two. His handicap is zero, which for someone who's not played for so long is actually better than it might sound."

"What's a handicap? Is it like in golf? And what do you mean number two and the other numbers you and Bill were rattling off last year? And what did Bill mean when he didn't question your skill?"

Matt's fired off questions made Ollie chuckle softly. "Handicaps are what you score in an average game, ten-goal being the highest. There are less than ten players in the *world* with that rating right now, and of course they're all professionals. Zero is actually quite normal in the world of club polo. Some people are minus one, or minus two." Ollie shrugged. "There are four players in the game, all numbered. One is a scorer, two is a feeder and defense for the other team's number three. Three is the tactical leader, playing both offense and defense, and four is the back, guarding the goal. That's the simplified description, but on the field, it can be different. All hands in and all."

Matt sat back in his chair. "And you play number three?"

Ollie nodded.

"And this makes you a better player than everyone else? Is that what Bill meant?"

"No," Ollie laughed and felt himself blush. "It just means you can't be a shitty player and play number three."

Matt nodded with a smile. "I'm guessing in your case it means you're a better player than everyone else, Mr. Humble." He scooped more chicken and onions from the bowl and added rice, pausing to take a big bite. "You're better than everyone at everything." He gestured to his plate. "In the kitchen, in business, and especially in the bedroom." He winked. "What was your goal count when you played?"

"Four," Ollie said quietly and held Matt's gaze. "Five and above are considered good enough to play pro."

Matt took a deep breath and let it out. "Of course you were that good. I can't wait to see you in action on horseback. Yet another field for you to conquer."

"*You're* better than everyone, at everything." Ollie smiled as his stomach fluttered. "I love you."

Matt cleaned the kitchen while Ollie went to his office to check on west coast business. He scraped the plates into the sink and loaded the dishwasher, lost in thought. Listening to Bill and David discussing private school and legacy and polo last year on the Cape had made him feel like a child again, listening to his wealthy peers discussing vacation homes, and boats, and private schools.

No one dared tease him for what he lacked because of his size and popularity, though everyone knew his family was solidly working class. His family, four sisters and his parents, lived in the smallest house in the neighborhood. It was a three-bedroom cape-style with one bathroom, and his parents' bedroom was the former den on the first floor. There were so many people living under a tiny roof, wearing clothes his mother made for them. His father drove a work truck and his mother a used minivan in a town of Mercedeses, and BMWs, and Range Rovers.

Discovering that Ollie had come from a life of privilege beyond the middle-class existence Matt had assumed had taken him by surprise. To find out that David had come from a legacy background like Bill, was also unexpected. Ollie had later assured him that their difference in upbringing didn't matter, and that he wouldn't play polo if Matt didn't want him to, which of course had made Matt feel like a prick; like he was so insecure he couldn't handle his boyfriend playing a sport of the wealthy.

Matt shook his head. He would never deny Ollie. It took a bit of getting used to, but the thought of seeing him play filled him with pride, and not a little bit of heat. He closed the dishwasher and washed his hands. He took the kitchen towel and dried his hands as he walked down the hall.

Ollie looked up from his computer as Matt came into his office. "I'm almost finished."

"Don't mind me," Matt replied and walked to the built-in bookcase. He opened a medium-sized box on the middle shelf and took out a small bottle from underneath some papers.   *Ollie wasn't wrong about one in every room*, he thought with a smirk as he turned to look at Ollie with a salacious grin. "I'm ready for my lap dance."

"Christ, Lieutenant," Ollie laughed. "How long has that been there? You really are *such* a perv."

Matt shrugged. "You love it."

"I do. I really do." Ollie stood aside as Matt sat in his chair and gave him an expectant look.

Matt turned his head to look at Ollie after pulling back on his sweatpants. "I'm shopping for a boat."

Ollie laughed still breathless and weak-kneed as he wiped the cum from his leg with the towel Matt handed him. "You want a vehicle for every travel scenario, don't you? Are you going to buy a train next?"

Ollie shrieked as Matt jabbed his tickle spot.

"Yes, and I'm going to make you wear a conductor uniform, complete with a silly little hat, and then, in a stunning reversal, I will punch your ticket." Matt tickled him again and pulled him against his body, running his hands down Ollie's naked back to cup his bare bottom. He gazed at Ollie's laughing face. "I love you, Oliver Turner."

"I love you, Matthew Dion."

10

Bad Pennies

OLLIE'S MIND WAS on the upcoming weekend trip to Truro and the first polo match of the season in Dover on Sunday. He felt a thrill in his belly knowing Matt would be there to see him play. The phone on his desk buzzed sharply, interrupting his thoughts.

"Yes, Kerry?"

"There's an Andrew Taylor here to see you, sir. Said he has an appointment. . . ." Her voice and the added 'sir' indicated that she knew there was nothing on Ollie's calendar.

Ollie frowned, his happy feeling disappearing abruptly as his stomach clenched. He stole a quick glance through the glass door into Matt's empty office. "Send him in." He pushed the button to end the call and stood, buttoning his suit coat.

The door opened and Andy, wearing a navy suit with a white shirt and maroon tie, came through, closing it firmly behind him.

"Hello, Ollie," Andy said with a cocky smile and shook Ollie's hand across his desk.

"Andy," Ollie said cautiously, looking at the folder in Andy's other hand. "Please, sit." Ollie gestured to one of the chairs in front of his desk.

Andy looked across the desk at Ollie as he sat down. "You moved offices. Took me a minute to find you."

"Sorry?" Ollie unbuttoned his coat and sat.

"Your business card you gave me at Christmas. Had your Kendall Square address, but now you're here in the Seaport." Andy looked around at Ollie's large, sunny office overlooking the Boston Harbor. "Nice fucking office, Ollie. Right next to the big boss." He nodded his head toward Matt's office next door. "Your secretaries sit across from each other. That's pretty cozy."

"What are you doing here, Andy?" Ollie ignored his comments. "You back in Boston for the summer again?"

"I'm here because you are dodging my emails," Andy replied pointedly. "And I plan on being in Boston, indefinitely."

"Oh, did you send me something? I never got it," Ollie replied somewhat truthfully. The business card he'd given Andy had his public email address; an account Kerry monitored. He had told her to mark them as spam after she forwarded him the first one.

"Fuck you, Ollie. You're a terrible liar." Andy pulled a face and leaned back in the chair. "But never mind. I'm here to apply for a job, and I expect I will be given one. It's not too much to ask. I really just want a visa."

"Andy. I think if you want a job, it's not wise to curse at and disparage the man you are trying to get to hire you," Ollie said coldly, irritated to his core.

"Ollie, I tried the nice route. I tried the HR route. And then I tried the direct route." He narrowed his eyes. "Now I have to try the brutal route."

"What do you mean?"

Andy pulled out his phone and began swiping through. "You said no one here knows you're gay. I'm guessing you would really hate for anyone to find out that you are." He looked up at Ollie. "And *emphatically so.*" He pressed a button on his phone and Ollie heard moaning as Andy held up the phone so Ollie could see the screen.

Ollie's stomach dropped and his mouth went dry. It was a grainy, but unmistakable, video of Andy fucking teenage Ollie, his body lean and smooth. Andy was just as young and just as lean, gripping Ollie's hips as he thrust in and out while Ollie moaned and panted Andy's name. Ollie couldn't look away. His breath shallow and panicked as he heard his tinny-sounding voice on the phone speaker, say 'flip me over. I want to come.'

Ollie gasped lightly. "When? I never gave you permission." He tore his eyes away to look at Andy with a frown.

Andy shrugged with a self-satisfied expression and turned the phone. He watched the screen, his eyes turning hot as he made a low sound. "Oh, this is the best part. I come all over your face." Loud moans came from the phone.

"Turn that off," Ollie commanded in a hard tone as his stomach burned with horror.

Ollie caught movement through the glass door out of the corner of his eye. Matt was back from his meeting and putting his suit coat on the back of his chair.

Shit! he thought desperately. "What do you want?"

"I want you to give me a job, pay me a lot of money in said job, and in return I won't show this to anyone." Andy turned his phone off with a smirk.

"I can't do that," Ollie said in a choked voice as he felt the walls closing in on him.

"Bullshit!" Andy said in a loud voice and sat forward in his chair. "You can do anything here. I know what a general counsel does. And you, here, next to the boss? Says pretty loud and clear your word carries weight. You've got your finger in every pot in this company. And speaking of fingers, and dicks, in pots. . . ." He bit his bottom lip and waggled his phone. "I'd hate to have to show this to anyone."

Ollie turned his head at the sound of the connecting door being opened. Matt came through and pulled up short at the sight of Andy. Matt was dressed in black suit pants, a lavender Brooks Brothers shirt, and a dark purple silk tie. He was wearing the trident collar bar that Ollie had given him for their first Christmas together through his tie and collar.

"Oliver. I didn't see a meeting on your calendar," Matt stated simply.

Ollie and Andy stood when Matt spoke. "Matthew, this is Andy—"

"Mr. Dion. Andrew Taylor." Andy didn't wait for Ollie to finish. He extended his hand.

Matt looked at it briefly and skimmed his eyes over Andy before glancing at Ollie. Ollie winced at the tightness in his expression.

"Sit," Matt ordered them both, looking back at Andy without shaking his hand. "Aren't you a waiter?" he asked in a derisive tone.

Andy looked slightly taken aback before sitting in his chair. "I was last year, while I was looking for other work. I have a degree, and I'm here to see Ollie about a job." He glanced at Ollie with a smile. "He told me to come see him."

Matt looked at Ollie. "Is that so?" he asked in a casual tone that was anything but.

"We knew each other during undergrad," Ollie answered stiffly, choosing his words carefully in front of Andy, so as not to sound like a defensive lover. The nervous knot in his stomach continued to tighten under Matt's simmering expression.

Matt raised his eyebrows and looked back at Andy. "Let me see your resume."

Andy pulled a piece of paper out of the folder he had placed on Ollie's desk and handed it to Matt.

Matt took it and ripped it in half before dropping it in the trash can next to Ollie's desk. Andy stared with wide eyes while Matt looked at Ollie calmly.

"You seem out of sorts, Oliver. Something the matter?"

Ollie slid his glance away, his stomach churning, the blood loud in his ears. He closed his eyes and swallowed roughly, then opened them to look at Matt.

"At university, I, uh, experimented." Ollie glanced briefly at Andy. "He filmed me, us, without my knowledge or consent. I'm not gay, Matthew," he added earnestly for the sake of the lie.

Andy snorted. Matt's eyes went to Andy like a whip and narrowed. He stepped in front of Andy, positioning himself between Ollie and

Andy. He leaned his hip against the desk, nearly looming over Andy in his chair and crossed his arms, his biceps bulging over his clenched fists.

"Is that right?" Matt asked.

Andy looked away briefly, clearly uncomfortable with Matt's proximity. "Yes. We had *sex*. Sometimes I filmed us."

Matt raised his eyebrows and began unbuttoning and cuffing the sleeves of his shirt, not taking his eyes off Andy as his biceps flexed menacingly under the material. Ollie saw Andy's eyes lingering on Matt's white gold, blue-faced, Submariner Rolex before turning back to Matt's face.

"You showed him, or told him this?" Matt crossed his arms again and gestured with a head nod over his shoulder at Ollie.

"I showed him."

"Show me."

"Matt, no!" Ollie said urgently. The knot in his stomach moved to his lower intestines and churned uncomfortably.

Matt turned his head toward Ollie without taking his eyes off Andy. "It's okay, Oliver." He raised his brows expectantly at Andy and held out his hand.

Andy frowned and then opened his phone with his thumbprint. He reloaded the video and turned the phone to Matt.

Matt took it from his hand and swiped the video away as it began to play, then he quickly swiped into the phone settings. He changed the auto-lock feature on the screen so it would never go to sleep and then went into Andy's cloud storage.

"Hey!" Andy exclaimed once he realized what Matt was doing and reached for his phone.

Matt grabbed Andy's hand without looking and twisted his arm, bending his wrist backwards painfully. Andy sat forward in the chair with a yelp. From Ollie's vantage point it looked as though Matt hadn't move at all.

"I need your thumb, thank you," Matt said calmly.

Andy squirmed. "No!"

"The phone doesn't care whether your thumb is attached to your body or not. Stop. Resisting," Matt commanded in a harsh tone.

Andy complied. Matt released his wrist after unlocking Andy's cloud account and began swiping through Andy's videos.

"Looks like you have a very illegal perversion, Mr. Taylor. I'm guessing none of these other men knew you filmed them." He met Andy's eye and held his gaze for a brief moment.

Matt then reached behind him for Ollie's desk phone and pressed the speaker button. "Kerry. Call security and have them wait by your desk."

"Yes, sir," Kerry said in her no-nonsense voice, as though she'd heard this command regularly.

Andy looked at Ollie worriedly and opened his mouth to speak.

"I don't hire criminals," Matt interjected. "And that you came to threaten Oliver in exchange for a job was a potentially fatal mistake." He stood and looked down at Andy. "Oliver is one of the best lawyers in the western world. He would crush you in a lawsuit. In a courtroom." Matt looked down at Andy's phone in his hand. "If you show this video to anyone or anything else you might have in your *spank bank* having to do with him, if I get a whiff of *anything* having to do with Oliver, whether it's from you or not, or if you try to contact him again, you won't be dealing with him." Matt gestured his head back at Ollie. "You'll be dealing with me. And I will crush you so hard, you will wish I put a bullet in your head instead."

Matt continued to stare down at Andy, his body calm, but Ollie could see his fury coiled within.

"If you doubt the sincerity of my threat, Google me." He pocketed Andy's phone and pulled out his money clip. He peeled off five, one hundred-dollar bills and passed them to Andy with his fingertips. "Now get out of my sight." He stepped back to let Andy stand.

"Give me my phone," Andy said in a quavering voice.

"It's mine now. I just paid you for it." Matt raised his eyebrows challengingly.

"You can't take my phone," Andy stated with indignation.

Matt walked to Ollie's office door. "Call the police. I'm having drinks with Commissioner Evans next week. I'm sure I could push the meeting up to today." He put his hand on the doorknob. "If you were smart, you would have done your research before even coming here, because now you've put yourself on my radar, and that is not anywhere you wanna be." He opened the door and nodded at the building security guard standing by Kerry's desk. He looked back at Andy. "Get the fuck out of here."

Matt closed the door behind Andy after making sure the security guard had a firm grip on his arm. He strode back to the door to his office.

"I'm sorry, Matt," Ollie said, swallowing the lump in his throat.

Matt made a disgruntled sound and walked through the doorway without looking at Ollie.

Ollie followed him. "Give me the phone."

Matt ignored him and opened the bottom drawer of the credenza under the window behind his desk. He pulled out a laptop, one of the few computers that wasn't hooked into the network. Working quickly, he connected Andy's phone and began backing it up, downloading all the data and media from it and from Andy's cloud account onto the computer. He scanned Andy's emails quickly.

Matt pressed the call button on his desk phone. "Stacey, send for Claudio."

He took out a piece of paper and wrote something down. There was a knock a moment later.

"Come in," Matt called.

Claudio, a recent grad from MIT with shoulder-length wavy brown hair, stepped through and closed the door behind him. He glanced at Ollie standing by Matt's desk before turning his attention back to Matt.

"We've got a client who wants to see how our product works. Send an email to this test address." Matt handed him the piece of paper across his desk. "Embed it with the worst malware we use for testing, the kind that destroys everything a person has on their computer and anything that connect to it. Put it in an email with a job offer that has visa sponsorship, from the company written below. Look up their logo, marketing, etc., make it look legit. Cover your trail, be a ghost, and let me know *in person* once it's been activated. Trace the clicks, then I can follow up with the client."

"No problem, Mr. Dion. I'll have it sent within the hour."

"Great. You'll have a bonus in your check this week. I want to show the client how easy it is to have your life's work destroyed." He smiled coldly.

Claudio closed the door behind him as Matt turned his attention to the phone whose contents had finished downloading. Matt disconnected it and swiped through to the videos.

No! Ollie jolted himself into action after listening to Matt lay out his retribution.

"Matt," Ollie said urgently. "Don't. Please."

Matt pressed play and the sounds of moaning played on medium volume. He watched, his face a cold mask, as Andy pounded in and out of Ollie. He swiped the video off and clicked on the next grainy video of Ollie sitting on the end of a bed as Andy undressed in front of him, and pushed his cock into Ollie's mouth. There was no mistaking that it was a younger, naked Ollie. His hair was shorter, and he had a stack of embroidered bracelets on his left wrist. Andy was moaning and talking quietly to Ollie as he ran his hands through his hair.

"Your technique has improved," Matt commented in a flat voice. "Did you suck your way through college?"

"Fuck you, Matt!" Ollie exclaimed and reached for the phone.

Matt grabbed his hand and twisted it like he did to Andy. Ollie inhaled sharply and bit his lip to prevent crying out.

"He's got quite a few of you on here." Matt looked up at Ollie. "You never once suspected that he was filming you?" he asked suspiciously.

"No. Let go of my hand." Ollie fought the urge to squirm, which would only make the pain worse.

"No."

"Ah, I see. Matt the Machine is here now. There go my feelings." Ollie shook his head angrily. "You know, that was *years* ago. You can see that for yourself. This has nothing to do with us."

Matt grimaced. "That man came here with these, looking to blackmail you, threatening to expose you. It very much has to do with us."

He began scrolling through Andy's message inbox. "This guy has amateur written all over him, but you better hope he doesn't have copies somewhere that I can't reach. If he surfaces again, if he so much as sends you a smoke signal, I'll kill him. He contacts you and you don't tell me?" Matt raised his eyebrows. "You and I are gonna have a problem." He let go of Ollie's hand and began swiping through the photos on Andy's phone.

Ollie felt a shiver of disquiet at Matt's tone. "I wouldn't keep that from you. Don't threaten me."

Matt's hand stilled over the phone. He expanded a photo and closed his eyes before holding it up for Ollie to see.

"Oh, no?" he asked in a hard voice.

On the phone was a photo of Ollie sitting with Ivan at the pub in Chelsea, taken from Andy's vantage point across the bar. George and Sahil had their backs to the camera. Matt touched the image and swiped to see four more photos of Ollie laughing and talking, and one with his hand in his hair, looking at George across the table from him. The date showed it was taken six months ago, when Ollie was home for Christmas.

Ollie's stomach sank. "Matt, you can see the photos were taken from another table. I spoke with him for less than five minutes. He asked me for my business card. You can ask any of the friends I was with, though you should trust me and my word. I've never lied to you," he implored. "We left the pub as soon as we finished our drinks. I couldn't wait to get out of there."

Just then the phone screen went black; Andy must have deactivated it remotely. Matt tossed it on his desk, closed the laptop and strode into the bathroom, slamming the door behind him.

Ollie felt his throat swell. He picked up the laptop and went quickly into his office. He typed in the password and began deleting the videos of him. He then went into the trash folder and permanently deleted them, but knew he needed to scrub it even further. Matt appeared in his underwear on his side of the door. He grabbed a t-shirt, shorts and a pair of socks from the top drawer of the credenza and dressed quickly at his desk. Ollie watched as he laced his sneakers and took his ear buds from his desktop. He saw Matt frown when he noticed the laptop missing.

He looked at Ollie through the door and came through. "Give me the laptop," he ordered with his hand out.

"No." Ollie shook his head. "I've deleted the videos of me."

Matt took a step forward. "Give me the laptop," he repeated angrily. "That wasn't a request."

"No. You didn't listen to me when I asked you not to watch the videos. I'm not going to listen to you." Ollie held Matt's gaze as his stomach quaked and churned. "Go for your run. I'll see you at home."

Matt stared at him with a fathomless expression. Something passed behind his eyes and he turned and left.

Matt didn't come home for hours. Ollie finally gave up waiting and hid the laptop between the sheet pans in the kitchen of his garden-level condo, where he knew Matt would never look, and went to bed.

Ollie woke in the dark to the strong smell of tequila and rolled over to find Matt laying on top of the covers looking at him. The light in the hallway outside the bedroom outlined Matt's shape but hid his face.

"Why do you smell like tequila?" Ollie asked sleepily.

Matt made an irritated sound. "You're the Oxford educated lawyer, with his MBA," Matt emphasized with an obnoxious tone. "You tell me, Mr. Smarty-pants."

"You said you don't drink it because it makes you angry," Ollie said as he came awake instantly and struggled to sit up. He found himself pinned under the sheets by Matt's heavy body and stilled warily.

"It does. But I drank it because I was *already* angry. I wondered if they would cancel each other out." Matt looked around the room in the dim light. "They didn't," he whispered in a hard voice.

Ollie felt a flicker of fear. "What's going on, Lieutenant?"

Matt looked up at the ceiling. "Where's the laptop?" He slid his glance to Ollie.

"No, Matt. Christ, what time is it? Please, come to bed." Ollie reached his arm out to touch Matt's face in hopes of calming him.

Matt grabbed Ollie's hand and squeezed the fleshy part of his palm near his thumb. Ollie let out a breath of air, refusing to cry out despite the excruciating pain. He was wide awake now.

Matt's eyes flared. "I love how you never make a sound."

He ran his other hand over Ollie's extended arm, pausing briefly at Ollie's elbow, while maintaining the pressure in Ollie's palm. He closed his eyes and released Ollie suddenly. He rolled away and left the room as silently as he'd entered.

Ollie strained to hear where he went, but was too disconcerted to get up and look for him. He fell asleep waiting for Matt to come back.

11

Round and Round

OLLIE'S ALARM WOKE HIM at seven and he looked at Matt's untouched side of the bed with worry. There was no note on the pillow saying that he was out for a run or that he'd gone to work.

"Matt?" he called into the hallway, listening for a response or movement.

He showered and dressed for work. He put on a navy Tom Ford suit with brown leather shoes, styled his hair with a small dab of styling serum and combed it off his face to let it dry with a sheen.

Downstairs, the coffee maker was cold and empty. Ollie frowned. Matt always programmed it the night before. He locked up with a sigh and got in his car, noticing Matt's Range Rover still in its spot. He wondered briefly if Matt was asleep in one of the guest rooms, but at that hour it was more likely that he ran to work.

He stopped in the building café for coffee and a breakfast sandwich after parking in the garage and went up to his office.

"Morning, Kerry, Stacey."

"Morning," they answered in unison, the dramatic events of the previous day going unmentioned.

Ollie closed his office door and walked the length of the room to look into Matt's office. There was no sign of him. He turned to his desk with a sigh and sat down to lose himself in emails.

Ollie had lunch at Del Frisco's with Bryan Green, their VP of Sales, and then had a meeting with his legal team in the large glass conference room down the hall from his office suite. There was still no sign of Matt.

"Have you heard from Matt?" he asked Stacey when he returned to their office suite.

"No." She shook her head.

Ollie frowned. "Did he have anything on his calendar for today? It looked blank when I checked."

"He had me clear his schedule yesterday."

Ollie walked into his office without responding as his mind raced. He got out his phone and dialed Matt, frowning when it went straight to voicemail. His mouth dropped open and a knot of worry formed in the pit of his stomach knowing Matt never turned off his phone.

"Lock up. I won't be back," he said to Kerry as he walked out. "And cancel my four o'clock, please."

He drove home in a blur, and parked next to Matt's car which was still in its spot. He went through the townhouse floor by floor, room by room, calling for him.

"Matthew?" His worry built steadily. He looked through his condo and paused to think. He crossed to the kitchen cabinet with the sheet pans, panic in his chest. The laptop was right where he left it. He exhaled with relief.

"You know, I was making myself crazy looking for that thing yesterday and this morning," Matt said from the doorway. He was wearing grey sweatpants and his favorite US Navy t-shirt. His jaw was dark with whiskers and his expression was ringing a warning bell in Ollie's head.

"Jesus Christ!" Ollie cried with a yelp, his heart nearly jumping out of his chest. "What the fuck are you doing sneaking up on me?"

Matt approached the kitchen island with an inscrutable expression. "And then I realized," he continued, ignoring Ollie. "I didn't need to look for it; I only needed to wait for you to. Clever hiding place."

Ollie swallowed and shook his head. "I've deleted the videos of me, I told you. And you shouldn't watch them anyway. Why are you doing this?"

"That asshole came to my place of business. He threatened my right-hand man," Matt said in a cold voice. "And you saw him over Christmas and never said anything to me." He shook his head. "That makes me very angry."

"There was no sense in mentioning it. I told you we spoke for maybe five minutes." He shrugged tensely.

"You gave him your business card!" Matt spat. "He asked you to help him get a job, one you knew you would never give him, that you knew I would never let you give him. If you had told me that I would have dealt with him preemptively." Matt thinned his lips. "Five minutes of investigating and I would have found all that shit and wiped it. And then I would have barred him from entering this country."

Ollie looked at him with shock.

"Ollie," Matt shook his head, "you're too naïve. Dealing with cock-suckers like him is what the US military trained me for. Don't feel any sympathy for that douche."

"I don't," Ollie replied. "I'm thankful that you handled it, because he frightened me yesterday."

Matt put his hands on the island, arms straight, and hung his head for a moment as he looked at the ground. "I wasn't scared of him," Matt replied and straightened to look at Ollie. "But he put fear in me." He pointed at the laptop. "That *whore* has quite the vast spank bank, and I don't recall seeing a condom in yours." Matt narrowed his eyes. "How many men have you let *fuck* you without a condom?"

Ollie felt the blood drain from his face. "Matt, we were eighteen. And I tested regularly."

"Answer my question," he snapped.

"I'm not going to answer that," Ollie said quietly. "How about you, Lieutenant? You live in a glass house then?"

"As a matter of fact, I do." Matt sneered. "You are the only person in my *entire* life that I fucked without one."

Ollie blew out a small breath at that heady revelation. "I've been tested. I'm clean." He took a step toward him. "Matthew, darling. I'm sorry, please."

"I knew you weren't a virgin," Matt closed his eyes, "but seeing that. Him. The reality—I don't care for it." He looked at Ollie and stepped back from the island. "Go get tested again."

"I told you, I'm clean." Ollie frowned. "That's his spank bank not mine. I think you're confusing the two of us now, Lieutenant. I haven't been with anyone but you since my last test, and that I only got as a formality, not because of worry. I like peace of mind too."

"I've never been tested as a formality."

"Well, you should. Straight people can get HIV too you know. Not to mention a slew of other STIs. You wear a condom for your blow jobs?" He raised his eyebrows. "Speaking of *whores*, you most assuredly have had more sex partners than I have," Ollie said harshly. "I've been with five other men, the last of whom I wouldn't even have been with if not for you dumping me for Sam. I prefer monogamy."

Matt rolled his tongue through his mouth irritatedly before leaving the room.

Ollie heard the front door close a moment later. He shook his head and opened the laptop, wondering what it was that Matt was so eager to discover. He went through and deleted the photos that Andy had taken of him, and made sure there was nothing else about him anywhere. He closed it, and left it on the island.

Ollie couldn't focus on work and eventually went to watch a show in the home theater on the third floor. He had made dinner and left it on the stove for Matt after forcing himself to eat a small plate. He turned the TV off at ten and went to brush his teeth.

Matt suddenly appeared in the doorway of the bathroom.

Ollie jumped. "Jesus Christ, Matt! Why do you keep doing that?"

Matt raked his eyes over Ollie's body and slowed as he scanned over his bare legs. He raised his eyebrows, his mouth in a thin line, and walked past him to the shower. He turned it on and stripped off his sweaty clothes while he waited for the water to heat. Ollie spit and rinsed his toothbrush as the hairs on his neck stood up before turning to leave.

"Where you going?" Matt asked from inside the shower. "Get in here," he ordered.

Ollie hesitated, his senses on high alert. "I have to work tomorrow."

"So do I."

"This feels like New Year's," Ollie said in a cautious tone.

Matt looked at the floor and then back at Ollie. "You can take tomorrow off."

Ollie closed his eyes and furrowed his brow. He wanted to say no but felt himself stir at Matt's tone. That New Year's incident was over two ago, and while Matt had been especially brutal that night, Ollie was more hurt by the damage to his heart than by the pain to his body. In fact, it was because of Matt that he'd discovered he actually liked a bit of pain during sex, though not all the time and certainly not when Matt was this angry. With a tiny sliver of fear, he stripped off his briefs and opened the shower door.

Matt was rinsing the soap from his body, the bubbles huddling together before escaping quickly down the drain like a herd of antelope running from a lion. Ollie ran his eyes over Matt's glorious physique. There wasn't an ounce of fat on his body, only muscle and veins under beautiful, tan skin. His chest had a light dusting of hair that narrowed to a strip under his bellybutton which led to a manicured nest around Matt's (fully aroused) treasure.

Matt's eyes were dark as they followed Ollie's every step. He turned on the steam, which warmed the large shower stall and waited for Ollie to come closer.

"Put your hands on your head," Matt commanded in his gravelly voice and waited as Ollie cautiously complied. "Turn around."

Ollie turned and waited, his fingers laced atop his head and goosebumps on his skin. Matt appeared silently behind him; the heat of his body and his breath on the back of his neck caused Ollie to shiver. He felt Matt touch the scar on his shoulder gently with one finger as he nudged Ollie closer to the wall and spread his legs by kicking the inside of Ollie's ankles with his foot.

"I'm gonna hurt you, Ollie, and you're going to let me. Okay?" Matt whispered, his lips touching Ollie's ear.

Ollie swallowed and nodded. "Okay," he breathed.

Matt took a deep breath and let it out with a moan. He licked Ollie's ear before spitting in his hand. Two fingers breached Ollie without warning and were quickly replaced by Matt's spit-slicked cock. In one hard thrust, Ollie's breath was stolen, and Matt's groin was flush against his ass. Matt paused with a grunt and gripped the back of Ollie's neck. Ollie struggled to breathe and realized that was what Matt was waiting for, because as soon as he managed two gasps, Matt began driving into him in short, bruising strokes.

It wasn't just the pain Ollie found pleasurable; it was how turned on Matt was. His bruising possessive grip, his grunts that were almost primal, and especially the angrily muttered Italian that rose in cadence as Matt got closer and closer to coming all went straight to Ollie's cock. He closed his eyes and pressed his ass out toward Matt, changing the angle just enough for Matt to pound his sweet spot inside.

"No, Ollie," Matt gritted out and nudged him straighter. He grabbed one of Ollie's wrists and twisted his arm back and up between them.

Ollie gasped sharply at the pain in his bicep. Matt put his other hand around Ollie's throat and squeezed.

"You get to enjoy it when I'm ready for you to, and not a second before." Matt bit the side of Ollie's neck, where his shirt collar would hide any mark, and sucked determinedly. "You're mine. And when I'm done marking you, and fucking you until you can't walk, you'll know it with as much certainty as I do."

Ollie would've moaned at that if he could breathe. He was beginning to see spots, which only heightened everything he was feeling. He was desperate for Matt's touch or permission to touch himself. Matt increased his pace, seemingly determined to fuck Ollie into oblivion, and his breathing grew ragged. He shifted his hand from Ollie's throat to his hip and squeezed brutally as he nudged Ollie into a more bent position. Ollie gasped for air and winced at the pain in his arm and then moaned as Matt's cock lit him up. It was dizzying from more than just a lack of oxygen.

"Give me your hand," Matt commanded, and Ollie eagerly complied. Matt spit into his palm. "I want fireworks on the marble, Oliver." Matt nudged Ollie's leg up onto the built-in bench and continued to drive into Ollie. "Tell me how no one can fuck you like I can."

Ollie fisted his cock eagerly. That it was Matt's saliva only fueled his desire. "No one can compare. Oh god, I'm so close."

"Come for me."

Ollie was coming in hot spurts, crying out Matt's name, before Matt even finished his command. It was a second later that Matt cried out and slowed as he leaned forward and bit Ollie's shoulder, right over the bitemark scar from last time. Matt thrust into him a few more times with the aftershock of his drawn-out orgasm, and released Ollie's arm, helping him straighten it before squeezing Ollie's back against his chest.

"*Sei mio*," Matt whispered, his lips on Ollie's ear.

"I am," Ollie replied and fought the urge to rub his sore arm. It felt like Matt had pulled something, but the pain was nothing in comparison to the pain in his ass, and shoulder.

Matt pulled away and stood under the shower, washing himself before handing the soap to Ollie and leaving the stall.

12

Willing Captive

OLLIE WOKE EARLY and everything was sore. He looked at the pillow next to him and saw a note.

Gone to work. Sleep in. I'll be home for dinner. —M

Ollie rolled over and did as he was told, not ready to get up anyway.

The next time he woke it was near noon. He got out of bed and took two ibuprofen with a big glass of water. The coffee was cold, the machine having turned itself off hours before. Ollie put some in a glass and added ice. He made himself a sandwich and ate while looking out the window at the cars and pedestrians that passed intermittently.

Matt hadn't said anything to him after the shower and then had woken him in the night, making a sound in his throat requesting consent, which Ollie had given freely. It wasn't quite the punishment of New Year's. This time Matt had been kind enough to use a dab of lube in bed, but it still hurt, and he used the same controlling restraints. The bed gave Matt more freedom of movement, more positions he could bend Ollie into, and Ollie felt as though he had run a marathon on his hands and knees. Every muscle was sore.

He left his dirty dishes on the island and went to take a shower, stripping his clothes off in the bedroom and dropping them as he walked. He turned on the water as he got lost in thought about the care Matt had taken after. Matt had cleaned him gently with a damp cloth, stroking him and kissing the bruises one by one as he whispered endearments in Italian. Then he held him tightly until Ollie fell asleep. It was weird, but strangely soothing even as it made him cry softly, and it helped keep the resentment about his arm at bay.

Claudio visited Matt mid-morning to report that the malware was accepted. Andy was clearly eager for a visa, and Matt was going to make certain he never got one. It was a slow burn virus designed to infect quietly so that it could spread to other devices before melting down.

Matt looked out his window at the harbor below; the boats and sunshine in stark contrast with the dark feeling inside him. His love and desire for Ollie overwhelmed him at times. The spark between them had ignited so quickly he never stopped to wonder, even for a moment, about Ollie's sexual history or responsibility. He never thought to ask for test results.

When he saw videos of that *bastard* with Ollie, and the plethora of other men, Matt had felt the cold blade of fear. He had nearly collapsed on his run as he thought about sexually transmitted infections. He was so angry when he got home, and the tequila shots only made it worse. The urge to hurt Ollie, to snap his arm, had overwhelmed and disturbed him enough that he fled.

Matt had been angry with Ollie, but he was furious with Andy, and Ollie was right: he was conflating the two of them. His anger had lessened a degree when he returned home after their argument and found that Ollie had left the laptop on the island for him. He went through it carefully, searching for insight in case Andy was stupid enough to retaliate. What had happened later with Ollie in the shower, Ollie in bed, with Ollie taking his anger and giving so much in return, calmed Matt's turbulent soul.

Matt blinked himself out of his musing back to the harbor view outside his window and powered down his computer. He stood, pocketed his phone and key fob, and left his office with a nod at Stacey to lock up. He was fully focused on Ollie, his *treasure*, the whole way home.

"Something smells amazing," Matt said as he came into the kitchen and put his folio down on the island next to his phone.

Ollie tapped the spoon on the rim of the pot and turned from the stove. He ran his eyes over Matt and found him to be confidently nonchalant but with something like apprehension behind his eyes.

"Hello, gorgeous. How was work?" Ollie smiled and ran his hand through his hair.

Matt crossed the room with a smile and tilted Ollie's face up with his knuckles under Ollie's chin. "Missed you, but I hope you got rest, sleeping beauty." He brushed his lips across Ollie's with a gentle kiss that stirred Ollie's emotions. He stepped back and then headed for the bar between the kitchen and the living room. "You want a drink?"

"I've got a beer, thanks. And there's wine with dinner."

"What are we having?"

"Seared tuna with a ginger, scallion, and soy dipping sauce, coconut brown rice with lime and cilantro, and charred broccolini with a chili garlic glaze. There's a spring salad mix with roasted beets and a lemon vinaigrette to start."

"Yum. I'm the luckiest guy in the world." Matt poured a bottle of Fever Tree tonic over his gin and ice and put the glass on the island after taking a sip.

Ollie watched Matt take off his suit coat and drape it on the back of one of the barstools. His shoulders rolled under his shirt with the motion and Ollie couldn't tear his eyes away.

What a specimen of a man. A crazy, mercurial, specimen of a man, Ollie thought as Matt stood in front of him. He had a five o'clock shadow dusting his jaw as it always did at the end of the day. Most men needed two days to grow what Matt produced in mere hours. Ollie needed at least a week, and it never filled in like Matt's.

Ollie wrapped his left arm around Matt's neck, his right too sore to lift, and leaned into Matt's solid body as Matt squeezed him around his waist.

"I love you, Ollie." Matt kissed him softly. "I will never let anyone hurt you or threaten you ever again."

Ollie touched his tongue to Matt's before sweeping it slowly into his mouth. He sighed in unison with Matt's hum. "Who's going to protect me from you, Lieutenant?" he whispered against Matt's lips.

He felt Matt's mouth quirk. "It's why I always ask permission. You can say no. Just remember, it's my job to make sure you never want to." Matt dropped slowly to his knees and pushed Ollie's lounge pants down as he did. "Commando," Matt growled. "You little slut." He grinned up at Ollie and then peppered kisses around Ollie's half-hard cock before taking him in his mouth.

Ollie rolled his head back and ran his hands through Matt's short, soft hair as he felt himself grow hard on Matt's tongue. He kept one eye on the stove, and one eye on what Matt was doing, moaning when Matt rolled his balls between his fingers.

"You need to stir that?" Matt asked, popping off Ollie's dick with a loud smacking sound.

He nudged Ollie's hip, mindful of the bruises there, and guided him to face the stove. Ollie picked up the spoon to stir the rice and nearly dropped it again when Matt spread his ass cheeks and dove in with his soft tongue.

"Christ, Lieutenant. Don't make me burn dinner," Ollie moaned.

"Just kissing you better, babe. I promise I won't let you burn my dinner." Matt squeezed Ollie's ass cheeks gently and went back to his reparations.

"You never talk about your father," Ollie probed later as they lay in bed. He studied Matt's face as he waited for the response.

Matt's brows moved toward each other. "What made you think of my dad?" he asked with a small laugh as his body tensed almost imperceptibly.

Ollie shrugged one shoulder and rolled to face him. He knew Matt was the man he was in large part due to this one-dimensional, mythical man Ollie had only seen in pictures.

"Not anything really. Just thinking that you never talk about him."

Matt put his phone down and turned to face him. "What do you want to know?"

"What was he like? What was his name? I can't believe I don't know his name." Ollie shook his head and frowned at the thought.

"Dominic, but everybody called him Del. Don't ask me why." Matt shrugged. "He was very handsome, very devoted to us, and a very strict Roman Catholic. Ruled with an iron fist."

"I know he was handsome; I've seen the photos. He looked a lot like you," Ollie interjected. "Please tell me he strode about all cocky just like you do."

"Even more so," Matt replied with a laugh, running his hand through his hair before tucking his arm behind his head. "Christ, he was a force. He was so confident, so macho, so 'strong-silent' type. He had a construction company you know, and was very talented. Pretty well connected, worked for a lot of powerful people. That's how I know so many people in high places, low ones too." Matt grinned down at Ollie. "And how I got into the Naval Academy."

"Didn't he want you to go into construction?" Ollie wondered quietly as he tried to picture their father-son relationship.

"He tried. I just didn't have a knack for it. I suppose I went the Navy route as a consolation for him, to really prove my manhood." Matt's mouth twisted ruefully. "He was super strict with my sisters. They weren't allowed to do *anything*. Not date, not go to parties, as I told you, but he was the opposite with me, his only son. Don't get me wrong, I caught the end of his belt a time or two, but with regard to my social and dating life, he really expected me to fuck around. So, I did." He shrugged. "Just not with whom I wanted."

Ollie looked away with a frown. He couldn't even begin to imagine what Matt's childhood must've been like. He was desperate to know more. "When did you lose your virginity?"

"Which one?"

Ollie chuckled at the distinction. "Both I guess."

"I was fifteen with a girl, and seventeen with a boy. Twenty-eight when I gave my first blow job."

Ollie pushed himself up on his elbow as the realization washed over him. "What?! Do you mean me?" he exclaimed.

"Yeah, Ollie. I wasn't sucking anyone's dick but yours." Matt scoffed. "I never wanted to before; it felt too . . . *gay*. Our first time together though, I couldn't fucking wait to taste you. I worried about my technique, but you came in like ninety seconds, so I figured I must have been doing something right," he added with a laugh.

Ollie laughed with him and lay back on the pillow, remembering that night. "Christ. It was *so* good, and I just couldn't believe it was you doing it to me. It was so hot I couldn't help but come."

"It was hot," Matt agreed and then looked away. "Speaking of first times, I told you my dad died never knowing about me. And, while that's technically true, he never *knew*, I think he might have suspected because of that first time for me."

"What do you mean?" Ollie asked as he felt Matt tense.

"It was in Italy. My family went for a few weeks every summer to stay with my father's parents. They had moved back when he graduated high school, like I told you. There was a boy my age, maybe a year younger, who took a shine to me." He shook his head. "I didn't encourage it, but I didn't stop it. It was thrilling." He slid a glance at Ollie. "Do you really wanna hear this?"

"Yes, Matt, I really do," Ollie said quietly, holding himself still, afraid to interrupt the moment for fear of Matt changing his mind.

Matt made a soft sound. "He lived up the street from my grandparents. He was all elbows, and bony knees, and brown skin. He was alright looking. Big doe eyes, lots of curly hair, and he wore these leather sandals that were a size too big." Matt chuckled lightly. "It's interesting the details you remember, because for the life of me I can't actually picture his face or remember his name. Anyway, it was more that he was gay, and made it very clear that he was interested in me, that I found appealing. He took me to some fucking place, I don't remember. I was too horny." Matt laughed, and maybe even blushed, Ollie couldn't tell in the low light. "I came rolling the condom on."

Ollie laughed in disbelief. "Oh, you little amateur."

Matt furrowed his brow with a laugh and pinched Ollie's nipple. "I was, with him. And because I was seventeen, I got hard again almost instantaneously, and I fucked him. God, it was heaven, to my little amateur brain that is. It just felt so right, in a way that the sex I was having with girls didn't.

"It's funny, I clung to those memories like they were religious experiences, even long past when I could actually remember them. Then I met you, and holy shit. It was as if my entire being was turned inside out and put right again. Our first time, I felt it in every cell of my body." Matt stroked Ollie's arm and held his gaze. "I almost came in your mouth the instant you touched me with your tongue," he said, his eyes turning smoky. "I wanted you so badly, and that our sex ended up being earth-shattering?" He shook his head. "I couldn't believe my luck. I still can't. It's only gotten better."

"Christ." Ollie sat up to kiss him, his stomach fluttering wildly with Matt's admission. It was moments and declarations like those that reinforced Ollie's love for Matt. "I want you to finish your story, and then I'm going to take that glorious cock of yours in my mouth and make you see stars."

Matt growled. "Then I'm going to give you the cliff notes version." He laughed as Ollie poked him in the side. "Fine. I guess I fucked him a dozen more times. We were never caught in the act, thank god. But one day when he came around, as he did every day, my dad was there. Usually, he was off visiting cousins and spending the days eating and catching up, but this time he was there. I was so nervous my dad would suspect something, and the boy, well, I guess he was smitten, and a bit obvious about it. My father . . . I'll never forget the look on his face."

Matt winced. "It was *awful*. I chased the kid away and promptly found some teenage girl to fuck around with."

A cloud passed over Matt's face. "When we went back the following year, the kid was gone. I mean *gone*. Apparently, he had disappeared right around when we left. His parents were beside themselves with grief." He closed his eyes. "I never knew if my dad had something to do with it, or maybe the kid hit on the wrong guy, or maybe he was just in the wrong place at the wrong time. But it scared the shit out of me. I was too scared to ask for details. I was too scared to feel sad. And I never fucked another guy, until you."

Ollie felt his eyes go wide as his heart fluttered with fear. He blew out a slow breath. "Holy shit. Do you really think your dad could've had something to do with it?"

Matt opened his eyes and searched Ollie's face with an inscrutable expression. "All I know is I applied for the Naval Academy and cemented Chuck to my side. My father was thrilled. Her family is the *crème de la crème* on both sides, as you know. She's everything he dreamed for me." He puffed out a breath and shook his head with wonder. "That Chuck went along with it, then helped me start my business. That she introduced me to you . . . ? Jesus, Ollie. I *really* hope you understand what a tremendous friend she is. I owe everything to her, and you are the crown jewel of what she has given me." He slid down his pillow and took Ollie in his arms.

Ollie hugged Matt tightly, overwhelmed by Matt's confessions, but single-minded in his need to soothe Matt as he slid even further down.

✳   ✳   ✳

Ollie woke the next morning shortly after Matt left for his run and decided to make coffee and sit on the roof with the newspaper. He pulled on the sheer white lounge pants that made Matt drool and left the stairway door to the roof deck open.

It was a beautiful summer morning, but the sun hadn't yet warmed the air. Ollie purposefully went shirtless, knowing Matt couldn't resist the sight of his puckered nipples and because he hoped for a 'yes' to his proposition. He set the insulated French press on the coffee table next to Matt's favorite mug from their first Christmas together that said, '*tastes like I need a BJ.*'

"You're up early," Matt declared when he appeared at the door, freshly showered and shaved.

"There's coffee. I knew you'd come looking for me," Ollie replied with a seductive smile and watched Matt pour himself coffee.

Matt looked utterly fuckable with his damp hair and clean sweats and tight t-shirt. Ollie's sore asshole twinged unhappily at the thought of sex, and he scowled into his coffee before remembering his plan. He swept his fingers absentmindedly over his nipples, drawing Matt's eye as he joined him on the sectional.

"Let's go to the beach. I don't want to wait until tonight," Ollie said and put the newspaper down. "You can work from there. Please don't say no." He adjusted himself in his pants to be sure the outline of his cock was visible before leaning back against the cushions.

Matt took a deep breath, his eyes shifting between Ollie's nipples and the front of his cotton pants and sighed. "I have a lunch meeting that I can't reschedule."

Ollie wrinkled his nose in disappointment but knew if Matt resisted all that he had on display, then it really was a meeting he couldn't reschedule. "Shite. Well, I don't, so I'll take the ferry. Chuck will get me, or I'll hire a car. We can stay through Monday; the weather looks grand. You come when you can. And then you'll come when you get there," he added suggestively and ran his tongue along the bottom of his upper lip.

Matt grinned. "I hope more than once."

"I will make you come as many times as you want. You know that. Just so long as I do too, and that my ass isn't involved," Ollie added.

Matt reached across the back of the sofa and rubbed his thumb at the base of Ollie's neck. "What about the polo match?"

Ollie looked at his coffee and quelled his rising disappointment. "I can't sit on a horse. And my arm . . . ." He looked at Matt.

Matt slid his glance away. "Well, then I'll come to next week's match." He stood and crossed the deck to the door. "You better call Bill."

Ollie watched him disappear down the stairs.

Would it kill you to show some remorse? To acknowledge that you hurt me? To understand I did nothing wrong?

Ollie put his mug on the table, swiped into his phone for the ferry schedule and thought about shopping with Matt's credit card in Provincetown.

13

Wild Horses

OLLIE WOKE ON SUNDAY to a perfect, sunny June day. Minimal clouds with temperatures expected to be in the seventies. He sighed and looked at the note on the pillow telling him Matt was out for a run, but heard the shower and saw a mug of coffee on his side table. He got out of bed, breaking with tradition because they still couldn't have proper sex anyway, and he was in no mood to give Matt the blow job he was likely expecting.

Ollie slipped on a pair of shorts and a t-shirt and took his coffee downstairs. He pulled out spinach, eggs, and cheese, and the leftover roasted potatoes, and went mindlessly through the motions of making breakfast for them both. He sliced three pieces of sourdough from the bread he bought the day before and put them in the toaster oven while he heated the potatoes with a diced onion and some paprika on the stove.

"Something smells amazing, and I am fucking starving," Matt declared as he came into the kitchen wearing shorts and a tight t shirt, his feet tanned and bare. "I forgive you for leaving the bed," he added with a grin and kissed the back of Ollie's neck.

Ollie smiled and put the omelet, some hash browns, and two thick pieces of buttered toast on a plate and handed it to Matt, along with a glass of grapefruit juice. Matt palmed Ollie's ass in thanks and sat at the big table between the kitchen and the windows overlooking the beach.

Ollie made himself a quick spinach and cheese omelet like Matt's but with two eggs instead of four and sat across from him.

"This is delicious. Thanks, babe," Matt said and covered Ollie's barefoot under the table with his own.

"How was your run?" Ollie asked, still a little too brittle to accept Matt's overtures.

"Perfect. Not a soul in sight. I ended along the shore." Matt finished his eggs and stole a potato off Ollie's plate. "The water is still too cold to swim, but I'm itching to get in."

"What about your wetsuit?"

"Maybe next weekend. I think I'll go to the aquatics center later, swim for a bit." Matt finished his toast.

Ollie swallowed the rising resentment about Matt's full range of motion and his own current physical restrictions and finished his breakfast. He left his plate and all the dirty dishes to Matt's care and went upstairs to brush his teeth and take a quick shower.

"Where you going?" Matt asked when Ollie came down dressed in flat front shorts and an Armani t-shirt.

"I have some errands and going to the market for dinner things. I was thinking vegetarian tonight." Ollie went to the cabinet to get the reusable grocery bags.

"Sounds great."

Ollie gave Matt a passing glance and took the Range Rover key off the hook by the door and left. He went to the garden store for new pruning shears and fertilizer for the roses, and then to Hillside Farms for dinner ingredients and pie for dessert. He made a quick stop at the regular market for what he couldn't find at Hillside and drove back to the house with an unsettled mind.

Matt took the car when Ollie came back, kissing him in passing. He swung his gym bag over his shoulder and closed the back door behind him as Ollie watched him leave with a sigh.

Ollie changed into clothes he didn't mind getting dirty and went to the kitchen to pull out all the ingredients he needed to make Matt's mother's recipe for eggplant parmesan. Cooking and transforming ingredients into a meal was something that always soothed him, gave him a task to take his mind off school, or work, or relationship drama, especially when he couldn't get that relief from physical exercise.

Ollie made a sauce of fresh and boxed tomatoes, garlic, shredded carrots, onions and basil stems on the stovetop and preheated the oven. He had made it enough times that he didn't need to refer to the handwritten recipe card Antonia had given him to know the quantities of each ingredient, the other seasonings needed, or when to add what. While that simmered on low in the oven, he breaded and fried the eggplant, bopping intermittently to the music playing through the speakers in the ceiling. When the eggplant was done, he added fresh mozzarella and grated Parmigiana Reggiano over each layer in the baking dish and covered it in the fridge.

After dumping the dishes in the sink for Matt to wash, he headed into the garden with his new pruning shears and fertilizer. He pulled the yard waste barrel alongside him as he pruned and weeded around the roses he had planted the previous fall. Ollie looked at his watch when the sun was above the trees behind him, and his heart was suddenly heavy at the thought of Bill riding onto the polo field without him to meet the opposing team.

That first day months ago that he and Bill met to ride, Ollie had been struck by how much he'd missed the smell of the horses, the leather of the saddles, and the feeling of the beast between his legs. It wasn't quite like riding a bike after years; he had to remember how to sync his mind and body with a horse, remember how to guide them and to get them to trust him, but he reveled in creating that relationship with the ponies Bill had found for him.

Ollie sat back on his haunches and then laid back in the grass, staring up at the sky like he used to when he was a small boy. His mind was a blur of thoughts and emotions and his focus shifted from horses to men. He thought about Andy, and he thought about Henry, the man he dated after Andy, and he thought about Matt. Three vastly different men; three very different relationships.

Dating Andy had been youthfully passionate, then confusing, and ultimately heartbreaking. Andy had been magnetic and attractive and incredibly shallow. He was a terrible boyfriend; the kind of handsome cad women needed rescuing from in the movies. Andy became the poster boy of what Ollie *didn't* want in a partner and was the reason Ollie dated Henry, his sweet and tender (but boring) knight in shining armor boyfriend, for just over two years. Ollie thought he wanted to be cherished in an uncomplicated way, and at first it was bliss and romance, the opposite of the angst and uncertainty he had with Andy. But it didn't last.

Henry was thoughtful and caring, steadfast and complimentary, and made Ollie's happiness his number one priority, even over his own studies. Henry had made him playlists, wrote him little love notes, and fawned over him to the point of being stifling. After a year, Ollie was secretly happy (while Henry was morose) about studying in France for the international law portion of his degree. He only saw Henry every few weeks and their reunions were sweet and passionate because of their infrequency.

For their final year at Oxford, Henry had convinced Ollie to move in with him and his flatmate. He and Henry barely made it to Christmas of that year before Ollie broke up with him. Henry was heartbroken, and had persisted, but there was no relationship to salvage and Ollie moved out. Ollie divided the remainder of his time before graduation between Ivan's couch and the couch at George and Sahil's flat.

Ollie waved a fly away as he shifted his thoughts to Matt. Beautiful, enigmatic, complicated Matt. His world had been forever changed that summer night in 2014 when he met Matt. Their first encounter had left him reeling. The electricity that had shocked him when they shook hands, met eyes, had affected him like never before or since. The chemistry they had was like something out of a romance novel and Ollie was torn between loving every bit of what Matt did to him, gentle or brutal, and feeling as though he should put a stop to Matt's unhinged response to jealousy.

Ollie turned his head to look at the barrel of dead stalks he'd snipped and then at the canes of new growth, the budding leaves red and full of promise and the flower buds just beginning to show. There was a metaphor there somewhere: cutting out the decay in order to cultivate the new. Roses thrived when tended to and weren't easy to maintain; there was always work to be done. But it was so worth the effort.

Is Matt worth the effort though? Andy was bad, but he never abused us, his brain interjected.

Ollie frowned at the unwelcome voice. There was a dialogue between his brain, his body, and his heart that only happened when he was particularly troubled and apparently now was one of those times.

Andy filmed us having sex, his heart replied indignantly. *He came to blackmail us for a job. That's way worse.*

Worse than the angry and brutal sex?! his brain cried incredulously. *You two might not see what Matt does to you when he's angry as abusive but isn't it?* his brain asked his heart and body.

Matt doesn't do anything we don't want him to, his body replied defensively. *It's hot. I like it.*

You like it because you're base, and all bloody hormones, his brain scoffed. *Matt is a user, and you and the heart can't see it because you're both so blinded by his beauty, his confidence, and his skill as a lover; both with his words and his body,* his brain added quietly.

Matt loves us, his heart defended in a rush. *He would be lost without us. He really is the luckiest man as he always tells us.*

He's never been with anyone who makes him feel what he feels when he's with us, his body bragged. *Not only does he say it, but his body can't lie any more than I can. He can't get enough.*

He pledged his undying love for us, in front of his mother, Chuck's father, our parents! his heart shouted. *He didn't fake that.*

No, he didn't fake that. But so what? That was a bullshit symbolic gesture that meant nothing, his brain scoffed. *It wasn't a marriage.*

He had custom charms made for our necklaces, thoughtful and romantic charms. He poured his heart out in his vows, Ollie's heart cried. *It wasn't bullshit!*

Oh, you're so naïve, his brain said darkly. *He just said what he knew you wanted to hear. It was a way to claim you as his, without actually having to do anything official. You're right, he can't live without us. We're a thousand times smarter than he is and he doesn't pay us what we're worth. You think it doesn't matter because he showers us with gifts and pays for everything, but it's a tax write-off for him,* his brain continued cynically. *Where is his apology for hurting us so brutally that we can't play polo today? Your ass? Your arm? We were really looking forward to playing. Bill was so disappointed when we called; you heard it in his voice.*

Ollie felt a tear escape from the corner of his eye and swallowed the lump in his throat, fearing that his brain was right.

Don't listen, his heart urged. *Matt loves us. He loves us with all his being. He is still new to love. He has been through so much. He's been to war. He's been shot! His father was a controlling asshole, who showed him no love or mercy. Forced him to be something he wasn't. His dad most likely had a child killed for the mere possibility of turning Matt's head. Matt's lived with that possibility. We have to help him grow. We have to be patient.*

We have to lavish him with love, surrender to him whenever he needs it, his body urged. *We know that is the most direct way to his heart and soul. He craves and needs us.*

His brain made a derisive sound in his head. *Just see if he'll apologize. I'm betting he won't. And if he doesn't, we should walk. Because if we don't, then we will be a fucking doormat, and we will deserve every swipe of his shoes.*

Ollie wasn't sure if he had dozed or was so lost in thought that he didn't hear Matt calling his name, but it wasn't until Matt's shadow fell across his body that he opened his eyes. He sat up and then stood, brushing the grass and dirt off his backside.

"I've been calling your name forever, off-world-Ollie. Didn't you hear me?" Matt looked at him with a bemused smile.

Ollie shook the cobwebs from his brain and bent to pick up his gardening equipment. He ignored Matt's comment as determinedly as he ignored his gorgeous physique. "How was the pool?"

"Nearly empty," Matt said happily and took the leaf barrel as they walked to the house. He dropped it by the shed next to the driveway and waited for Ollie to wipe his shears with rubbing alcohol, watching as he dunked them in the bucket of sand and mineral oil before wiping them with a rag. It was the only thing Ollie ever cleaned; he took his roses *very* seriously.

Matt followed Ollie into the house and watched him wash his hands at the sink. Ollie saw him look around and sniff the air.

"Something smells amazing. What did you make?"

"Your mother's eggplant parm," Ollie replied distractedly, still lost in his thoughts.

Ollie dried his hands on the towel next to the sink and used it to take the enameled cast iron pot out of the oven. He stirred the sauce and removed the basil stems with tongs.

Matt's face spread into a slow smile. "Jesus, Oliver. Will wonders never cease?"

Ollie smiled, blowing out a quiet breath, and turned the oven temperature up. He got the prepared eggplant out of the fridge and ladled steaming sauce into the dish, shaking the sides so the sauce would fill into the layers. He added more cheese, covered it back up with foil, and put it into the oven before filling the big spaghetti pot halfway with water.

"Salt it," Matt said from over his shoulder.

"I know, Lieutenant," Ollie scoffed as he reached for the box of salt. "Don't you start telling me how to cook."

"Right." Matt grinned and put his arm around Ollie's waist. He ghosted his nose up the side of Ollie's neck, raising goosebumps with his breath.

"You smell like a pool," Ollie said and turned out of Matt's arms. He was still feeling out of sorts and didn't want to fall prey to Matt's charms. "And I smell like dirt. I gotta get cleaned up."

"I'll join you," Matt said as he followed Ollie up the stairs. "Since I apparently smell so offensive."

Ollie bit his tongue and wished he could confront Matt with the anger he felt about being punished for something he hadn't done, yet again. He felt as though he was being pretty obvious with his displeasure, so Matt was either ignoring it or just being completely and willfully oblivious.

Ollie turned on the shower and stepped back. Matt pulled Ollie against his chest with his palm on Ollie's stomach and ran his hand under Ollie's shirt. His large hand spanned possessively across Ollie's flat stomach and then his fingertips pressed in.

"You smell so good," Matt murmured against Ollie's ear. "Like a wood nymph with undertones of sex and naughtiness." He ran his other hand over the length of Ollie's body, from his collarbone to mid-thigh. "I know I still can't fuck you, but my tongue won't hurt you." He met Ollie's eye in the mirror.

Ollie's body responded naturally, and unwillingly, to Matt's hands and voice and lips. His cock thickened and he turned in Matt's arms before Matt's hard cock pressed against him clouded his judgement.

"I wish it wasn't so hard for you to say sorry to me," Ollie said and held his breath.

Matt stilled. "What am I apologizing for?"

Ollie's temper flared and he stepped back. "Hindering my ability to play in today's match. I had people depending on me. I let Bill down," Ollie said angrily. "And before you go on about free will, I know I let you. I don't know what that says about either one of us, but I'd like to hear some remorse on your part. If you can't apologize for what you did to me, then the answer next time, and of *course* there will be a next time with you, Lieutenant, will be a resounding no."

Ollie searched Matt's face for emotion. "I'm fairly certain I can live the rest of my life without it. How about you? Would a meaningful sorry be so hard for you that you would risk your future pleasure?" Ollie raised his eyebrows and watched Matt roll his tongue through his mouth, his jaw flexing with the motion.

"I'm sorry. I mean that," Matt said quietly, his eyelids flickering. "I'm sorry you missed the polo match today, and *part* of me is sorry for hurting you." He touched Ollie's face gently and held his gaze. "But the other, much bigger part isn't. So, get naked, get in the shower and I will make it up to you. All the while imagining myself hurting you again for even suggesting that you would say no."

Ollie let out a breath as his body flooded with heat as he stripped off his clothes.

$$\text{———}$$

14

$$\text{———}$$

Wait for Me

OLLIE WAS READY to play polo again on Wednesday and met Bill at his barn in Dover.

"We really missed you Sunday; the other team beat us by two points," Bill said and shook Ollie's hand with a smile. "What did you do to your arm?"

Ollie flexed his arm and rolled his shoulder as he thought of an excuse. "Tried to keep up with Matt. I'll never have his strength," Ollie replied sardonically. "It's all better now."

"Good, because we're up against Don and his team, and he and I have a long-standing rivalry." Bill grinned. "Is Matt coming?"

"Maybe Sunday," Ollie replied. He put his bag of gear in the trunk and folded himself into Bill's vintage Jaguar. He looked around the immaculate leather interior. "You restored this one yourself too, yeah?"

Bill turned the key, and the engine came to life with a quiet roar. "Yup. This is the second Jag I restored and, including the sixty-three Stingray I worked on with Finn, it's the eighth car I've refurbished."

"I don't know when you find the time."

Bill put the car into first and turned down the driveway. "It's been a while since I've done a full restoration, and this is the only car I've kept. I gave Finn the Stingray and sold the others. Each one was a labor of love that took a couple of years to work on, less when Finn was old enough to help. I'm itching to do another one. I'm keeping my eyes open for a sixty-seven Camaro."

"I don't know what that is, but I'm guessing it's a beauty," Ollie looked at Bill. "Judging by this one and Finn's."

"It is. I'll show you a picture." Bill turned between the tall stone pillars marking the entrance of the Sentry Polo Club and took care navigating the cobblestone road.

The woods were thick on either side, until the canopy thinned and the road cut between the flat polo field on one side and the stable and paddocks on the other. He drove through another tree lined path to where their horses waited in their holding paddock and turned off the car.

Ollie got out and followed Bill to the trunk of the car, where they put on their knee pads, gloves, and helmets. Bill followed Ollie through the paddock gate to greet their grooms, Xander and Philip, who had readied their ponies for the match.

Bill brought four ponies and Ollie had three, each of them hearty enough to play two chukkers of a non-tournament game. After shaking hands and making small talk with their two teammates, and a few of the players on the other team, they mounted their horses and headed for the field. It was overcast but with a breeze, so the temperature remained at a steady seventy-six degrees.

Of the four players that make up a polo team, Ollie played number three and Bill played number two. As number three, Ollie was the captain of the team despite his young age, and while Bill had played longer, he was happy to defer leadership to Ollie. Ollie took his role as captain very seriously and called constantly to his teammates on the field, particularly to his number one as he hit the ball hard in her direction. It shot down the field and Ollie charged after it with the other team's number two racing alongside him.

Ollie's ears were filled with the sound of hooves thundering and horses chuffing and snorting. He was hyper-aware of the beast between his thighs; the horse like an extension of himself. He directed with the reins, with his knees, but the horse always seemed to know which way Ollie wanted it to go, as eager to follow the ball and outrun the other horses as Ollie was. He dodged mallets and other horses as he remained fully focused on the little white ball bouncing in the grass.

The three chukkers before halftime went by in a blur of charging up and down the field and switching horses between each. There was a break before the last three chukkers which was spent chugging water and discussing plays. Ollie watched Philip and Xander wipe down the horses and give them water as he listened to his teammates strategize.

"Matt's here," Bill said to Ollie as he came to refill his insulated water bottle at the cooler.

Ollie straightened and looked around with a sudden flutter in his stomach. "Really? I didn't see him."

"I don't know how you missed him. But he's in my spot to the left of the announcer's booth. He's with Naomi."

Playing on Wednesdays was different from Sunday matches in that the field wasn't lined with spectators, though often players had friends and family, and other club members who would come watch. Ollie only happened to miss Matt among the sparse crowd because he was so focused on the game, and because he hadn't been expecting Matt at all. He wondered briefly at the 'why' Matt was there before gesturing to Philip for a horse.

Ollie mounted his horse from the first chukker and followed Bill back to the field. He scanned the sidelines and found Matt sitting next to Naomi in folding chairs near the empty announcer's platform. He smiled when Naomi waved, her lean arm swinging happily above her blonde head. Matt held up his can of seltzer in greeting and smiled his knee-buckling smile that was visible from midfield. Ollie returned that smile and waved his raised mallet. He imagined himself trotting over and collecting a favor from Matt like a knight at a joust before being snapped out of his reverie by Bill who was shaking his head with a grin.

The match started again, and Ollie quickly slipped into game mode, fully focused on the little white ball that kept disappearing under the horses' hooves. Midway through the fourth chukker he dodged the opposing team's number four and scored his third goal of the game. Bill came up beside him and whooped happily as he guided his pony next to Ollie's. Ollie looked to his left after giving Bill a fist bump and beamed with pleasure at the sight of Matt and Naomi on their feet cheering.

A few times during the remainder of the game the horses ran along the boards in front of Matt and Naomi. Each time they did Ollie was only peripherally aware of them, so focused he was as always on that little white ball. He was too busy making sure the other team's number two didn't hook him again, or too concerned with the plays he was calling across the field to his teammates to truly notice what Matt or Naomi were doing. In the last two minutes of the match, he hit the ball away from the boards and turned from the line to head toward the middle as he called to Bill who took up the ball and scored.

Ollie's team won the match four to two and they rode back to the paddocks with broad smiles. Ollie passed his reins to Philip and took off his helmet and gloves. His hair was sweaty and plastered to his head and he wiped himself down with a towel before taking off his knee pads. Bill handed him a water bottle and they stood drinking quietly.

Bill smiled at Ollie. "Great game. It's gonna be a fantastic season. You're playing in the tournament in August, right?"

"Absolutely. I've already blocked it off in my calendar, and am looking for more horses. I may buy two, and continue to lease the others. I don't want to get ahead of myself. Work is still so busy."

Bill nodded in agreement. "I know, though I always told Diana it was better than golf. Just a couple hours as opposed to the whole day."

Ollie laughed and pulled a US Navy baseball cap he had swiped from Matt's collection over his sweaty hair. "Very true. Matt was thinking of taking up golf but realized how much of a time suck it was and changed his mind. Not to mention he has no patience for it. There are other ways to make a deal in business."

Bill agreed with a laugh as they made their way up to the field and over to Matt and Naomi, who were talking to another couple holding a golden retriever on a leash. Naomi left the small group and walked quickly to Ollie. She hugged Bill before grabbing Ollie in hug and kissing him enthusiastically.

"Ollie! Amazing game," she exclaimed. "You are like a god on a horse. Just like I knew you would be."

"Thank you, lovey." Ollie smiled and stepped back. "I'm sorry I'm a sweaty pig."

"No worries. It's very sexy." Naomi grinned. "Matt thought so too. He couldn't take his eyes off you."

Ollie's stomach flipped with pleasure, and watched Matt excuse himself to make his way to them.

"Great game, Ollie. You were on fire out there." He shook Ollie's hand and squeezed it firmly, his eyes discreetly appreciative.

"Thanks." Ollie smiled and let go of Matt's hand with a drag of fingertips.

Matt turned to Bill as he appeared at his side a moment later. "I want to take you winners to dinner or drinks. What's good around here?"

"Not much in Dover. How about Chloe's in Wellesley?" Bill answered and looked at Ollie. "But he and I are gonna need to get cleaned up. You can follow us to the farm or we can meet you at the restaurant."

Matt looked at Naomi. "We'll follow you. It could be an entire dinner service before Ollie's done with his hair." Matt grinned at Ollie.

"Sod off." Ollie laughed. His body was thrumming with the thrill of winning and he couldn't wait to celebrate.

Matt followed Bill into the driveway of a small Cape-style house off a winding country road. The two large horse trailers were already backed up to the stables behind the house, and two guys that Matt assumed were Bill's horse caretakers, or whatever they were called, were unloading the horses. Matt had never been to Bill's farm though he'd heard about it from Finn over the years and he paused to take it all in.

He followed Naomi into the cottage behind Bill and Ollie and looked around. They came in through a mudroom into a modest-sized kitchen and Matt could see a hallway at the opposite end that presumably led to a bathroom or maybe a basement. Bill continued leading them through a wide archway into a large living-dining room that had a staircase along one wall and a book-lined library through an open door on the other. There were two bay windows on either side of the front door and furniture that looked brand new and barely used.

"This is nice," Naomi admired, scanning the space with her designer's eye.

"It was the caretaker's cottage for my grandparent's farm which is over the hill and belongs to someone else now." Bill gestured toward the back of the house with his free hand. "It was in bad shape so I had it gutted and renovated a few years ago." He headed for the stairs with his bag. Ollie followed him close behind with a bag of his own. "Have a seat." Bill gestured to the white sofas. "And there are drinks of all kinds in the fridge, help yourselves."

Matt watched Ollie go up the stairs, wishing he could follow and watch him shower. He turned with a sigh and poked around instead as he fought the urge to pace. He scanned the old maps and photos on the walls as he made his way around the periphery of the room. Many of them were yellowed with age. There were several slightly faded photos of young children, which, judging from the clothes, must have been Bill and his siblings in various locations. Some were posed and stiff and others were carefree and taken outside. There was a black and white photo of a regal looking man on horseback that caught his eye. He was dressed in a hunting coat and breeches with a top hat and there was a pack of dogs milling about the horse's legs.

"You want a soda or water?" Naomi interrupted him from the kitchen archway.

"I'll take water, thanks." Matt turned from the wall of pictures and looked at his watch and then at the ceiling with a sigh.

Naomi passed him a bottle of water and sat on the couch with her phone. "Go upstairs and hurry him along. I'm getting hungry."

Matt didn't need to be told twice and took the stairs two at a time. He found himself on a small landing between two closed doors.

Shit, he thought. *Which one is Ollie's?*

Both suites appeared to span the top floor, and presumably had views of the front yard and the fields behind, so there was no preferential, primary suite. He knocked lightly on the one to the left of the stairs and hearing nothing he peeked in. He saw a picture of Finn's late mother on the side table next to the large bed and quickly pulled the door shut. He strode to the other door and entered quietly, seeing Ollie's clothes in a heap on the floor. He shook his head with a small smile and picked them up. He wrinkled his nose at the strong smell of horse. He folded them and stacked them in the wooden chair under the window overlooking the horse paddock as he heard the water turn off. He crossed to the bathroom door and peeked his head inside.

"Christ!" Ollie jumped as he was toweling off and gripped his chest. "What are you doing in here?"

"Naomi sent me to hurry you along," Matt answered and swept his eyes over Ollie's beautiful naked body. He leaned against the door frame and drank in the sight. "She's hungry, and my eyes were starving."

Ollie chuckled low as he continued to dry off, wiping his face and arms. His chest was smooth, muscular and hairless, thanks to regular waxing appointments, and his bush was trim and manicured. His soft cock twitched under Matt's scrutiny and Matt tore his eyes away.

"You were amazing out there today, not that I had any doubt that you would be." Matt straightened and stepped into the bathroom. "You had many admirers, including the woman I was talking to. I almost decked her for eye-fucking you."

Ollie tilted his head back and laughed. Matt ducked his head and kissed the exposed column of Ollie's throat and then his collarbone. Ollie's skin smelled of the expensive sandalwood-scented body wash he favored and was warm under Matt's nose. Ollie stopped drying off and closed his eyes as Matt pulled him close and kissed his waiting lips. Matt ran his hands over the smooth skin of Ollie's ass and squeezed.

He wanted nothing more than to bend Ollie over the sink until he was blathering mess begging for an orgasm but restrained himself.

"You have to do your hair and get dressed. This will wait. But we're skipping dessert; I won't have the patience for it." Matt smacked Ollie's ass lightly and stepped back with a grin. He lifted Ollie's bag from the long granite countertop and put it on the floor. "Leave the door open and don't put any clothes on until after you've put on all your lotions and whatnot."

Matt went back into the bedroom, turned the upholstered chair in front of the fireplace to face the bathroom and sat down.

Ollie watched him questioningly and then went back to what he was doing. With a sigh he bent over to get out his hair dryer and bag of moisturizers and hair crème.

"Turn this way," Matt commanded softly to Ollie's profile.

Ollie paused and then shifted his feet. "You are such a perv," he said with a laugh when his back was to the door. He shook his ass briefly before continuing to rummage in his bag for his clothes.

"That's right. Really dig for it, Ollie. But skip the dryer; I love your hair when it's wild."

Ollie looked over his shoulder with a chuckle and put his hair dryer back in the bag. "You're ridiculous."

"Ridiculous? Or genius?" Matt asked and raised his eyebrows with a shrug as he scanned his eyes over the crack of Ollie's ass and the backside of Ollie's perfectly sized balls. "I just created a masterpiece of a view."

Ollie laughed again and turned to the mirror. "I love you, Lieutenant."

They caravanned to the restaurant and sat at a table in the front, Bill and Matt with their backs to the wall, and Naomi and Ollie facing them. Bill ordered appetizers to go with their cocktails while Naomi told them about her latest design project in Orleans on the Cape.

"I have to thank you guys, and Finn, for letting me do your houses and take such spectacular photos. Everyone wants your house in particular." She nodded at Matt.

Matt grinned. "You are the wizard who made that happen, so don't look at me."

"I'm thinking some of the bedrooms and the cottages on Nantucket need an overhaul, Naomi." Bill smiled. "When you have a free moment."

"Seriously?" Naomi asked with wide eyes. "I would love to. I love your house there and to be honest, I've already thought of ideas." She raised her glass with a grin.

"Terrific." Bill smiled and clinked his glass to hers, and then shifted his gaze to Ollie. "Tell me about Lyon, and why you won't be here for the July tournament."

"I usually go in August, at least before I moved here." He flashed a glance at Matt. "But I'm going in July because I have a meeting set up and will hopefully have a contract signed. We've been negotiating with this company for over a year now."

"Why Lyon?" Bill asked.

"It's a property that's been in my Aunt Clare's family for over a hundred years. There was an aging, unproductive vineyard when my aunt inherited it, and my Uncle Lloyd, my dad's older brother, restored it, with a tremendous amount of help of course, and got the vines producing again or whatever. I'm not a vintner, so I don't know what they did, but now it's a viable vineyard again and produces about seventy thousand cases a year, but don't quote me. I just show up and drink and eat apricots from their orchard. It's truly spectacular."

"Sounds amazing," Naomi said and clinked her glass to Ollie's.

Matt flicked his glance between Ollie and Bill with a sudden desperate need to change the subject. "So, you're amazing at polo, naturally," Matt said and waved his hand. "How much is it going to cost me? You need your own horses now obviously."

Matt watched Ollie shift his gaze to Bill. "Thank you, but I'll pay for my own horses. My boss pays me a *fairly* decent wage. I think I can manage, as long as Bill has room in his stables for my ponies."

Was that a dig? Matt wondered as he studied Ollie's body language.

"I have plenty of room, and room to expand if need be." Bill looked at Matt. "You would be great on a horse, by the way. I can easily get you a school horse to start. And don't look at me like that; you can't get on a thoroughbred or a quarter horse your first time out. No one can." Bill shook his head at the face Matt made. "Put aside your pride."

Matt shrugged nonchalantly and ate a mussel while looking around the restaurant. The thought of having to be on a school horse like a twelve-year-old around his boyfriend, who was so accomplished he looked like a centaur, was humiliating.

Matt raised his finger to the waiter to get the check. "When are you headed to Nantucket, Bill?"

"Sunday night. I'll be back to play in the July tournament. And then I'll take two weeks off when Finn is here; she said she'd come out to stay for a bit. I'll be there until the August tournament and will be thrilled to see Ollie again." Bill raised his glass and clinked it against Ollie's.

"*Slainte*, Bill." Ollie smiled.

Matt looked between Bill and Ollie and smiled to himself at how close they'd become, especially considering their tumultuous introduction.

BUD

15

Red, Red Wine

OLLIE GOT OFF THE TRAIN in Lyon and looked for his car service. The meetings in Paris had gone as well as Ollie had expected, and he had used the two hours of travel to review their changes to SharkFinn's contract proposal. He saw an O. Turner sign being held by a man standing next to a black Mercedes and greeted the driver in his flawless French. Ollie handed him his suitcase, which the driver took with a smile before opening the back door for him.

The ride to the chateau, southeast of Lyon, took just under an hour. Ollie had three phone calls: one with Fred, one with Krish, and one with Kerry. When the car slowed and the sound of crunching gravel under the tires drew his attention, Ollie looked up to see the familiar chateau: a large, three-story, cream-colored stone structure with white shutters and a reddish-brown roof.

One of the tall, aqua blue double-doors opened in the center of the house as his driver brought the car to a stop in the circular drive and Ollie's Aunt Clare, a strikingly beautiful, former model with curly brown hair appeared with a smile on her face. Ollie gathered his things as he waited for the driver to open his door and then strode happily to greet her.

"*Olivier!* It is so good to see you," she exclaimed in French.

"*Tante* Clare! How is it you are looking even younger than ever?" he replied in French as he kissed both her cheeks and then hugged her warmly.

She patted his face. "You are my favorite nephew."

Ollie turned to the driver and pressed a generous tip in his hand after taking his bag. "*Merci,*" he said and then followed his aunt into the cool of the chateau.

His parents were already there, sitting with his uncle on the expansive patio that spanned the back of the house and overlooked the rolling hills with the Alps in the distance. Ollie smiled at the similarities between his uncle and his father, the only differences being his uncle's slightly longer hair and that his father wore glasses.

After hugging and kissing everyone hello, Ollie took off his linen suit coat and sat down at the long wrought iron table next to his mother. He draped his arm on the back of her chair and squeezed her shoulder. Clare called for their housekeeper, Amelie, a local woman in her late sixties, to bring Ollie a spritzer and more charcuterie for the table. Ollie raised his glass in salute to everyone and looked out over the low stone wall at the view as everyone resumed conversation and settled back in their seats.

The scent of the house and the air and the food brought him right back to his childhood. He suddenly and vividly remembered the time he was eight years old, chasing Guy on the patio. Ollie had tripped on one of the bluestone pavers and skinned his knees. The gravel that was between the stones had to be picked out of his wound by the very housekeeper who just served him his alcohol.

"Ollie, *Tante* Clare just asked you a question," Maggie interrupted his musings in heavily accented French.

"*Pardon.*" He looked at his aunt. "I was just lost in happy memories of here."

Clare smiled. "I'm so happy you're here to make more. I was just asking how work was and how things in Paris went."

"Things went really well. I think we should be closing the deal very soon. Unfortunately, that means I have to work tonight and tomorrow if I want a response before the August holiday. But there's a strong chance we could be sealing a multi-million-dollar deal in the next week or so."

"Wonderful, Oliver," his uncle said appreciatively.

David raised his glass and smiled at Ollie. "You're doing great things for your company. I know Matt realizes that he would be lost without you."

"Thanks, Dad. He does," Ollie replied, happy that his dad was no longer snarky or distrustful of Matt. He looked at his aunt and uncle. "I have a great boss, and tons of autonomy at my company. He's sorry he couldn't come to France this time around but said to say hi to everyone." Ollie smiled. He looked at his aunt. "Is Sophia coming?"

"She can't make it this week. Viktor can't get the time off, but they'll be here in August with the twins. Sorry that you'll miss her."

"Oh, that's too bad; I wanted to see her. I can't believe she has babies." Ollie shook his head with a smile. "When is Guy getting here?"

"Within the hour. He's at the winery now," Clare answered. "He stops there on his way home from work."

"Did I just hear an obnoxious Englishman inquire about my whereabouts?" a deep voice, similar in cadence to Ollie's, asked in French from the doorway.

Ollie stood with a grin for the handsome man stepping onto the patio. Guy was almost the same height and build as Ollie, with the same balanced mouth and slightly square jawline, but had dark brown hair and hazel eyes. He was his father's clone, as Ollie was to David, but with his mother's coloring and nose. Ollie hugged him tightly and exchanged cheek kisses.

"Look what the cat dragged in," Ollie responded in English. "Did you have to sneak in under a mower to get here? What the hell happened to your hair?"

Guy ran his hand over his short, Caesar hairstyle. "I have a life and a *real* job; two actually." He smiled at his dad. "I don't have time to style my hair every day. I see you're still putting in the effort. So, no life in America yet?" he teased.

Ollie smiled. "Nope."

Guy sat down next to Ollie and took some cheese from the board as Ollie's sister Cassie and Guy's sister Genevieve propped their bikes against the stone wall. They came up the steps onto the patio, wrapped in towels and carrying their clothes. Their hair was wet and hanging down their backs in contrasting shades of blonde and brunette.

Genevieve's face broke into a smile. "*Olivier!*" she exclaimed and hugged him when he stood.

"Genny, great to see you." Ollie smiled and kissed her cheeks. "You're looking as beautiful as ever."

"Nice to see you, brother. You're quite tan," Cassie hugged him when Genevieve stepped aside. "You spending time at your boss' fancy beach house?"

"Yes, and playing polo," Ollie replied sitting back down.

"You're playing polo again?" Lloyd asked.

"Oui. My friend Finn's father, Bill, he's also SharkFinn's board chairman, belongs to a club and we both picked it up again. There's a small but vibrant polo scene on the East Coast."

"*Mon dieu,*" Guy shook his head. "Do you work at all?"

"I have excellent time management skills," Ollie countered and gave Guy a small shove.

Guy snorted disbelievingly.

"You girls want to get showered or dried off for dinner?" Clare interrupted in French, looking at Cassie and Genevieve. "We're eating in twenty minutes."

After dinner Ollie and Guy walked the paths of the grounds with their wine, catching up and laughing about the things they did as kids. The apricot trees were heavy with fruit and the nut trees were just beginning to turn.

"Christ, the smell of this orchard takes me right back, every time." Ollie shook his head. "First, I couldn't even look at an apricot because we ate so many, and then I couldn't because none could ever compare. These are perfect." Ollie picked one and bit into it, the juice running down his chin. He swiped at it with his sleeve and looked at Guy.

"I know what you mean," Guy grinned. "It's good to see you, Ollie." He looked over the treetops as they came around the slope and gazed at the Alps in the distance. "I missed you. I thought you went to America and forgot all about us."

"Oh, right. Were you crying yourself to sleep?" Ollie took another large bite of the apricot and then threw it as far as he could. His muscled polo arm made the fruit disappear far into the distance. "I bet you use it as a pick-up line. 'My *incredibly* gorgeous cousin went to America and forgot all about me. Love me tonight; I'll most likely kill myself in the morning,'" Ollie teased.

Guy threw his head back and laughed, his rich voice echoing across the hills. "I don't need pick-up lines, and neither do you." He looked at Ollie appreciatively. "You have a boyfriend in Boston?"

Ollie chuckled. "Of course I do. How about you, Casanova? You got a bevy of girlfriends in rotation?"

Guy looked at the chateau on the hill. "I'm dating two women now. The older I get the pickier I am; I have to be. Women get a whiff of this," he gestured around the estate, "and it's no longer just my pretty face."

"I get it. If only you had a decent personality to keep them by your side."

"You're a wanker, Ol." Guy punched his bicep. "I think you have to date men because no woman would have you."

"Introduce me to your girlfriends and let's test that theory of yours," Ollie said with a cocky grin.

"I'd tell them you're gay. You wouldn't get anywhere with either one."

"Au *contraire*, mon frere," Ollie laughed. "Women love gay men, and the thought that they could turn one straight? Forget it. I'd have their panties off in heartbeat, and I'd fuck them better than you. I've seen your moves, don't forget."

Guy laughed. "That was years ago, I have all the moves now, mon frere. And you can't turn someone straight, or gay, that's pure fantasy."

Ollie raised his eyebrows as they turned back toward the house. The sky was dark around the bright silhouette. "Oh, my boyfriend was as straight as a Roman road when I met him. It can be done."

Well, not quite, but to the world he was, Ollie thought.

Guy threw his head back again with a hearty laugh. "Oh, Christ! You move to America and get delusions of grandeur. How very American of you. If he told you that and you believed him, then I have some ocean front property in Lyon to sell you."

Ollie smiled smugly as he thought of Matt. "Let's find our sisters and play some cards."

*   *   *

Matt looked up at the sky at the sound of a plane overhead as he rinsed the shampoo from his hair and thought of Ollie. He looked at his watch and guessed Ollie was eating lunch, taking his little bites and chewing thoughtfully. He sighed. It was lonely at the beach, but it beat being alone in the city. At least in Truro he had Finn next door.

He turned off the water and looked through the gap under the wooden door at Finn's German Shepherd chewing on her bone with alert eyes. She sprang to her feet when he emerged with a towel slung low on his hips and his sweaty running clothes in his hand.

"Come on in, Jayne," he said and waited for her to go through the slider in front of him. Matt poured himself a mug of coffee and went upstairs to get dressed with Jayne on his heels. "To your bed," he commanded with a snap of his fingers.

Jayne quickly crossed the room to a large dog bed near the glass door to the balcony and laid down. Matt's eyes scanned the tidy room and the empty bed, and he sighed again as he felt a twinge in his dick thinking about Ollie and his beautiful body. He walked into the equally tidy bathroom and wished for Ollie's crumpled towel or discarded underwear to be there to remind him of his whirling dervish of a boyfriend. There were no styling products or lotions on the counter either and Matt couldn't believe he actually missed the mess. He turned his back to the empty space and hung up his towel.

Dressing quickly to escape the quiet, he picked up his laptop from the shelf of his side table and headed to Finn's with Jayne bounding ahead to the path through the tree line. He let himself in, turned on her coffee maker and sat on the couch facing the ocean while he waited for Finn to wake up. She emerged from her room thirty minutes later with Jayne dancing happily around her legs as she came through to the kitchen.

"Good morning." She smiled. "Have you eaten?"

"Morning, Chuck." Matt hit send on the email reply to Ollie and closed his laptop. "Nope. I figured you'd like the company."

"You mean you didn't feel like having cereal," Finn corrected.

Matt grinned and stood. "What are you making?"

"You want French toast or eggs?"

"Ollie usually makes eggs and bacon. You got any leftover potatoes? He makes those sometimes too with onions." Matt pulled out a stool and sat at the island.

Finn rolled her eyes. "Oh my god, you're so fucking spoiled."

Matt shrugged, and held his tongue. Finn was the only person he accepted an eyeroll from. He watched her pull out ingredients and then dip slices of bread into the whisked and seasoned bowl of eggs.

"When does Ollie get back?" Finn asked ten minutes later as she put a plate of French toast with fruit in front of Matt and sat next to him.

"Sunday night. I'm going to meet him at the airport."

Finn groaned. "So, I get this joy and stimulating conversation all to myself for the next five days. You sigh dejectedly every two minutes. I feel like I should remove the sharp objects from your house." She twisted her mouth at him.

Matt scoffed. "Don't be ridiculous. I'm fine. I just don't sleep great when he's not home."

Finn looked at him with a soft expression. "Stay here tonight. I'd have you all week, but Glenn is coming tomorrow for a few days, and you can't be here," she said pointedly.

Matt rolled his eyes at the mention of Finn's high school boyfriend. "Christ, is he gonna be doing drills on the beach? What's the hostess gift gonna be? A signed copy of the 2007 *Wellesley Townsman* featuring his big football win?"

Finn laughed. "You're such a dick. He didn't even play football."

"Well, he wasn't on my swim team, so whatever sport he did or didn't play, doesn't matter. Don't get too attached, Chuck. I don't approve."

She shoved his shoulder and took a bite of her breakfast.

* * *

Ollie worked late after the card game and then again in the morning before taking a break. He opened the windows in his room, and then the shutters to let the light in. His room overlooked the orchard, and with the window open he could smell the ripening fruit. It was a heady scent that made him nostalgic.

He always stayed in this room when he visited. It was next to Guy's, and had a small double bed, two simple nightstands, and a dresser with three drawers. The parquet floor was bare, as were all the floors in the chateau with the exception of the living room and the dining room. His bedroom shared a balcony with the guest room on the other side, the one his parents usually stayed in, but they were in one of the recently renovated bedrooms on the other side of the house. He marked the page of the contract he was reading and went downstairs in search of coffee and food.

He had a quick breakfast with his dad and uncle, where they discussed the weather and business and what the plans for the weekend were. Ollie asked his uncle about the possibility of sending his mark-ups back to the client in Paris.

"I have a scanner here, if you can believe it," Lloyd said in English with a smile. "Sixteenth century building, with twenty-first century amenities."

"Fantastic. I need to send it to Matt, and then back to the client." Ollie nodded happily. "Point me in the right direction, Uncle."

Ollie played tennis with his father on the grass court next to the orchard after he sent the documents, knowing all there was left to do was wait. He checked his email after the match and saw that Matt had approved the contractual changes. His language was all business, and nothing more. Ollie sent the mark-ups to the client in Paris with a brief state-ment of finality and hit send.

He was pensive over dinner about his lack of contact with Matt. He knew that work at home wasn't busy; it was July and the only month deader than July for work, was August. It reminded him of when they were first dating and Matt had stopped calling every day, saying at the time that he was too busy, but admitted later he just couldn't stand hearing from Ollie without being able to touch him.

Ollie participated peripherally in the dinner conversation, and begged off after just a few hands of cards. He texted Matt from bed, knowing that it was late afternoon at home.

I miss u. How's the beach?

It took Matt an hour to get back to him.

> I miss you too. I was just out for a
> swim, and have some emails to
> catch up on. I'll call in a few hours
> if you're still up

Ollie sighed, apparently Matt wasn't missing him as much as Ollie was.

I'll try to stay awake Lt. xoxo

16

Voulez Vous Coucher Avec Moi?

OLLIE WOKE THE NEXT DAY, Thursday, to a blank phone screen. He sighed disappointedly as his morning erection deflated along with his mood. He dressed in shorts and a t-shirt, brushed his teeth and went downstairs for coffee and croissants.

"*Tu veux nager?*" Guy asked after they finished eating.

"*Pourquoi pas,*" Ollie replied and went to change into his swimsuit.

Ollie and Guy biked to the river and lost themselves in the day as if they were teenagers. They spent hours floating, swimming, and swinging into the cool water from a rope some locals had tied to a massive tree on the bank. Ollie took a break and spread out his towel on the grass while Guy flirted with a group of girls who were over eighteen but still far too young for them. The girls were persistent and had descended upon them with the single-minded focus of youth and hormones. Guy finally indulged them with some banter, while keeping them at arm's length.

Ollie checked his email on his phone and saw that the Paris company had responded positively, indicating the go ahead for the business. Ollie smiled triumphantly and looked at his watch. It was past noon and he knew he couldn't be dressed and driven back to Paris in time for their closing but he replied immediately that he would be there to sign the contract on behalf of SharkFinn in the morning, and copied Matt in. He looked at Guy who had left the girls and was headed toward him.

"What are you so happy about?" Guy asked as he picked up his towel and began drying his fit and lean body. "Did you finally get a response to your fan letter to Harry Styles?"

Ollie snorted and shook his head. "I just negotiated a fifteen-million-Euro deal," he boasted. "Not our biggest by a long shot, but something I did here on vacation, so I feel pretty good."

"Bloody hell, Oliver. That's quite impressive, especially for a twenty-five-year-old slacker." Guy slapped him on the bicep and then went in search of his dry clothes.

Ollie napped before dinner, exhausted from staying up late with the contract and from the time spent at the river. He showered and put on a pink linen shirt and dark blue linen pants, freshly ironed by Amelie, and cuffed his sleeves lightly. He left the top two buttons of his shirt undone and checked his reflection in the mirror. He straightened the trident pendant dangling from the silver chain around his neck and then ran a small dab of styling cream through his hair.

Ollie looked at himself in the mirror and thought about cutting his hair like Guy's. He then decided to skip the hair dryer because who cared what his unruly waves would do on the patio. He wasn't at work, and it wasn't as though Matt would be there to admire him. He threw his shoulders back and headed downstairs.

He found everyone on the patio and took his usual seat next to Guy. Guy poured him some Cotes du Rhone from the vineyard and clinked his glass to Ollie's before putting his arm on the back of Ollie's chair. The sun was still shining over the hills but beginning her fiery journey to bed. The family chatted and laughed as they decimated the charcuterie boards on the table while waiting for dinner.

The hairs on Ollie's neck raised suddenly at the same time that Amelie came out of the doors from the main part of house, not the one off to the side that led to the kitchen. He saw Lloyd and Clare straighten in their chairs and followed their eyes over his shoulder, standing reflexively as if he were jolted and his chair nearly toppled in his haste.

"Matt!" he exclaimed softly as Matt appeared in the door behind Amelie wearing his Ray Bans and a white linen suit with a dark blue shirt underneath. The top two buttons were undone like Ollie's and exposed the matching silver chain with the dime-sized moon pendant around his neck. "What are you doing here?" Ollie puzzled stupidly as his mouth went dry at the sight of him.

Matt grinned his sexy grin as his gaze flitted around the faces at the table, lingering on Guy's before landing back on Ollie. "Hello, Oliver. I hope I'm not intruding." He took Ollie's hand firmly in his own, a happy jolt passing between them before letting go.

David had stood at the same time as Ollie. "Great to see you, Matt," he exclaimed welcomingly as though his arrival wasn't a surprise, and came forward for a hug. "So glad you could join us." He turned to his brother. "This is Ollie's boss, Matt Dion. Matt, this is my brother Lloyd, his wife Clare, his son Guy, and daughter Genevieve." David made the introductions, and Matt shook hands with everyone, kissing Maggie and Cassie on their cheeks.

Amelie reappeared with another place setting and set it in the empty spot next to David. Matt sat down as Guy poured a glass of wine and passed it to him. Ollie wanted to stare openly at Matt across the table, but was mindful of the eyes all around them. His stomach fluttered happily at the sight of him, so beautiful in his suit and his Ray Bans, his hair tousled from his running his hands through it, and a five o'clock shadow bruising his jaw. He looked like a movie star and the women at the table couldn't keep their eyes off him.

Matt took off his sunglasses and put them in his chest pocket. He turned his shining blue eyes on Ollie. "To answer your question,

I had a contract to sign. Thank you, Oliver." He raised his glass and smiled at Ollie before looking around the table. "I don't know if Ollie said, but he just closed a deal we've been working on for more than a year."

"Congratulations," Guy said and raised his glass, drawing Matt's eye. Guy looked at Ollie and switched to French. "Maybe you would've gotten it done sooner if you didn't take so long with your hair."

Everyone laughed as Matt looked at Ollie with a quirked eyebrow.

"He's making fun of me, Matt. It's not worth repeating because he's an idiot." Ollie shook his head and elbowed Guy.

"Ah, but you love me, and I'm not wrong." Guy put his arm around Ollie's shoulder and kissed the side of his head.

Amelie interrupted the banter by putting down the big platters of food in the middle of the table and clearing away the nearly empty charcuterie boards.

Night fell around them, and Ollie helped clear the dishes after dinner, primarily to keep from staring at Matt. He was finding it nearly impossible to keep his eyes off the way Matt's cheek folded when he smiled, the perfect curve of his ear as he turned to look at David, and the hollow of his throat just above the moon pendant when he swallowed a sip of his wine.

It was thrilling to have him on the patio, sitting with his family in a place so dear to him. It had been a huge shock when Matt appeared in the doorway, and to have him within reach but unable to touch him was nearly unbearable. Ollie cleared some plates to distract himself and went into the house. He saw a giant bouquet of flowers in a tall vase on the hall table and a large shopping bag next to Matt's suitcase, on his way back from the kitchen.

Matt appeared silently in the doorway to the patio. "Bring that out please, Ollie." He swept his eyes over him in that way that always made Ollie's blood hum, before disappearing. Ollie picked up the bag as he plotted his midnight visit to whichever room Matt was staying in.

The bag was filled with host gifts, including a bottle of Macallan eighteen-year scotch, a Blanton single barrel bourbon, and a jug of Vermont maple syrup.

"I would've brought wine but. . . ." He gestured to the vineyard that stretched down the hill with a smile.

"*Merci beaucoup*," Lloyd said happily as he and David eyed the scotch. "Amelie, please bring five tumblers for whisky, *s'il te plait*."

The table was cleared of plates and food after dessert was finished and the men were left alone at the table talking and drinking their whisky. Matt had spent the better part of dinner keeping his eyes off Ollie, partly because he didn't want to give anything away to the group, and partly because he had been so impressed by the house and grounds. He hadn't known what to expect when Ollie spoke of the chateau, but it certainly wasn't a house that was more like a castle than a country estate, with a vineyard that stretched into the horizon.

"This is quite something," Matt said gesturing down the slope with his hand. "Did you restore the vineyard?"

"Yes and no. It's been in Clare's family for more than a hundred years, but it was Clare's father who began the restoration of the house and vineyard. We ramped it up and kept it going, and Guy has expanded the operation. He has quite a knack for business," Lloyd smiled at his son.

Matt looked at Guy next to Ollie, and was again amazed at how much they looked alike despite the different coloring. Guy was handsome but not nearly as beautiful as Ollie, whose hair was so wavy and sexy, Matt's fingers were tingling with want to touch it. He had to keep his hands clenched and eyes off him entirely for fear of acting on his urge. "Did you study business?"

"I studied finance at Cambridge, and just finished my MBA at the London Business School last year. I'm helping with the winery, but I have a 'real' job working in private equity," he responded with just the tiniest bit of a French accent to his British English, only noticeable with certain words.

Ollie tuned out the conversation while watching Guy and Matt, reading Matt's body language and feeling as though he was being ignored. He could tell Matt found Guy attractive, and felt a tiny stab of jealousy. He ran his hand slowly through his hair which drew Matt's eye and smiled inwardly. He looked at his dad, who was watching him, and grinned happily with a blush.

David finished his scotch and looked at Lloyd. "I'm headed in. We've got tennis tomorrow morning, right?"

Lloyd stood with his empty glass. "Oui. Matt, wonderful to meet you, so glad you could join us. Thank you for the whisky." He smiled as Matt stood and shook his hand. "See you in the morning."

"My pleasure. Thank you for letting me drop in unannounced. I can just bunk in with Ollie. I don't want to be any trouble."

"Nonsense. David told me you were coming, and we've plenty of room. I'll find out where Clare put you and leave your suitcase outside the door. *Bonne nuit.*"

Ollie shot his dad a look and David just shrugged and grinned mischievously. He should've guessed that his father had something to do with Matt's appearance.

"*Buona note,*" Matt replied before sitting back down and watching as David and Lloyd disappeared into the house. Matt looked at Guy. "Ollie told me you guys would swim somewhere around here."

"Oui. There's an offshoot of the river that comes down from the Alps. Do you swim?"

Ollie watched Matt nod with a grin.

"Well then we should go tomorrow."

"Matt was a Navy SEAL, Guy. He's got gills," Ollie said proudly with a light laugh.

"Is that right?" Guy looked at him with new appreciation. "That's pretty hardcore. Did you spend any time in the Middle East?"

"Some," Matt answered vaguely.

"Were you a sniper?" Guy asked, putting his elbows on the table and folding his hands in front of his mouth.

Ollie saw Matt's eyes flit to Guy's hands and then mouth, and wondered if Matt was remembering when Ollie had done the same thing the first time they were alone together, when he had asked about Matt's military service. Of course, at that time Ollie had been flirting and had run his thumb over his bottom lip as he imagined that it was Matt's cock, while Guy was just rubbing his hands together distractedly.

Matt cleared his throat. "No, I was a special warfare officer."

"Guy has seen too many movies," Ollie teased.

"*American Sniper* was about a Navy SEAL. It's not out of the realm of possibility," Guy argued.

"I had snipers under my command, but that wasn't my specialty."

"Oh. What was?"

Matt chuckled. "I can't say."

Guy sat back in his chair with a smile. "Fair enough."

Matt looked at his watch and then at Ollie. "Is there a road or direction you recommend for a run in the morning?"

"Oui," Guy answered before Ollie could respond. "It's about five kilometers to the larger part of the river. Ollie and I bike, but it's a good run, and we could swim and come back. What time do you want to go?"

"He's up at the crack of dawn," Ollie replied. Guy looked at him questioningly. "We travel for work together all the time. He's always up before the rest of us," Ollie lied smoothly and didn't dare look at Matt.

"I think with jetlag I'll be a little later than usual. Maybe six-thirty. You up that early?" Matt tilted his head, also avoiding Ollie's eye.

"I will be. I know this one won't." Guy gestured with his thumb to Ollie. "If he didn't get his eight hours of beauty sleep every night in the summer, we'd all pay the price."

"That was you," Ollie countered primly, while inwardly acknowledging that Guy was right.

Guy laughed. "Still projecting. Some things never change." He stood along with Matt and Ollie. They cleared the glasses and bottles and brought them to the large modern kitchen before going upstairs.

"Ah, you're next to Ollie. I'll knock on your door in the morning," Guy said, looking at Matt's suitcase on the floor outside the bedroom that shared a balcony with Ollie's room.

Ollie guessed that his mother had arranged that and smiled to himself. He watched Guy put his hand on the doorknob to his room on the other side of Ollie's.

"I'll knock on yours," Matt said simply. "Where's the bathroom?"

Ollie pointed across the hall. "There, and there's another down the hall, first door on the left when you turn the corner." He looked at Guy and then at Matt. "Goodnight, everyone."

All three doors closed.

Ollie used the bathroom (and the bidet), brushed his teeth, stripped down to his underwear and put on his well-worn Oxford t-shirt. He paced for ten long minutes and strained to hear Guy through the thick walls but heard nothing before finally opening his windows and then the shutters. He climbed out into the dark to find Matt waiting in the shadows of the balcony. He smiled shyly.

"I was just about to come into your room and drag you out here by your glorious hair," Matt whispered and stepped back through his window and waited expectantly. He pulled Ollie into his arms the minute he stepped off the ledge.

"God, I missed you," he said before kissing him deeply. He tasted of mint and whisky, and smelled like heaven. Ollie hugged him and ran his hands down Matt's back as Matt ran his fingers through Ollie's hair with a moan. "It's almost like you were expecting me with this slutty hair," he breathed against Ollie's lips, tightening his fingers and pulling Ollie's head back. Ollie closed his eyes at the feeling of Matt's lips and whiskers on the column of his throat and couldn't wait to feel them between his legs.

Matt ran his hands down Ollie's back and then up under his shirt. He moaned as his hands roamed Ollie's skin. Ollie slipped his hands under Matt's shirt and smoothed his hands over the hardened planes of

Matt's chest. He mapped the ridges of Matt's washboard abs and then teased Matt's nipples into points and captured Matt's soft moan in his mouth as he kissed him again.

Matt's kisses were insistent and full of need. Ollie knew exactly how Matt felt as he returned them with his own barely contained desire. He angled his hips and brushed his erection against Matt's with a moan. He lowered his hand and palmed Matt's cock over the front of his underwear. Ollie felt a wet spot, one that matched the dampness on his own underwear, and squeezed.

"I missed this magnificent thing," Ollie murmured against the column of Matt's throat.

Ollie slipped his hand under the waistband of Matt's boxer briefs and dropped to his knees. He pulled the front of Matt's underwear down and licked a stripe up the front of Matt's cock. He smelled musky and heavenly, and Ollie's cock twitched in response. Ollie ran his tongue around the wide head of Matt's cock under the foreskin the way he knew Matt loved and then took him halfway into his mouth.

Matt moaned and then caught himself before he got too loud as Ollie jacked him slowly and sucked. He lifted the front of his shirt so he could watch what Ollie was doing.

"Get your dick out. I wanna see it," Matt commanded in a gravelly whisper.

Ollie pushed his underwear down with his free hand and began stroking his aching cock in sync with the hand on Matt. Matt buried his fingers in Ollie's hair and titled his head back slightly so their eyes could meet.

"You look so beautiful with your lips stretched around my dick." Matt pushed deeper into Ollie's mouth and then drew all the way out, leaving a string of saliva connecting them. "How much of a racket do you think that bed makes?" Matt pulled Ollie to his feet.

"Let's get on it and see," Ollie suggested and wiped his chin.

They took off each other's shirts and stepped out of their underwear, pausing to admire each other's nudity in the moonlight before laying down. The bed groaned slightly under their weight and then was quiet.

Ollie rolled and stretched his body along the length of Matt's. They kissed and touched with urgent lips and hands, the desire building as Matt lifted Ollie's leg over his hip and circled Ollie's pucker with the tip of his finger.

Ollie felt a jolt of pleasure at Matt's teasing touch and gripped Matt's cock in his hand stroking him with a soft moan. He shifted forward and lined his cock up with Matt's and then stroked them both, their pre-cum providing enough lube to keep from chafing. Matt groaned in response.

"You'll have to be quiet, Lieutenant. The walls are thick but the windows are open," Ollie murmured against Matt's lips.

Matt rolled on top of Ollie with a sigh. "Fine." He settled between Ollie's legs. "How do you want it?"

"Let's test the bed for motion first," Ollie replied. Matt pressed up and back, listening to the frame creak.

He rolled off Ollie and grabbed the small bottle of lube from the nightstand. "Looks like it's going to be the floor or against the wall." He grinned his eyes smoky. "Or both."

"I'm so glad you're here," Ollie whispered, tucked into his spot under Matt's arm as they laid in bed after their passionate tango around the room. "What made you change your mind?"

"I missed you, and I got your email with the contract revisions. I knew they would accept them. I saw it as the perfect excuse to come." Matt kissed him and rolled Ollie onto his side so he could spoon behind him in the queen-sized bed. "I also decided I wanted to see this place, meet your family."

"I can't believe you told my dad, and he kept it a secret." Ollie stroked Matt's arm. "Makes me want to slay him at tennis."

Matt grinned and kissed the sweet spot behind Ollie's ear. "I made him swear to secrecy, and I'm glad to know he's a man of his word."

Ollie made a thoughtful sound, and chose his words carefully. "You seem very taken with Guy. Should I be worried about the two of you, nearly naked, swimming with each other tomorrow?"

Matt chuckled lightly on an exhale that was warm on Ollie's neck. "He's very handsome. I can't believe how much you look alike, but, Ollie, he is nowhere near as beautiful as you are. No one is. I love you; you are my treasure." Matt kissed the scar on Ollie's shoulder for emphasis.

Ollie closed his eyes happily, and fell asleep a moment later.

17

The View From the Balcony

MATT KNOCKED ON GUY'S DOOR the following morning at six-thirty and waited. He had his bathing suit on underneath his shorts, and one of his usual Navy t-shirts. He had left Ollie sound asleep in his bed with a kiss, knowing he would go back to his room along the balcony when he woke. He knocked again more firmly and heard the door behind him open. He turned with a start to see Guy coming out of the bathroom, dressed and ready to go with a broad smile on his handsome face.

"What is it you say? Hut, two, three, four?" Guy grinned and smacked Matt's stomach with the back of his hand and led the way down the stairs. Matt smiled at Guy's back and, with a glance at his closed bedroom door, followed.

The weather was perfect; just over seventy-five degrees with a light breeze. They ran down the long driveway, their feet crunching over the gravel and then on the grassy shoulder of the road. Matt ran alongside Guy and pressed him to run faster, until finally Guy begged to slow down.

"What's your pace?" Guy asked breathlessly.

"I usually do about a five-minute kilometer. How 'bout you?"

"Jesus, not that fast," Guy gasped. "Probably six to seven minutes on a good day."

"Let's split the difference. I want to see you push yourself," Matt said with a grin. "Earn your swim, cadet."

They made it to the river, and Matt pulled his shirt off as he admired the lush greenery and banks lined with willow trees and wildflowers. "Wow. This is beautiful." He looked back at Guy. "How many young ladies did you and Ollie seduce on these banks?"

"A fair number," Guy said, still catching his breath as he pulled off his shirt and he kicked off his sneakers. He looked over Matt's tattoos and muscled physique. "Though it turns out Ollie's heart wasn't as into it as mine was." He quirked his eyebrow, his words full of meaning.

Matt made a thoughtful sound and looked away, then turned his attention to removing his sneakers and socks. *What was it with these Turner men being so open with everyone's business?* He stripped off his shorts and walked to the water in his navy-blue trunks. He knew his swimsuit wasn't the 'norm' in America, but he hated the extra fabric of regular men's swimsuits ('bro-suits' he called them). They slowed him down, and every male swimmer he knew avoided them. He looked at Guy in his similar trunks and thought of Ollie and his even smaller swimsuits (the tan lines those left were too delectable for words) and smiled before turning to look at the crystal-clear water.

The slow-moving river looked to be about two hundred yards wide and was lined with rocks and pebbles. He waded in and sank to his neck, luxuriating at the feeling of the cool mountain water on his hot skin. He took a deep breath and disappeared under the surface where he hoped to both lose and find himself in the depths. He came up for air near the far side and looked back and searched for Guy.

"*Sacre bleu!* I thought you drowned," Guy called from waist-deep water on the side where they left their clothes. He dove under and swam to meet Matt.

Matt did laps as he waited while his soul regenerated in the cool water. He thought about Ollie, and how many people knew about his sexuality. Obviously, everyone in Ollie's family knew that he was gay and that knowledge shot a flare of anxiety through Matt. He winced at the thought of anyone in his own family knowing about his less-than-straight sexuality and marveled again at Ollie's ability to live freely within his skin as he ducked under the surface at Guy's approach.

None of Matt's sisters, or his brothers-in-law, thought he was anything but straight, or suspected that he was with Ollie. Only Matt's mother knew, and he wanted to keep it that way, *forever*. It seemed easier for parents to keep their children's secrets safe in a way siblings couldn't or wouldn't. He knew Ollie's parents, like his mother, would never say a word about him and Ollie, and felt relief.

He watched Guy from under the water as he approached and grinned to himself as Guy spun around looking for him. He admired Guy's body (he couldn't help himself) before surfacing silently behind him.

"Boo," he said in a calm, deep voice and then laughed when Guy splashed and turned with a cry.

"They teach you that in your SEAL classes?" he cried.

Matt smirked and shrugged.

Guy looked at him and wiped his face as he treaded water. He watched Matt for several moments. "You ever kill anyone?"

The question caught Matt off guard. "Would that impress you?"

Guy looked away briefly. "I don't know. *Non*."

"Have you?" Matt held his gaze.

"No," he laughed nervously.

"How would it make you feel if you had?" Matt asked, the words out of his mouth before he could call them back. He did not want to have a philosophical discussion about the things he had done for the US government.

Guy blew out a breath. "I guess it depends on why I did, or how it happened."

Matt blinked and thought of how to change the subject. "Is Guy short for Guillermo?"

Guy laughed. "No. It's just Guy. G-u-y. The Brits and the Americans butcher it when they see it written, especially when it's followed by 'Turner,' and not something like Aubert or Dubois."

A smile of realization spread on Matt's face. "Ah. I would have too. I didn't realize there was any other way to pronounce your name."

"*Pas de soucis*," Guy waved his hand and made a face so like Ollie's.

Matt caught his breath at the resemblance and kept his eyes off Guy's mouth. "Wanna see something cool?" he asked, and dove under the water without waiting for Guy's response.

Matt searched the depths for what he was looking for, and kept one eye on Guy cycling his legs.

Matt surfaced next to Guy a moment later, holding a two-foot trout, and beamed enthusiastically, not sure why he wanted to impress Ollie's cousin, but couldn't help himself.

"Holy shit!" Guy exclaimed. "Did you just catch that with your bare hands?"

"No. I was upriver fly fishing. Didn't you see me?" Matt grinned, kissed the side of the fish and let it go.

"How in the bloody hell did you do that?"

Matt shrugged; happy he had succeeded in his mission. "I'm full of surprises, Guy." He disappeared under the water again and surfaced near the middle. "What are you waiting for slow poke?" He smiled to himself and was feeling at ease in a way he hadn't anticipated. There was something relaxing about Guy that he was learning was the essence of the Turner men.

Guy shook his head and broke into a fast crawl. He arrived at the other side to find Matt sitting on a wide flat rock in the shallow water, the current running over his calves. He pulled himself up onto the rock next to Matt.

"You really are a fish. Ollie wasn't kidding," Guy laughed, slightly breathless. "How did you meet Ollie? Did he apply for a job or something?"

Matt ran his hands back and forth over his hair, shaking the droplets out and leaving it in disarray. "My friend Finn introduced us. She knew Ollie at Oxford."

"Oh, Finn," Guy said somewhat reverently. "I met her once. She's bloody beautiful, and so smart. I tried to get her to go out with me, but she said she was getting over a broken engagement. What kind of idiot would let her go?" He scoffed with a smile and looked across the river. His smile fell. "Oh, *merde*." He looked back at Matt after a moment. "She said he was in the service. Christ, was that you?" Guy smoothed his hair nervously.

Matt pulled a face for effect in order to sell the lie. "Yeah. I was the idiot who let her get away. Don't worry; I admit I was an idiot, and she and I are best friends. I don't know what I'd do without her. Like I said, she introduced me to Ollie, who is the smartest person I have ever met, and my company has thrived because of him."

Matt caught movement out of the corner of his eye. "Speak of the devil." He grinned at Guy. "How long do you suppose he took on his hair this morning?" he asked, knowing that it couldn't have been long because the waves were visible and unruly, just the way he liked them.

Guy threw his head back and laughed as Ollie got off the bike and propped it against a tree. The basket was full of towels and there was a box strapped to the back.

"I brought you assholes towels, and you're laughing at me; aren't you?" Ollie looked pointedly at Matt.

Matt winked when Guy's head was turned. "Thank you, Oliver. I don't know what I'd do without you."

"Don't you forget it." He stripped off his shirt and shoes, took the box off the back of the bike and waded out to them.

"Did you bring food? I'm starving." Matt quirked his brow and kept his eyes off Ollie's smooth bare skin. He might not have spent time on his hair, but he had on using that lotion that made his skin all shimmery, to Matt's great delight.

Ollie deposited the box in Matt's lap. "Of course I did. Share that though; it's from Amelie for both of you." He looked at Guy. "Being a general counsel isn't glamorous, especially not for this demanding bastard. Don't let anyone tell you otherwise."

Guy laughed lightly as he looked between them, and Matt caught something in Guy's expression that made him turn away.

Matt ran back to the chateau ahead of Guy and Ollie who pedaled slowly alongside Guy. Ollie scanned the familiar fields on either side of the small road and then turned his face to the sun with a smile, his heart light and happy.

"You have the hots for your boss don't you," Guy breathed in French, his feet crunching in the gravel of the road.

"Non," Ollie scoffed and opened his eyes. "I mean, oui. He's gorgeous, but I just really respect him and am in awe of what he has achieved in his short life. He's only thirty you know."

"Really?" Guy puzzled. "He's an enigma. Sometimes he seems young but most of the time he seems positively ancient and uptight. Should we get him drunk tonight?" he asked mischievously.

"You could try. But he never gets blitzed. I think he has a hollow leg."

"Just be careful, Oliver. You have always worn your heart on your sleeve, and I don't want anyone to take advantage of you and your feelings. There's no way he doesn't know how you feel."

Ollie watched Guy with a smile, touched by the concern he was showing him. "Matt would never take advantage of me. He depends on me too much. He'd be lost without me. You heard him."

Matt and Ollie played cards after dinner with Guy, Cassie and Genevieve, laughing and drinking as the hours passed. Guy refilled Matt's bourbon with purpose, until Matt covered his glass with his hand and switched to water. Genevieve was flirting openly with Matt. The more drinks she had the more she touched his arm and laughed at his comments. She was beautiful like her mother, all eyes and lips and curly hair, with a willowy frame and perky breasts.

Matt looked at her over his cards, and flirted lightly in return. Before he met Ollie, he would have encouraged her, *definitely* would have fucked her, she was his type then. But once he met Ollie, it was as though a switch rerouted his train, and his destination became Ollie and only Ollie. The other trains on the tracks he used to run on still flashed by like beautiful scenery, but his eyes never lingered on or longed for anything he saw out the window; he was singularly focused on where his train was bound.

Matt waited in his Tom Ford underwear by the window for Ollie to come. The smell of the orchard filled his nose and the whisky buzz still hummed through his blood. There was certainty deep in his bones that Ollie would come to him like he had the night before. He closed his eyes and exhaled the breath he didn't realize he was holding when he saw Ollie's beautiful face appear in the open window frame. He helped him step down and pulled him into his arms.

"Another day of longing and not being able to touch you and your absurdly soft skin. I don't know how I survived," Matt murmured against Ollie's lips as he kissed him, sweeping his tongue passionately through Ollie's mouth. "What is it about you?"

"You taste like whisky. A *lot* of whisky," Ollie breathed with a low chuckle. "Did Guy get you drunk?"

Matt hummed briefly. "I'm drunk on you," he said slowly as Ollie pressed him back against the wall.

Matt pulled off Ollie's shirt and ran his hands through Ollie's hair before running his hands slowly down his back. He ghosted his nose along Ollie's jaw and then neck, breathing in Ollie's heavenly scent. A bit sandalwood, a bit fresh air, and a bit indescribable. Matt nibbled and licked his way to where Ollie's neck met his shoulder as he lifted his hand to Ollie's mouth and pressed a finger between Ollie's lips.

Ollie swirled his tongue around Matt's middle finger and then sucked gently with a moan. He knew what was coming and Matt couldn't help but smile at his needy man.

Ollie's skin was warm under his fingertips and Matt's free hand roamed unabashedly before stopping and pinching one of Ollie's nipples. Matt pulled his finger out of Ollie's mouth and captured Ollie's gasp with his lips. He pulled the waistband of Ollie's underwear away from his body and slipped his hand inside. He ran his wet fingertip over Ollie's tight hole and tapped twice before pressing lightly.

Ollie exhaled a moan into Matt's mouth and pressed back, and then forward to rub his hard cock over Matt's. "Yes. Put it in."

Matt's finger eased past the first tight ring of Ollie's pucker while his other hand gripped Ollie's ass cheek. He thrust gently in and out in sync with Ollie's hips rocking back and forth for a few moments before stepping back.

"I want your beautiful mouth on me," Matt whispered, kissing all the soft and hard spots between the dimple on Ollie's cheek and his beautiful neck.

Ollie licked Matt's upper lip and began kneeling. He kissed his way down Matt's chest and lowered Matt's underwear with a murmur of delight when Matt's cock slapped back up against his stomach. Matt groaned and spread wide as Ollie licked him, it felt like his tongue was everywhere, between his legs and on his balls, before he took him deep. Matt was dizzy from the sensation of Ollie's warm mouth, his swirling tongue, and his firm grip.

Matt pressed his head back against the wall to steady himself, not sure if he really was more buzzed than he thought and took a deep breath. He looked down and was mesmerized by the sight of Ollie bobbing on his dick with gusto. He then moaned when Ollie looked up with eyes that were dark with desire.

Matt suddenly couldn't decide if wanted to come in Ollie's mouth or take him to the bed so he could come all over him and then feed the resulting splatter to Ollie with his fingers. Or if he wanted to come deep inside him, Ollie's legs splayed, one arm folded behind his head and the other hand on his cock. The fantasies battled inside his brain until finally he seized Ollie by both arms and hauled him to his feet. He kissed him passionately and tasted himself on Ollie's tongue with a groan.

"You've got me so close I can barely walk," Matt murmured. "But I need to decorate your body. Have a seat."

Matt steered him silently to the low bed and sat him down. He watched as Ollie took him into his mouth again and buried his fingers in Ollie's glorious waves. Matt thrust in ever quicker strokes as his heart raced. He held Ollie's head tightly in his grip as his dick hit the back of Ollie's throat and caused him to gag and drool. He felt the pleasure build because of Ollie's soft tongue and his insistent fingers that were stroking behind his tight balls. He suddenly let go of Ollie's head with an exhale and gripped his dick.

"Fuuuuck." Matt nudged Ollie's shoulder and watched as he fell back on the bed.

Ollie folded his arms above his head in the way Matt loved and he groaned as he stroked himself through his orgasm.

"God, I love you, Ollie," he cried out quietly, watching as the splatters hit Ollie's chest and chin like paint on the most beautiful of canvases.

Matt eventually unlocked his knees, his breath coming in short gasps, and knelt between Ollie's legs. He pushed them into Ollie's chest and dove in for his dessert.

* * *

Ollie woke to a note on the pillow next to him, same as the one the day before:

Gone for a run, go back to your room—M

He smiled and wondered if Matt packed the notepaper and pen with him as he got up and searched for his underwear on the floor before finding them neatly folded on the foot of the bed. He stretched on the balcony, the passion of the previous night at the forefront of his mind and marveled at the early morning beauty of the orchard like a lovesick teenager. He inhaled the scented air and listened to the faint buzz of insects with a dopey smile. It was going to be another incredible day without a cloud in the sky, and Ollie felt like singing.

Ollie brushed his teeth and dressed for breakfast in shorts and his favorite navy-blue Armani t-shirt. He greeted his parents and aunt and uncle on the patio with a broad smile and sat for soft boiled eggs and fruit. Cassie and Genny breezed through to have coffee and a bit of fruit before leaving for town.

"Any sign of Matt or Guy?" Ollie asked between bites of food.

"Matt ate and disappeared into the study, and Guy hasn't been down yet," Clare replied in French.

Guy appeared at that moment and said his hellos. He looked at Ollie with a grin and sat for coffee.

They ate and discussed the weather, the vineyard, and the plans for the day.

Ollie got up to leave the table when he finished his coffee, and Guy stood. "Walk the vineyard with me, cousin."

Ollie shrugged. "*D'accord.*"

He followed Guy off the patio and down into the vineyard noticing the gnarled stems and the branches that were heavy with fruit. Guy paused from time to time to check the grapes and to caress the globes gently. He led Ollie from the vineyard to the orchard and came to a stop in the middle of one of the rows, just under the balcony outside Ollie and Matt's rooms.

Guy looked up at the house. "So," he said simply in French.

Ollie paused waiting. "*Et alors?*"

"I didn't believe you about your straight boyfriend. That sounded like *such* a gay boy fantasy," Guy laughed and waved his hand. "Until I saw it with my own eyes."

Ollie frowned. "*De quoi parlez-vous?*"

"I went to your room last night, like I always did when you were here, when we were kids. I wanted to show you a silly video." He held Ollie's gaze, as Ollie stomach sank. "Your window was open, and I thought you were on the balcony maybe smoking some *weed* or something, and I went out." Ollie swallowed. He waited with his mind racing.

"*Je t'ai vu.*"

"What did you see? I'm sure you're imagining things." Ollie blushed a deep red as he remembered Matt's cock in his mouth, Matt's tongue in his ass. Then his cock in Matt's mouth and Matt's cock in his ass before going back in Ollie's mouth.

Guy laughed. "I didn't imagine seeing his rather *sizable* cock in your mouth, or him coming all over you. Please. I'd rather I didn't. Some things once seen can never be unseen." He shuddered dramatically.

Ollie's heart was pounding as his eyes scanned the orchard. He was searching for an excuse, a way out, while thanking god that was the only bit of the evening Guy had witnessed.

"I can explain. He was drunk. You got him drunk. I took advantage of him. You said it yourself I have a crush on him. It's never happened before."

Guy twisted his mouth and scoffed lightly. "He said 'I love you, Ollie,' as I turned away. Must've been *quite* the blow job for him to have said that the first time." He chuckled. "I also noticed that new necklace of yours looks suspiciously like that tattoo of his.

"You know, I was only worried because it seemed like he was taking advantage of you. It appears I was wrong."

"*S'il te plaît.* You can't say anything to *anyone.* Not your parents, not your sisters, no one. My parents know, but not Cass," Ollie pleaded. "He was straight, is straight. I mean he won't acknowledge that he's gay. Guy, he broke up with me for months because someone saw me leave a closet after he did. They didn't even see anything and he freaked. I love him. If he knew you saw us? Doing *that?*" Ollie shook his head rapidly in a panic. His breakfast churned and made ready to escape the confines of his stomach.

Guy pulled him into a hug with a face full of concern. "Christ, Ollie. I love you. I won't say a word. I only brought it up to tease you. I mean, it was like a porn, you perv." Guy threw his head back with a laugh and then stepped back dramatically. "You showered, right?"

Ollie hit Guy's chest with the back of his hand and exhaled with relief. "You're the perv for watching. How long were you standing there with your hand in your pants?" he said shakily, his adrenaline still surging.

"For a second, but it felt like hours. I couldn't turn away. It was like a train wreck. I'll be seeing my therapist three times a week now thank you very much."

"Don't be such a prude. Like you've never come all over someone." Ollie rolled his eyes and paused. "But seriously, thank you for keeping quiet about it. He's very private."

"No one knows? No one at work knows? How do you hide it there?" Guy puzzled as they continued walking among the trees.

"Our friend Finn knows, her best friend, Naomi, and Finn's dad and Matt's mom, but that's it aside from my parents. I'm Matt's right hand at work so it makes sense that we're always together, and I don't moon over him there. I'm far too busy," Ollie said emphatically.

"That sounds insane, Oliver. But we do crazy fucking things when we're in love, don't we?" Guy shook his head. "Let's bike into town," he suggested, effectively changing the subject.

"I sure as shit do a lot of crazy things for that man. You have no idea." Ollie looked away. "Let me just check on Matt, and we'll go."

Ollie followed Guy back to the house and headed to the study while Guy went to the bike shed. He knocked on the closed study door as he turned the knob and stepped into the room. Matt looked up from his laptop and smiled.

"Morning, sleeping beauty. You just getting up now?" Matt looked at his Rolex and then laced his hands on his head as he sat back in his chair.

"No," Ollie answered with a laugh. "I had breakfast with my parents and everyone, and then took a walk with Guy. Now we're biking into town. Do you need anything from me for work? Or want anything from town?"

"I forwarded you a few emails but they can wait until you get back. Go have fun."

Guy peppered him with questions about Matt and work as they rode their bikes into the walled town. Ollie answered them cautiously, and made sure to return the favor on the trip home with their purchases strapped onto the back of Guy's bike and in Ollie's front basket.

"What about the two ladies you're dating? You going to pick one and settle down?"

"It won't be with either one of them," Guy shook his head. "Isabelle is beautiful but needy, and Renee has babies on the brain, and I'm not ready for that. You know, Matt reminded me about Finn. She was something else. Is she single?"

"Yes, last time we spoke anyway. But Matt is incredibly protective of her. I wouldn't recommend it."

"He had his shot with her," Guy laughed. "Why did they split? Is she secretly a horrible person? A terrible lay? Is that why she's still single?"

Ollie laughed. "She is the most remarkable woman. And while I can't speak to her prowess in bed, I can tell you they weren't *really* engaged. His father was dying so they pretended. They've never been *together*."

"Well, that's a relief. I'd hate to be the man who follows that cock. I mean, mine's plenty big but, Christ." Guy widened his eyes.

"Trust me, I know. There are none who compare. It was awful when we split." Ollie shook his head. "Anyway, they're just best friends, and she's his business partner, owns nearly half of SharkFinn."

"Oh, so she's rich?" Guy beamed.

"She was rich before that." Ollie told him Finn's mother's maiden name.

"*Merde*." Guy shook his head in wonder. "Do you think she'd move to France? I'm serious, *Olivier*. She's beautiful and smart, *and* has her own money? Sign me up!"

"Then you had better be nice to Matt. *He's* why she's still single."

Amelie served a feast of grilled chicken and vegetables from the garden, with grilled apricots and romaine for Matt and Ollie's last night in Lyon. The weather was perfect, the conversation was lively, and the scent of grapes and apricots wafted sensuously around them. Ollie couldn't keep his eyes off Matt as he relaxed in his chair after dinner.

Matt was listening to the conversation, which was mostly in English but peppered with French, and shifted his gaze between all the people at the table. Ollie watched Guy turn his charm onto Matt who was oblivious to the knowing smile Guy wore all night. If Matt was suspicious, he hid it well, probably because he was pleased with all the attention. Ollie suppressed stab of jealousy, again, as Matt laughed at yet another one of Guy's jokes.

"What time is your flight tomorrow?" Aunt Clare asked Ollie at their end of the long table, drawing his eyes away from the scene of his annoyance.

"We're flying on the company jet. I believe the flight is around noon."

"Matt has his own plane?" Genevieve asked, looking speculatively at Matt.

"Oui. He never flies commercial anymore."

"Is he single?"

Ollie laughed. "Yes, but he prefers women, not little girls."

"I've got dibs on him anyway, Genny, so look elsewhere," Cassie warned with a gleam in her eye.

Ollie shook his head with amusement and looked out at the last of the sunset, the sky burning red and gold just over the tops of the grapevines.

Guy followed Ollie to his room after their parents said goodnight. Matt had excused himself after dinner to work in Lloyd's study but as they passed the room on the way to the stairs, Ollie saw that it was empty. Guy flopped on Ollie's bed, and made no signs of leaving until Ollie figured out he was delaying his visit to Matt's room intentionally.

Guy laughed as Ollie prodded him off the bed. "Took you long enough to figure out I was fucking with you. I was running out of things to talk about."

"Yeah. I was just being polite, and clearly forgot I don't have to be with you. I knew when you started on about software updates that you were playing me. Now shoo." Ollie made to shove him out the door.

"You so eager to get drenched in cum again?"

"I'm eager not to hear your voice anymore." Ollie shut the door on Guy's laugh.

Matt was on his phone typing out an email when Ollie climbed through the window. He looked up with a smile and tossed his phone on the nightstand.

"Took you long enough."

Ollie smiled to himself at the echo of Guy's words. "Guy was sobbing about my departure tomorrow. I had to console him."

"I got something for you to console." Matt gripped himself over his underwear.

Ollie chuckled and stripped off his shirt. He tossed it toward the chair in the corner but missed and bit his lip at Matt's slow blink.

They ended up on the floor because of the creaky bed. Matt prepped and fucked Ollie until he was breathless and then paused with a gasp.

"My knees are killing me."

"Maybe if you didn't run so much your knees wouldn't bother you," Ollie panted. "I really think you should just shut up and keep fucking me. I'm not complaining about the splinters in my palms."

"Aren't you though? Stop talking, Ollie. I'm trying to fuck you." He squeezed Ollie's ass for emphasis. "I'd smack this beautiful thing if it wouldn't make so much noise."

"You can smack it 'til it's raw when we get home, Lieutenant. Just fuck me harder."

Matt pulled out and rolled onto his back. "This will save my knees and your precious palms. Hop on, cowboy."

Ollie scooted over and straddled Matt. He leaned down for a kiss and sank back onto Matt's cock with a sigh. "Fuuuck, you feel incredible. I'm not gonna last. You know I never do when I'm riding your cock." Ollie rolled his hips and moaned.

The floor was hard under his knees, as was Matt's chest under his hands but Ollie couldn't feel anything other than Matt's cock rubbing against that heavenly spot inside him. Matt gripped Ollie's hips and drove up into him with his eyes locked on Ollie's.

"I know that look," Matt growled as he continued to pummel into Ollie. "You're close."

Ollie nodded, incapable of speech as he focused on keeping hips angled just right.

Matt's warm hand fisted his bobbing cock and Ollie was undone. He gripped Matt's shoulders as he ground down and rolled his hips. "Oh, god . . . just like that. . . ." he cried softly, rolling and riding Matt until his orgasm burst free of his body.

Matt cursed in Italian as he came, his hips stuttering as he filled Ollie's ass in sync with Ollie filling his hand. A few splatters hit Matt's chin, and Ollie leaned forward to lick them off as he caught his breath.

"Holy fuck. I'm not walking anywhere for a while." Ollie grinned.

Matt squeezed Ollie's ass. "Good. Because I have no intention of letting you leave my bed."

18

Back to Life, Back to Reality

MATT AND OLLIE said their goodbyes in the driveway as the driver put their luggage in the back of the SUV. Ollie's uncle invited them both to return next year as Guy caught Matt off guard by hugging him tightly. He then turned to Ollie and hugged and kissed him emphatically on both cheeks.

"I'll be visiting you and Finn sometime soon," Guy said in French. "Let her know I can't stop thinking about her."

Ollie scoffed. "I'm not telling her that. She'll change her identity and go into hiding, you stalky freak."

Guy threw his head back and laughed. "Okay, then just tell her I said hello."

"What was that all about?" Matt asked once they were under way, the car bouncing along the dirt road.

"Guy fancies Chuck."

Matt made a thoughtful sound and looked out the window. "That's why he was laying on the charm so thick last night. You said something to him about me didn't you."

"Oui," Ollie replied with a laugh. "You are her gatekeeper."

"He's a nice guy, good job, *great* family," Matt said with a pointed look at Ollie. "Maybe," he added with a shrug.

Ollie looked at him with surprise. "Really? He would never live in America."

Matt frowned. "He'd have to move. If he really loved her he would. You did for your love," he added with a smile.

Ollie grinned. "Best decision I ever made."

* * *

"Remember, my parents are coming soon with Cass. They'll come to watch the tournament, I hope you can too," Ollie said the next day on the deck as they sat in the shade, waiting for the sun to come over the house. "And other than that, what are we doing? I'll have to take Cass to the city while she's here."

Matt sighed. "They'll stay at Chuck's. She and I talked about it this morning. She's happy to have them. But, Ollie, you're sleeping here. I can only be so accommodating."

"Oh, is that so? What if I want a week of not being groped?" Ollie replied, not meaning a word of it.

A small smile spread on Matt's face. "Fine. I dare you." Matt licked his lips and ran his hand slowly over the front of his shorts. The outline of his soft cock was clearly visible, and Ollie forced his eyes away. "But that means you can't grope me either," Matt added coyly.

Ollie pursed his lips and faked that he was considering it. "I should take that dare."

Matt scoffed. "You would never last."

"You project like nobody's business."

Matt quirked his brow with a grin. "Not in this instance. But no matter, I have a key to Chuck's. I'll drag you out by your hair."

Ollie gasped with a little thrill at the thought. "You really are a caveman."

"You love it," Matt said and turned his face to the ocean, leaving his hand draped provocatively in his crotch.

"I do. I really do, you sexy bastard." Ollie shook his head and studied Matt's perfect profile.

* * *

Matt and Ollie spent one day at the office upon their return to Boston, and then worked from Truro while they counted down the days until Ollie's family arrived. Ollie left every Sunday to play polo and returned at night, smelling faintly of horses.

Matt woke Finn early, as he did every couple of days, for a run around the warren of the streets of their private neighborhood and then returned along the beach. Jayne ran alongside, off-leash, and kept up with them easily.

"Did you have an overnight guest the other night?"

Finn slid her glance at Matt and then away. "Are you spying on me?"

Matt grinned. "So, the answer's yes. Who was it?"

She sighed. "Glenn again. His family has a place on Harding's Shore, and he came for drinks. It's a long way back to Chatham at night with tons of cops, so he stayed over."

"Did you make him keep his letterman jacket on?" Matt teased. "What was the hostess gift this time? A signed football from his Pop-Warner days?"

"No, but he did bring his A-game," Finn laughed and ran away from Matt.

"I still don't approve," Matt called after her, and then easily caught up. "I met Guy. He raved about you."

"Oh, is that right?"

"Yeah, and you know what? I actually like him. He's infinitely better than that bozo, Glenn."

Finn snorted and looked at Matt. "What's happening right now? Are you playing matchmaker?"

"Why not?" Matt asked defensively. "You set me up with Ollie and look how well that turned out."

"Yeah, but I was following your rule about not getting involved with friends' friends, and certainly not their family." Finn stopped running. "I wanted Ollie for you, and when Guy hit on me, I declined because I didn't want messy in case things didn't work out between him and me."

Matt wiped his face with his shirt and looked around. "Yeah, but I think you guys would be good together. And if it doesn't work out, he'll be in France."

Finn eyed him. "And if it does work out? He won't leave Europe. . . ."

Matt shrugged his eyebrows. "He'll have to." He took off running without waiting for a response.

19

Brilliant Disguise

MATT BROUGHT OLLIE'S PARENTS and sister to Finn's beach house in Truro and then parked his car in his driveway and took the path through the wide tree line to join them for dinner. After dodging Cassie's kisses so they landed on his cheeks and not his mouth he helped Ollie get his parents settled while Finn gave Cassie the tour.

After dinner, Ollie took Cassie next door and gave Cassie tour of his and Matt's house where he skipped showing her the primary bedroom and his home office on the first floor. Matt was such a neat freak there weren't many personal possessions left lying around (outside of those two rooms) so Ollie didn't worry about Cassie finding out the house was half his.

"Christ. This place is amazing!" she exclaimed. "I don't know whose house I like better. And they live next door to each other?" Cassie mused to Ollie. "I bet his skinny model girlfriend dumped him because he's still close with Finn. I wouldn't care. He could have tea and crumpets with her every day, I'd just sit on this deck in the sun, and wait for him to come home." She waggled her eyebrows. "He's so bloody gorgeous, and so fucking rich. You still pining for him?"

"No, Cass. I have a boyfriend, and he's perfect."

"Oh, but he's not here?"

"No. He's traveling." Ollie turned and left Cassie on the deck.

Ollie took his parents and Cassie to Carnival in Provincetown, where he was eye-fucked and flirted with nearly the whole time. There was a particular group of men dressed identically in brightly colored, see-through kaftans over gold lame Speedos, who had stood near Ollie when he had stopped to watch the parade on Commercial Street. They peppered him with compliments and suggestive remarks which spurred a conversation, much to his sister's amusement.

"Oh my god, your accent!" One of the men exclaimed and turned to look at his friends. The giant floral arrangement on his head bobbed excitedly and Ollie had to bite his cheek to keep from laughing. "He's gorgeous, has knock-out legs," he said dramatically, "*and* the accent of a duke?"

The man turned back to Ollie and scanned his eyes over Ollie's linen Prada button down and flat-front tennis shorts with a five-inch inseam. He reached out to touch the trident on Ollie's necklace and then trailed his fingers lightly over the skin that was exposed by the two buttons Ollie had left undone. Ollie was thankful in that moment that Matt had decided against coming.

"Are you single?" the man asked coyly.

"Who cares?" One of his companions chimed in. "That never stopped you before, Steve. What happens in P-Town stays in P-Town!" He snapped his fingers.

"I'm not single." Ollie smiled. "And my boyfriend does care."

A lot.

"Come on, Ollie. I'm hungry," Cassie interrupted as the men groaned.

Ollie waved goodbye and led the way to the restaurant that Matt loved. Ollie had enjoyed the exchange but wished he'd been with Matt. Ollie was always proud to be seen with Matt, even if it was under some ruse or as coworkers, but he also wished they could walk the streets arm and arm, or even hand in hand, like the lovers they were.

When they got back to the house, Ollie helped Finn with dinner while his parents had a cocktail with Cassie on the deck. Ollie cooked the lobsters in sea water, just as Matt had taught him, and grilled the veggies while listening to his family laugh on the large sectional on the far side of the deck.

Matt joined them just as they were sitting down to eat and sat in his spot at the head of the table. He was wearing the same linen pants and linen shirt that he had on when Ollie left, and it was rumpled from sitting at his desk for most of the day. Ollie ran his eyes over him and noted how tired he looked. He wanted to remark on it, and he wanted to chastise Matt for working too hard but couldn't because of his sister. He glanced at Cassie with irritation, and then got mad at himself for resenting her presence.

Don't be mad at her. It's really Matt's fault that you can't be yourself, a chiding voice in his head chimed in.

"How was P-Town?" Matt interrupted Ollie's thoughts as he passed David the corn.

"Crowded. Colorful. Fun," Ollie's father replied with a smile.

"I warned you." Matt grinned and shifted his gaze to Finn. "What did you do all day?"

"I worked on my paper about a recent discovery of a Babylonia era tomb in Iraq." She took a sip of wine. "Really wish I could go see it in person."

"Not a chance, Chuck." Matt cut her off with his eyebrows raised.

Ollie looked between them and noticed how Finn deferred to Matt's commands just like he himself did.

"Have you been?" Cassie interrupted.

Ollie watched as Matt turned his eyes to her. "Yes."

"What's it like?"

"Depends on where you go. Baghdad is like any city and the mosques are beautiful. But then there's a lot of deserts. It's hot, and it can be dangerous. Particularly for Americans." He looked back at Finn with a set jaw. "You'll have to make do with the pictures."

Finn held his gaze and Ollie watched her features soften. "I know."

Ollie looked at Matt and saw the tightness around his eyes. Matt hardly talked about his time in the service, and what little he had said was terrifying and stressful. He knew Matt's protective 'wall' was about to go up and that it would undoubtably be misconstrued as rudeness by his family. Ollie searched for something to say to change the subject.

"Well, I could've used the warning for P-Town today," Ollie interjected and looked from his parents to Matt with a mock-serious expression. "Quite dangerous for men. I now understand why you don't go. I wonder how many kidnappings take place during Carnival week."

Matt's eyes went to Ollie like a whip. There was something behind them as he grinned, and Ollie didn't know if it was relief at the change of subject or ire at the thought of men ogling him. "Is that right?"

"Oh yeah." Cassie laughed and tossed a lobster shell into the big metal bowl in front of her. "Ollie was a big hit. Especially with a bunch of guys in gold Speedos and floral headdresses. They nearly ran off with him."

Ollie hid his grin as Matt raised his eyebrows and shook his head. The tightness was gone from his face and replaced with another look entirely. Ollie exhaled and couldn't wait for the inquisition later.

After dinner, Matt and Ollie carried the firepit down to the beach. Ollie watched the breeze catch Matt's linen shirt, as if it too were irritated with how rumpled it was, and waited for Matt to bring up the conversation from dinner. Matt was silent but brooding as a gust of wind blew Ollie's hair into his face. Ollie exhaled a burst of air to get it out of his eye and waited for Matt to speak.

"How many guys would I have punched out today, Ollie?" Matt raised his eyebrows at Ollie's short shorts as they followed the boardwalk to the hightide mark.

"Quite a few, Lieutenant," Ollie replied in a light tone. "Though only a couple were bold enough to grab my ass."

"What?" Matt snapped and stopped with a scowl.

Ollie stumbled slightly. He knew Matt was jealous (over-the-top jealous some might say) but he didn't think it would extend to harmless strangers.

"You know Carnival." Ollie shrugged nonchalantly. "I stopped to chat with some of the more colorfully dressed men and several wanted pictures with me. Naturally," Ollie said with a cocky grin to lighten the mood. "One or two of them put their hand on my ass instead of my waist. It was harmless."

Matt made a displeased sound and his nostrils flared. "You're not going alone next year."

Ollie laughed as they resumed walking. "Oh. Are you going to fight them all, whilst declaring to have no feelings for me whatsoever?"

Matt frowned. "Sexual harassment is sexual harassment, Oliver."

"Then I better speak to HR." Ollie made a dramatic face and bit his cheek to hide his smile.

Matt chuckled low in his throat. "Any complaints you have could be easily shot down with evidence against you. I save all my receipts."

"So do I. Of course, I save the texts and pictures you send me for *other* reasons, but I could present them as evidence if need be."

Matt shook his head with a laugh and held Ollie's gaze as they paused at the end of the wooden walkway.

"I'll always remember my first time here with you," Ollie said softly, changing the subject as they stepped into the sand, their bare feet sinking sensuously into the cool softness. "It was amazing. It's been amazing ever since. I love you," he whispered.

"I love you too, Ollie," Matt replied quietly, his eyes locked on the trident pendant glinting at the top of Ollie's chest muscles which were flexed pleasingly with exertion. "Should we have sex outside tonight? Since we're reminiscing about our first time here." Matt smiled and quirked his eyebrow.

"If you think you can keep it down. My parents sleep with their windows open."

Matt narrowed his eyes in thought. "I told you, Ollie. You feel too good. I can't help myself. But I managed to be quiet in Lyon."

Ollie thought about Guy. "Yes, I supposed you did, for the most part."

Finn, Cassie, and Ollie's parents appeared on the walkway with folding beach chairs, interrupting them. Finn had a shopping bag of long sticks, and treats, and opened a bag of marshmallows when she sat down. Matt filled the firepit with wood and driftwood, then lit it and fanned the flames. The wood crackled and popped satisfyingly while the resulting sparks floated above the smoke and then drifted away as smudges on the light breeze. They roasted marshmallows for s'mores while the chocolate bars and peanut butter cups on the graham crackers softened on the wide rim of the fire pit.

"These are fantastic," Maggie exclaimed. "Why have we never made them before?"

"They're messy," Ollie replied with his eyes on Matt, who was sitting back in his chair with his whisky, watching everyone else eat. Ollie knew how Matt hated the stickiness of the hot marshmallows on his fingers, and the dripping of the melted chocolate on his clothes. "But so worth it." Ollie took a bite and grinned when the chocolate trickled down his chin.

Matt smiled at Ollie and looked heatedly at the drip of chocolate. "I suppose messy things often are." He met David's eye and grinned as David laughed.

"I hope you didn't mean me when you were talking about messy things," Ollie said as he rolled on his side to face Matt. "I've gotten tidier."

"You're a slob, Ollie," Matt responded with a gentle grin.

"I am not," Ollie said defensively, his voice shrill.

"I love you, baby. But if I didn't follow you around with a hamper, our homes would be overrun with your panties and t-shirts and dirty dishes."

Ollie threw his head back laughing. "I don't wear *panties*, you perv."

Matt rolled on top of Ollie, tickling him, Ollie's shrieks filling the room. "Your sexy briefs are tiny enough to be considered panties. I hope you don't wear them in the locker room at the polo club. The WASPs would faint. The horses would faint. I don't dare mention your jock straps, or those undies with the mesh panels."

"Stop, stop! I can't breathe!" Ollie gasped as he laughed.

Matt stilled his hands and stared down. "You are so beautiful and so smart. I don't care how messy you are. I live to clean up after you, especially when you wear your sexy panties. Your ass is phenomenal in them."

My ass is phenomenal in them, Ollie thought, as he opened his mouth to Matt's tongue.

20

Games People Play

OLLIE WOKE EARLY to make breakfast at Finn's the following morning. He was waiting for the bacon and frittatas to finish cooking when Cassie came down the stairs. Jayne greeted her with a woof and a wagging tail.

Cassie gave Ollie the side eye. "Where were you last night?"

Ollie frowned. "Why do you ask?"

Cassie stirred milk into her coffee. "I went your room to ask you something and your bed was made. Still is," she added pointedly.

Ollie rolled his eyes. *Jesus, she really is as nosy as Matt worried.*

"Matt and I had a conference call last night with Australia. I didn't want Jayne to wake the house barking at me when I came back so I crashed at his place." Ollie shook his head. "Just wait until you join the real world, Cass. Work isn't nine to five." He stood as the timer beeped and pulled breakfast out of the oven. "Are you coming to my polo match? I have a tournament at three."

"Right. Hot fields, smelly horses, I hated watching you play when I was kid, why would I want to come watch you now?"

"We've got some Argentinian players coming to the tournament. It's a twelve goal, which is a big deal this far north."

Cassie made an appreciative sound. "I do love the Argentinian players, but I'm gonna stay here with Finn."

Ollie turned at the sound of the deck door and saw Matt appear in shorts and a tight US Navy t-shirt. His feet were beautiful and bare as they always were at the beach. Jayne greeted him with a happy woof and wriggled against him as he headed for the kitchen.

"No cereal at home, Mr. Dion?" Ollie asked teasingly.

Matt slid his glance at Cassie, and discreetly waggled his fingers at Ollie in warning. "Someone left the box open; it's all stale." He shrugged nonchalantly.

Ollie made a thoughtful sound. "But you live alone. Do you think someone broke in and left all your cereal open?" Ollie gasped dramatically. He pushed the big bowl of cut fruit in Matt's direction with a small bowl and a fork. "You can eat this while you wait for the police to conduct a full investigation."

Matt widened his eyes and looked threateningly at Ollie's tickle spots and then back at Ollie's grinning face with a stern expression while Cassie was distracted by her phone. He dished himself a full bowl of fruit with a shake of his head and then sat at the long farmhouse table.

"What time's the tournament?" Matt asked between bites.

"Three, I think we'll leave here around one."

Cassie looked up from her phone. "Where's the match?"

"Dover. It's about thirty minutes or so west of Boston."

"And how far is that from here?" Cassie asked as she dished herself a bowl of fruit. "It took an hour or more on the ferry, and I recall you saying it was shorter than the drive."

"Dover is about two-hours without traffic, but we'll be going by helicopter." Ollie looked at Matt. "Matt is letting us use SharkFinn's."

"Cor," Cassie breathed. "I've never been in a helicopter." She looked at Matt with a longing glance. "I promise, I would make sure the cereal boxes were fully sealed at *all* times," she said to Matt with comically wide eyes.

Ollie watched as Matt chuckled and shoved a forkful of fruit in his mouth.

It was a quick and scenic ride in the helicopter to Bill's farm, where they transferred to Bill's SUV and drove the short distance to the Sentry Club. Ollie led his parents to Bill's spot next to the announcer's booth and left them to set up the chairs and the table Bill had packed in the car for tailgating while he and Bill went to meet their grooms and check their horses.

He and Bill both had six horses which were tethered to the side of the trailers, four in full tack and two with just bridles and reins. Xander and Philip were responsible for swapping the saddles and wiping the horses down between chukkers while Ollie and Bill just focused on the game.

Ollie was excited that one of the Argentinian pros, Lucas, who was making the rounds of tournaments, was on their team for the match and was already suited up in the Caribbean-blue SharkFinn team polo. Lucas resembled the famous Argentinian player with the tex-mex appetizer nickname and played nearly as well. Ollie managed to keep his fan-boying to a minimum as he shook Lucas' hand with a smile and then greeted Sharon, a regular teammate from the club.

Ollie and Bill were playing their usual positions, as were Lucas and Sharon, playing one and four respectively. After a brief strategy discussion, they mounted their ponies and took the field. The game day energy was high, and the stands were nearly full. There was a light breeze that fluttered all the flags around the perimeter of the field and Ollie felt a pulse of anticipation as they lined up to be announced. His horse shifted and chuffed, as anxious to be underway as Ollie was. Ollie met his parents' gaze as he waited for his name to be called. It was thrilling to have them there, watching him and he didn't want to disappoint.

Once the match began, Ollie lost himself in the game. Tournament matches were that much more intense and competitive because of the cash prize. Each chukker was the equivalent of putting the horses through three Kentucky Derbies in seven and a half minutes, and everyone competing had at least six horses with them.

The other team was good. Ollie knew they would be, but it had been years since he had played in such a competitive match and his adrenaline surged. He played with single-minded focus, only categorizing the players around him as either teammates or adversaries. He charged after the ball, ever mindful of the other team's number two. In one play, Ollie used his horse to block a hook and drove the ball twenty yards before turning away from the line as Lucas raced after it. He roared with triumph as Lucas scored and beamed at his parents as they cheered with the crowd.

By halftime he and Bill were drenched in sweat, as were the horses. They stood in the shade with Sharon and Lucas, wiping sweat, drinking water, and discussing plays. Bill explained a pick play strategy, and then Ollie recommended that Lucas communicate more during the match, as the noise of hunting horns and hounds barking came down on the breeze.

"You're the highest goal. Any suggestions and encouragement you have for us brings us up to your level. Whether we perform there or not, at least we're thinking like you do." Ollie smiled at Lucas. "I can tone down my chatter."

"We'll both call out suggestions then. You've had good plays." Lucas nodded at Ollie, whose stomach warmed with the compliment, and then turned to Sharon. "A bit of advice, if I may, is don't watch the ball, instead watch the players. Watch your man and where his eyes are. You'll hit the ball more, trust me," Lucas replied in his smooth accent.

Sharon agreed and tossed her empty insulated water bottle into the bucket on the ground. "Let's close the gap and win this," she said determinedly and bumped their fists.

They went back into the second half with fresh horses and fresh strategy and won the match, ten to nine. Ollie rode happily past his parents with a broad smile before leaving the field to help hose down the horses.

Matt picked Ollie and his parents up at the Provincetown airport and took them to a celebratory dinner at Delphi's in Wellfleet after Ollie's text declaring their win. Ollie wished Matt had been there to see it, but was so high from his win he decided not to let it bother him. He focused instead on the surprise he had planned for Matt later. Ollie waited until everyone had gone to bed at Finn's, pacing the guest room he was fake-staying in before sneaking next door to the house he shared with Matt. He found Matt in the kitchen prepping the morning coffee.

Ollie scanned his eyes over Matt and his cock swelled in his sweatpants. Matt was wearing shorts and a t-shirt, but he may as well have been naked from how turned-on Ollie was.

Ollie took a breath, and tried to remain nonchalant as he closed the distance between them. "Cass and I leave tomorrow, but I'll see you in four days, when you bring my parents to town."

Matt groaned. "Four days? Can't you stay another day at the beach?"

Ollie leaned into Matt's body, sniffed his neck and sighed at the scent of the ocean he found there. "Cassie is champing at the bit to see the sights, probably hoping to net herself a Boston man just like I did."

Matt chuckled, his chest rumbling against Ollie's as he lowered and tightened his arms around Ollie. "She can't live here so please don't let that happen." He slid a hand free and titled Ollie's chin up slightly with his finger to drop a kiss on his lips. "Now, I believe I owe you some tickles for your comments at breakfast." He poked Ollie's side. "Don't think I forgot."

Ollie shrieked. "No, Lieutenant. There's a statute of limitations." He laughed and scrambled backwards around the kitchen island.

Matt shook his head and stalked after him. "No, the beach is out of jurisdiction. Private property, private rules," he said with a serious expression and inhaled through his teeth. "Punishment will be swift and judicious."

Ollie chuckled with his heart in his throat, still in motion as he continued to avoid Matt. "You can't be serious." He shook his head. "You going to tickle me 'til I pee?"

Matt coughed out a laugh, and regained composure. He stopped walking and feigned left before dashing right to try to catch Ollie.

Ollie, anticipating such a maneuver, dodged easily out of grasp. "Oh, Lieutenant. I play football. You'll have to do better than that."

Matt stopped short and then ran after Ollie with determination. Ollie shrieked again and dashed for the stairs as he laughed. He tripped halfway up and with a surge of adrenaline, ran for the bedroom trying to close the door behind him as he gasped with laughter. Matt followed close behind and tackled him on the bed where he tickled Ollie's sides with his strong fingers.

"Stop! Stop. I can't breathe. I'm the one who left all the cereal boxes open." He gasped, his body alive in a new and exhilarating way.

Ollie wondered if Matt felt the thrill of the chase too.

Matt stilled his hands and stared down into Ollie's face before straightening and removing his shirt.

"Because no one over twelve should eat cereal," Ollie burst out and scrambled to get away, the chase not over yet. "Especially not Cap'n Crunch. Christ!"

Matt pounced and pinned Ollie's body easily. He gripped Ollie's wrists raised them over Ollie's head. "You can't get away. But I love it when you try."

Ollie wriggled and writhed and tried to buck Matt off as his fingers dug into his sides.

"That's it, Ollie. Keep squirming," Matt said breathlessly. "It's working."

Ollie tried to stop as he gasped for air. He felt Matt's erection against the inside of his thigh. "You are such a perv, Lieutenant!"

"You love it," Matt said huskily, kissing Ollie's laughing mouth.

"I do. I really do," Ollie sighed as Matt stopped tickling him and relaxed into his body with a deep kiss.

Ollie shuddered with desire as Matt lifted Ollie's shirt over his head and moved his hands over his nipples. He tilted his chin to give Matt better access to his throat, wanting Matt's lips everywhere on his flushed body. He ground his hips into Matt's and gasped with the resulting pleasure.

"My god, you're horny." Matt bit Ollie's nipple then licked it as Ollie rolled his hips another loud moan.

"Big wins always make me horny. And then to come home to you. . . ." Ollie replied and ran his fingers through Matt's hair.

Matt hummed in agreement and eased Ollie's sweatpants down and stood to remove his shorts. "Hmmm, new jock?"

Ollie nodded, his stomach fluttering as he waited for the rest of Matt's discovery.

"What's that look for, Oliver? You swallow a canary?"

Ollie shook his head and sat up. His dick twitched enthusiastically in his jockstrap as he leaned forward to pull Matt into a straddle over his chest. He licked a stripe up Matt's cock and caught the drop of pre-cum at the tip, smearing it over his lips before taking Matt deep.

"Oh, god, baby. Just like that." Matt pushed himself gently in and out of Ollie's mouth. "So warm. So beautiful with my dick in your mouth."

Ollie rolled Matt's balls through his fingers and then sucked them into his mouth one at a time, while jacking Matt slowly. Matt moaned and pulled out of Ollie's grasp.

"I need a taste of your sweet ass, and then I'm gonna fuck you into the mattress so hard you won't be able to leave me tomorrow." Matt climbed off Ollie and maneuvered him into the middle of the bed. "Jock on or off?"

"Off. I wanna come on your chest. I'm so close."

Matt's chuckle was cut off with a sharp intake of breath when he bent Ollie's knees.

"What the fuck is this?" he asked in a low voice, raising his eyes to meet Ollie's with a look of wonder.

Ollie bit his lip and smiled. "Surprise."

Matt ran his finger over the navy-blue butt plug imbedded in Ollie's ass. He gave it a poke and then a tug, and Ollie couldn't help the moan. "Fucking hell," Matt whispered and pressed it back in, fucking Ollie with it slowly. His other hand went to his cock, and he stroked himself in sync with the dildo. "I love the trident."

Ollie wrapped his hand around his aching cock and put his feet on the bed as he squeezed to stave off the orgasm. Matt was hitting his sweet spot, and the stars were beginning to sparkle behind his lids. "I special ordered it," he gasped. "I uploaded a picture of my pendant. It's the ssssaaaammme," Ollie moaned as he began stroking himself with just two fingers and thumb.

Matt swatted Ollie's hand away and he groaned. "No, Oliver. You can't do that until I'm inside you. But I promise, I won't keep you waiting."

Ollie groaned in disappointment and then cried out when Matt leaned forward and licked around the outside of Ollie's hole.

"Mmmm, coconut," he praised before diving back in.

Ollie's heart was racing and if Matt didn't stop torturing him, he was going to expire from an overabundance of lust. He was alternating between gasping and moaning, and pumped his hips off the bed, craving friction. Finally, Matt pulled the plug, literally, and Ollie was left feeling empty, but only for a second. He felt the head of Matt's cock graze his hole before plunging deep inside.

Matt bent Ollie in half and fucked him ruthlessly as he kissed him with oil slicked lips. "You're a naughty boy, Oliver. How long were you wearing that?" he asked between thrusts.

"I put it in after my shower at Chuck's," Ollie answered breathlessly, his lungs compressed by his position. "I don't know what made me hornier, the way it felt or the anticipation of you finding it."

Matt chuckled, his throat raspy with exertion and need. "I fucking loved it. You were so ready for me, so turned on." He pulled out and flipped Ollie over like he weighed nothing.

Matt put one hand in the middle of Ollie's back and lifted his hips with his other and slammed back in, taking Ollie's breath. "Maybe next time I'll make you wear it to work." Matt lowered himself to bite the back of Ollie's neck as Ollie protested the suggestion. "God, you feel so good. You were made for me. I. Own. This. Hole." Matt pounded into Ollie, emphasizing each word.

"You do. Fuck yeah," Ollie whimpered and lifted his hips.

Matt eased back on his haunches and pulled Ollie with him. "Fuck yourself on me," he commanded, and took Ollie's dick in a firm grasp. "You're getting me close . . . I can't wait to fill your ass."

Ollie shuddered as the pressure built at the base of his spine. His thighs were burning from the polo match, but he didn't slow. He was so close, he could taste it on his tongue. He rotated his pelvis forward and cried as Matt's cock slid over his prostate, lighting him up. "Oh, god. I'm gonna come." He threw his head back onto Matt's shoulder as he gasped and blathered nonsensically through his orgasm.

Matt slowed his stroke but gripped Ollie's hip in his other hand and began pounding into him. "Holy fuck, babe. Oh, Christ." He groaned loudly as he came. His hips moved in short jerks that were punctuated with grunts as he continued through his aftershocks.

Matt turned his face into Ollie's neck and placed open mouthed kisses in the warmth there. "I love you so fucking much," he panted as he tightened his arms around Ollie's midsection.

Ollie caught his breath as Matt squeezed. "I love you too." He turned his head to kiss Matt, their mouths fitting together perfectly despite the awkward angle. "That ought to tide you over for the next four days."

Ollie grinned as Matt groaned and rolled them forward onto the bed.

* * *

Ollie took Cassie sightseeing the next two days, where they sweated through the August heat. They hit all the Boston tourist spots and ate at restaurants along the waterfront and in the many small neighborhoods around his condo in the Back Bay. On the second evening, after dinner on a large deck overlooking the harbor, Ollie took Cassie to SharkFinn to see his office.

"Cor, Ollie. This is fantastic," Cassie shook her head. "This city is beautiful. You're really something here, aren't you?" She looked at him as they stood in his office looking out the window at the water. "You know I tease you, and I will always tease you, but this is really amazing. That you're here, with your fabulous flat, and you're a bloody general counsel at your age." She shook her head with wonder. "God, it's remarkable."

Ollie smiled as he led her from the building. "Thank you for saying that. I really love it here. It's a beautiful city."

Cassie looked at him as they waited for their rideshare back to the condo. "Can I meet your boyfriend? I mean does he know I'm here? Have Mum and Dad met him?"

Ollie cleared his throat uncomfortably. "No, Mum and Dad haven't met him, and he's away for the week." He glanced at her. "Maybe next time, Cass. Or maybe if he and I get serious, I'll bring him home to meet you all."

The ride back to the condo was quiet, as Ollie wished he could just tell his sister the truth. He was certain he could get her to keep it a secret, if only he could convince Matt. He stared out the window while Cassie scrolled through the photos she had taken, until they arrived on Marlborough Street.

He was still lost in thought as he opened the door under the exterior stairs and pulled up in shock when he found his parents having a drink in the living room.

"What are you doing here?"

"Oh, Matt said he had some work to do and offered to drive us," Maggie answered with a smile. "We leave the day after tomorrow anyway, so it made sense. I wanted to have dinner in the North End before we go. That restaurant there is my favorite in the city."

Cassie looked around. "Is this couch a pullout? Where will you sleep?" she asked, clearly worried she would have to give up her bed.

"Don't worry, Cass, you can stay put. Mum and Dad will take my room. I have a fold out sofa in my study."

Cassie smiled with relief. "Great."

They had drinks, recapped their day sightseeing, and then said their goodnights.

"Have fun on the sofa bed, Ol," Cassie teased.

Ollie quickly pulled out the bedframe in his study and made the bed hastily. He laid down to rumple the blanket and then climbed the stairs two at a time all the way to the top floor.

Matt was waiting for him with a smile. "Jesus, Ollie. I was just about to come down and drag you up here by your hair."

"You're so needy, Lieutenant."

"I wasn't the one taking the stairs two at a time." Matt grinned his sexy grin. "The bed's too big without you. Get your sexy ass in there." He smacked Ollie on the bottom as he walked past. "Driving home with your parents was awkward. Knowing that the reason I needed to be here was so I could fuck their son. A lot."

Ollie's stomach flipped in anticipation. "I'm glad to hear that you missed me as much as I did you. My hand is like a fumbling fool in comparison."

Matt closed the bedroom door behind them. "Ollie, don't take another step clothed," he commanded huskily with his back pressed against the door.

Ollie stopped with a small sound and smiled slowly.

*　*　*

Ollie's phone buzzed next to him on the sectional the following day, and he answered it with a questioning frown.

"Yeah, Dad?"

"Your sister's awake and full of questions as to your whereabouts. Your mother mentioned the roof and now she's curious."

Ollie sighed. He'd hoped she'd stay asleep a bit longer. "I've got coffee up here if you'll bring the muffins and some mugs. Oh, and leave the lights off, I don't want her looking around."

"Will do."

Ollie turned the music on low and put his t-shirt back on. He was glad Matt had already left for the office, or he'd be furious with the thought of Cassie on their roof. He stood as his parents came out followed by Cassie.

"Morning." Ollie gestured to the carafe.

Cassie looked around, taking in the row of arborvitae for privacy and the wrought iron pagoda in the corner with a round daybed and privacy curtains tied to the posts. Maggie and David poured their coffee and split a muffin before joining Ollie on the couch.

"This is nice," Cassie remarked as she poured herself coffee. "Beautiful flowers. Who takes care of all of this, and why didn't you bring me up here before?"

Ollie shrugged. "It's technically the other unit's space, and I look after it when they're away. Admire the view and then have a seat."

"Yeah, it's okay," Cassie said sarcastically. "So, you can just wander through their space? The staircase is wide open. That's not very secure."

Ollie looked away briefly. "I only come up here when they're away, or if I ask." He looked at his parents. "So, what do you want to do today, and where shall we have dinner on your final night here?"

$$21$$

Lost in the Fire

"I HEAR YOU'RE GRACING THE UK with your presence again for Christmas," Guy said with a smile in his voice when Ollie answered the call from his cousin in December.

"Oui. Are you crossing the channel this year?" Ollie responded in French as he sat back from his desk. He looked at Matt's empty chair through the glass door, and then looked out the window at the harbor.

"No, sadly, but I will be crossing the *pond* in the new year. Your guest room available?"

"My whole flat is available! When?"

"Second weekend in January. I have meetings in New York City, and can take the train after and then fly out of Boston."

Ollie checked his calendar and then Matt's. "Perfect. I'm in Dallas the Wednesday of that week and have no weekend plans. What do you want to do?"

"I don't care," Guy paused. "Is Finn around or does she stay in Baltimore?"

"She's usually here for winter break, but I can find out for sure."

"Great. Let's all have dinner."

Ollie hung up and texted Finn before leaving for the sales meeting in the conference room.

> **Call me when u get a chance**

Ollie followed Matt out of the conference room after the stressful meeting and matched Matt's long stride perfectly, while Fred had to double his effort to keep up. They reconvened in Matt's office at his glass conference table where Matt took his spot at the head and Ollie sat at his right as usual.

"Run the numbers by me again," Matt commanded in his gravelly voice. "Is Bryan's sales team hitting their targets?"

Ollie listened as Fred and Matt discussed sales and then the new software that was in development. Matt stood and opened his office door. "Stacey, get me a meeting tomorrow with Krish and Bryan. Fit it in my calendar before lunch please."

"Yes, Matt."

He turned to Fred. "Have Stacey add you if you'd like to hear about the new tool for yourself." He held the door open, dismissing Fred.

Fred stood, accustomed to Matt's curtness. "I'll be there. Thanks."

Matt looked at Ollie with his eyebrows raised expectantly. Ollie stood and followed Fred out, hearing the door click behind him.

Ollie looked at his watch and headed back to the conference room where he had a meeting with his legal team in thirty minutes. Matt was in a mood and Ollie was only too happy to avoid him.

The rest of the week passed in a busy blur. Matt was optimistic after his meeting with Krish, Bryan and Fred, but he was quiet and brooding at home. Ollie dodged around his mood, as Matt divided his time at home between the gym, his office, and the bedroom.

"We have that fundraiser tomorrow with the girls," Ollie said quietly when Matt came out of the bathroom. "Do you want to cancel? Order food in?"

"No."

"You know we're on target to hit all our numbers by year-end?" Ollie said carefully as he plugged his phone in on the side table.

"That's not good enough. We've been blowing our numbers out of the water every year, and this year we're just hitting them. I need more. I need more . . . from *everyone*."

Ollie sat back on his pillow with a frown. "What exactly does that mean?"

"It means I expect everyone to work harder, especially my right-hand man. The man who directly benefits from my company's success."

Ollie took a breath, wondering if he wanted to stick up for himself and have a big blow-out fight this late in the night, or whether he would just let Matt lash out. He gritted his teeth and chose the former. "I work my ass off for you, in *every* way, and I take a lot of shit from you without pushing back. Don't you dare."

Matt pulled a face. "What fantasy world do you live in? You sleep late, you play tennis, soccer, and now *polo*. You leave work early. I see a tall stack of contracts on your desk constantly. You don't work nearly as hard as you think you do."

Ollie felt an adrenaline surge as he leaned forward. "I work seven days a week. I get up like a normal person. I'm at work when you are or just after. I leave work like a normal person, so that I can have dinner on the table for you. You get up earlier so you can have a fucking run, you work out and swim nearly three hours a day, *every* day. I play tennis maybe once a week and am at the barn maybe twice a week, with your bloody Chairman of the Board or my assigned beard. Football is once a week, on the weekend, and not year-round just like polo matches. Each and every contract is reviewed by me well under deadline, and I keep my eyes open for new work or new companies to acquire each and every day. On top of that, every night I'm here in bed eager to please you, *Matteo*. I do things for you no one in their right mind should or would. I bet there are a lot of people out there who would think I am weak, or spineless with you, but I do it because I love you, not because I'm some swanny pushover." Ollie paused for a breath. "I get that you're upset about the numbers not being record-breaking, but don't you dare take that out on me, or I swear to god it will be all work and no play for this Jack." Ollie thrust his thumb at himself. "And you will regret it."

Matt held Ollie's gaze and wanted to remain indignant, but knew Ollie was right. He was taking out his frustration on him, and the way Ollie was defending himself was such a turn-on. Matt looked away, knowing if he reached for Ollie, he would have his hand slapped or his head bitten off.

He looked back at Ollie and nodded once. "Okay. I didn't mean it."

Ollie gritted his teeth. "I know, but it doesn't make it any less hurtful. I hope you don't believe those things about me. I work hard because I am just as invested in this company as you are. Just as invested in you. It's bloody insulting."

"I know, babe. I don't think that of you," Matt said contritely. "I just need the numbers to be better, and we have two and a half months to make them so."

"I'm on it." He turned his bedside lamp off and rolled away from Matt. Silence stretched between them as Matt weighed his options.

"Ollie," Matt said softly as he sidled up to Ollie's back and ghosted his lips over Ollie's shoulder.

"What?" he asked in a slightly pissy tone.

"Nothing," Matt answered innocently and trailed his finger lightly down Ollie's bicep. He waited and watched Ollie's back tense before sagging as he rolled into Matt's arms with a sigh.

"You bastard."

Matt kissed him and kept his triumphant smile to himself.

* * *

It was nice to have Matt walk on eggshells for a change, Ollie thought. He kept his normal routine, not altering a thing in his work schedule, because he knew that he already busted his backside for SharkFinn and for Matt. He had Kerry book a meeting with Krish to review some companies that Ollie had his eye on.

"Stacey. Does Matt have time in his schedule today for fifteen-minutes with me?"

Stacey looked at her computer and then back at Ollie. "I'll check." She picked up her phone and buzzed Matt's office. "Oliver would like fifteen minutes. You have time now or after your three o'clock, which do you prefer?" She looked up at Ollie as she listened, and then hung up. "He's free now."

"Thank you, Stacey." He strode into Matt's office with a small stack of write-ups on struggling companies and sat at the conference table, all business.

Matt stood, leaving his suit coat on the back of his chair, and came around his desk. "What d'you got for me?"

Fifteen minutes later Matt was smiling broadly. "Take these three to Fred, see if we can swing it before year-end. The rest I want on deck for next year, see how they perform in the meantime." He stood and put his hand on Ollie's shoulder. "I love you," he said quietly and walked back to his desk, dismissing him.

22

Let it Will Be

MATT PICKED UP OLLIE at the airport the day after Christmas and squeezed his knee once he was seated in the passenger seat next to him.

"I missed you."

"I missed you too, Lieutenant." Ollie smiled and ran his eyes over Matt.

God, he's so fucking gorgeous.

"When was the last time you shaved?" Ollie asked as he resisted the urge to brush his knuckles against Matt's short beard.

"The twenty-third. I've been busy." He shrugged and pulled into traffic.

"Guy is coming."

Matt looked at Ollie and then back at the road. "To stay with us? When? Why am I just hearing this?"

Ollie nodded. "Yes. And speaking of being busy, I haven't had a chance to tell you. He'll be here on the twelfth, after dark I think. I'll get him from the train, and he'll stay with me."

Matt hummed thoughtfully and followed traffic into the Ted Williams Tunnel. Ollie wondered if Matt was looking forward to seeing Guy again and scoffed at himself for the twinge of jealousy.

Well, it'll be good to see him." Matt reached over and ran his fingers through Ollie's hair once they were out of the tunnel and in the dark. "I got you something," he said changing the subject.

"What? We already exchanged gifts."

"Yeah, well, I came across your little *toy* while you were away, and it got me thinking." Matt exited the highway and followed the roads to Marlborough Street. He moved his hand to the trident at Ollie's throat and touched it through Ollie's shirt, before returning to the steering wheel. "You've got a trident on your butt missile, a trident pendant on your chain, but you're missing a third one, and with tridents it's only fitting that you have three."

Ollie furrowed his brow as he studied Matt's profile. "What?"

Matt turned into the alley entrance and followed the narrow, mostly paved strip to their driveway. He stopped behind the neighbor's cars and looked at Ollie with a broad smile. "That." Matt nodded with his chin at the windshield.

Ollie followed Matt's eyes and gasped. "What the fuck?!"

"Surprise." Matt laughed and put something in Ollie's hand.

Ollie looked down at the key fob that had a trident top on it and then back up at Matt, feeling as though his heart had stopped. "You bought me a *Maserati?*"

"Do you like it?"

"It's bloody beautiful, Lieutenant!" He turned instinctively to kiss Matt.

"Whoa." Matt held up his hand and looked around. "You can thank me inside." Matt took his foot off the brake and pulled into the spot next to Ollie's new car.

"Right," Ollie replied, managing to keep the disappointment from his tone at Matt's constant vigilance in public, even at night. "I can't wait to see it in the daylight. It looks fantastic. Thank you."

Ollie climbed out of Matt's car as Matt got his bags from the back. He walked around the outside of the Maserati and admired the shiny newness before following Matt into the back door of their townhouse. Matt held the elevator open and pushed the button for the fifth floor. He swept Ollie into a tight embrace.

"I'm so glad you're home. I hate being here without you."

"I'm glad to be home too." Ollie buried his face in Matt's neck, his beard scratching Ollie's cheeks, and breathed deeply. "What did you do with my Audi?"

Matt chuckled and stepped back. "I cleaned it out and traded it in. Don't worry, I got your Troye Sivan *Flower* CD from the player," Matt replied and stepped off the elevator with Ollie's bags.

Ollie followed him down the hall to their bedroom as he puzzled over Matt's words. "Do you mean *Bloom*?" he asked, his smile broadening as he watched Matt's broad back and head nod. "That's not a song about flowers. It's about bottoming. He's singing about his asshole."

Matt turned around with a shocked expression and Ollie couldn't help but snort with laughter. He could see the gears turning in Matt's head as he thought about the lyrics.

Matt smirked. "It's still an annoying song, but now I won't mind when you sing it to me. And I never mind when you *bloom* for me." Matt dropped Ollie's bags and took him in his arms.

He took off Ollie's suit coat and worked on the buttons of his shirt as he steered him to the bed. "In fact, I not only want to see your beautiful bloom, I want a taste. It's been over a fucking week." Matt slipped his hand down the back of Ollie's pants and tapped Ollie's hole with his middle finger. "Take off your pants." Matt stepped back and hurriedly removed his clothes while watching Ollie with predatory eyes.

Ollie waited for Matt's pulse to slow to normal, knowing it was the optimal time for open discourse. "Guy knows about us," he whispered and felt Matt's body still.

"What? You told him?!"

Ollie ran his hand down Matt's chest, holding him in place. "No. He saw us through the window back in Lyon. Saw you come all over me. Just like you did a minute ago." He swept his fingers through the mess on his chest and sucked them into his mouth with a grin. "And you know what? He doesn't give a shit. He only worried that you might be taking advantage of me. He wouldn't—won't— breathe a word of us to anyone. He loves me."

"He *saw* us?" Matt sat up and blew out a breath, his skin flushed. "Why didn't you tell me? Oh god." He rubbed his forehead with both hands.

Ollie looked at him with his eyebrows raised. "Seriously, Matt? It's really to prove a point darling. He knew days before we left and never said a word or treated you any differently. He laughed about it; *marveled* over your cock," Ollie added salaciously. "I chastised him for being a prude, about making fun for letting you come all over me. I'll never apologize to anyone for that, I love it when you do. Every splatter is a delicious triumph." He swept more of Matt's cum into his mouth.

Matt exhaled a laugh with a frown and chewed his lip. He looked away and then back at Ollie after a moment. "I guess that means I can fuck you all I want while he's here," he said with a guarded grin. "We don't have any balconies; he's not going to scale the bricks looking for you. Right?"

Ollie laughed and pulled Matt's arm so he would lay back down. He kissed him slowly and then pulled back. "He's not Spiderman, and he'll be too focused on getting into Chuck's pants to worry about us."

Matt frowned with the thought and then kissed Ollie again. "He really marveled over my dick?"

"Yeah. Said he'd never seen anything quite so small." Ollie shrieked as Matt tickled him. "Stop, stop! Yes. He marveled over it. Couldn't believe I fit it in my mouth. You cocky bastard, who wouldn't marvel over it?" Ollie grinned against Matt's lips. "It's fucking *magnificent*, and you know it."

"It is, and you love it," Matt said huskily.

"I do. I really do, you sexy bastard." Ollie kissed him and rolled with him onto his back.

23

French Knot

OLLIE PICKED GUY UP at South Station and put his suitcase in the trunk.

"Nice bloody car, Ollie," he said when he got in.

"Thanks. Matt gave it to me for Christmas."

"You're a kept man, aren't you?" Guy laughed and switched to French.

"You're just jealous that no one has ever thought you were so phenomenal, *so* good in bed they wanted to buy you a Maserati, or a Rolex, or a fucking two-bedroom flat in one of Boston's most expensive neighborhoods." Ollie smirked and headed toward Copley Square.

"*Merde,*" Guy shook his head and gave Ollie a shove.

"This place is nice. Sushi was delicious." Guy nodded as he looked around the bar and sat back in the banquette after they finished. "So, where's Matt?"

"We're not conjoined twins," Ollie laughed. "Would you have preferred he picked you up? Took you out for dinner?" Ollie quirked his brow. "You been dreaming about his cock?"

"Definitely not," Guy laughed. "That thing could choke a horse. No, thank you. I prefer pussy. And speaking of pussy, we're having dinner tomorrow with Finn?"

"Don't you dare be a pig about Chuck. Matt would have your head," Ollie chastised and looked around.

"Who's Chuck?"

"It's Matt's nickname for her: Chuckleberry Finn. Should indicate to you just how much he loves her. Seriously, Guy, you had better be on your best behavior about her. Matt wouldn't think twice about beating you senseless, cousin of mine or no," Ollie warned.

"Okay, *okay*. I know what you mean. Matt is an intimidating *mec*," Guy held his hands up defensively. "I don't know how you fuck him. I mean, aside from the gigantic cock. Do you sleep with one eye open?" he laughed. "Worried that he'll kill you?"

"No, I sleep like rock. *He* sleeps with one eye open, protecting me." Ollie shot Guy a smug smile and thought of just how safe he felt with Matt.

"*Mon dieu*," Guy closed his eyes and shook his head.

* * *

Finn got off the elevator into the first-floor foyer of their townhouse at six o'clock the following evening. She was dressed in dark jeans, a brown leather jacket and had a tan cotton scarf wrapped loosely around her neck. Matt watched as Guy looked her over appreciatively.

"*Bonsoir*, Finn. It's wonderful to see you again." Guy kissed both her cheeks. "You look beautiful."

"Thank you. It's nice to see you too."

Matt fought the urge to roll his eyes as Finn swept her eyes blatantly over Guy's body. Yeah, his jeans fit him perfectly, and the lavender paisley shirt he wore under his black leather blazer enhanced the hazel of his eyes in the most delectable of ways, but Matt wasn't quite ready to hand her over to Guy just yet.

Don't be ridiculous, Lieutenant. She's not yours, and you don't even want her like that, the voice in his head chastised.

Yeah, but I still want to protect her from getting hurt, he thought as he unfolded himself from the couch.

He straightened his pant legs and stepped forward to kiss Finn hello. "You look stunning as always. I'm glad you like the bag," he added with a smile, nodding at the soft brown Birkin bag on her arm.

"I love it. Thank you. You look gorgeous; new shirt?"

Matt couldn't help but catch Guy's stunned expression at the extravagant gift and smiled to himself before turning his attention back to Finn. "Ollie gave it to me." He smoothed the Dolce and Gabbana button down shirt over his flat abdomen.

"Speaking of Ollie, where is he?" Finn looked around.

"Fussing over his hair, I'm sure," Guy laughed.

"Fuck you. I was looking for my shoes," Ollie said as he came from the stairs. "They weren't where I left them."

"That's because you left them in the middle of the bedroom where you walked out of them," Matt scoffed. "I nearly tripped."

"You should watch where you're going." Ollie shrugged and kissed Finn hello.

Matt shook his head and wished he could tackle Ollie onto the sofa and tickle him breathless for that sassy response. He led the way out to his Range Rover instead.

"Where we dining, Lieutenant?"

Matt pulled out into traffic. "Cinquecento's."

"Yum. I haven't been there in ages," Finn chimed in happily.

They sat in a booth with views of the bar; Matt and Finn on one side and Guy and Ollie on the other. Guy made a toast when the drinks arrived and then promptly began flirting with Finn. Ollie met Matt's gaze from time to time as he watched Matt watching them, his eyes speculative as he ran them over Guy. Ollie wondered what Matt was thinking and supposed it had something to do with the idea of Finn dating someone he approved of.

That has to be a hard concept for him, Ollie thought with a snort.

Matt shifted his gaze to Ollie and quirked his brow. Ollie just shook his head and took a sip of his beer as the server arrived with their food. After a few bites, Matt helped himself to food from Finn's and Ollie's plates with his fork. Ollie thought nothing of it, Matt always ate nearly half of Ollie's meal no matter where they were, but he caught Guy's look.

"I don't know whose dinner I like the best." Matt grinned in response to Guy's raised eyebrows. "And you ordered the same thing I did otherwise I'd be picking off your plate too."

Guy shook his head with a laugh and drank his wine. "Well, I certainly wouldn't be stopping him if he did," he said to Ollie in French. "I mean, I don't know what prospect frightens me more: him choking me with his bare hands or with his massive cock."

Ollie threw his head back with laughter. "Guy!" he admonished. Finn's eyes widened as she looked from Guy to Matt.

"What is he saying, Oliver?" Matt looked at him expectantly.

"I can't repeat it here. I'll tell you later." Ollie wiped his eyes.

"You will not," Guy admonished in French. "You can't tell him. You said he can't know I saw."

"*Je lui ai dit*," Ollie replied and then looked at Matt.

Guy looked at Matt with wide eyes and smiled sheepishly.

"Don't worry. You'd be very pleased," Ollie reassured Matt with a grin.

"*Je parle français, Guy*," Finn said in perfect French with a laugh.

Guy's mouth dropped open. "You little sneak."

"She has a gift for languages, especially dead ones." Matt put his arm around her shoulder and kissed her cheek.

Finn and Guy summoned a rideshare to go for drinks after dinner, while Matt paid the check and begrudgingly said goodbye to them at the curb. He watched their car drive away like a concerned parent before taking Ollie home.

He looked at Ollie while they waited at a stop light. "So, what was so funny? Am I going to have to torture it out of you?"

"Ooh, I was going to tell you, but now I think I want you to torture it out of me." Ollie bit his lip and raised his eyebrows.

Matt chuckled and looked back at the road. "I've been trained by the US military. I know how to get the information I want. You sure you're up for it?"

Ollie felt a little thrill in his belly and exhaled. "When you put it that way, I'm *certain* I'm up for it."

Matt chuckled and adjusted himself in his pants.

*   *   *

Ollie texted Guy in the morning.

> I'm making brunch.
> It'll be ready by 1030.
> Will there b 2 of u?

Guy responded an hour later

> Oui ☺

Guy and Finn came up for brunch, freshly showered and smiling. Guy looked cautiously at Matt who raised his eyebrows but didn't say a word. Matt smiled to himself thinking about what Guy said at dinner, and how he got that information out of Ollie. Ollie's cries for mercy and moans of pleasure were still ringing in his ears.

He watched Ollie, gorgeous in his grey joggers and blue t-shirt that stretched tightly across his muscular torso, working his way around the kitchen, plating food and making sure everyone had everything they needed, and he sighed quietly. Ollie looked at Matt, conscious of his eyes on him, and gave him a secret smile.

"Where'd you guys end up going last night?" Matt asked Finn as he tore his eyes away from Ollie and popped a piece of bacon into his mouth.

"Well, I took him to Faneuil Hall, because you can't come here and not see it. We had overpriced drinks at Frost Ice Bar, and then I took him to Dick's Last Resort for some over-priced punishment, before heading to Parla for a proper drink," Finn answered with a smile.

"Oh yeah? What'd his hat say?" Matt asked with his eyebrows raised.

"'I miss prison food, and showers,'" Guy answered with a laugh, furrowing his brow. "People pay for that kind of abuse? The drinks were shite."

Matt laughed. "That's a good one. What'd yours say, Chuck?"

"'Fake blonde, real dumb.'" She laughed.

"What are you on about?" Ollie puzzled. "What do you mean hats?"

Finn looked at Ollie and pulled out her phone, swiping to the photos. "They make cone hats out of butcher paper then the server writes some insult on it and you have to wear it." She shrugged and showed him pictures of Guy with his cone hat on.

"Christ, I'm with Guy. People pay money for that? And the drinks suck?" He frowned at the photos.

"It's funny, Ollie. We're going, I can't wait to see what they write for you." Finn smiled.

Matt laughed as he imagined Ollie cringing in horror at the thought of putting a cone hat on his perfect hair.

"Oh, I'll go if he goes." Ollie gestured with his chin to Matt. "And I can't wait to see what they write for you, Lieutenant. And you have to wear it."

"Not gonna happen, Oliver." Matt finished his eggs.

"Oh, he's just mad because the last time we went he got 'Bruce Jenner stole my idea.'" Finn collapsed in peals of laughter.

Guy laughed. "Oh, Christ. They couldn't write that now. It'd say Caitlyn."

"You guys are fucking hilarious. Why don't you take your comedy troupe on the road?" Matt scoffed with a grin. It had been embarrassing wearing that, but it wasn't the worst one at the table.

"Thank you for brunch, Ollie." Finn kissed Ollie and handed Matt her plate. "I've got to go rescue Dad and Kodi from Jayne." She grinned and turned back to Guy. "Enjoy the rest of your day. It was great seeing you."

"I'll walk you out," Guy said with a smile and followed her, leaving his plate on the island.

Matt looked at the plate. "Jesus. You don't just look alike; he's a slob too."

"We don't do it on purpose." Ollie smiled and left the kitchen.

Ollie drove Guy to the airport at four o'clock for his flight. "You and Finn have fun?"

"Oui. She is something else. God, I wished she lived in France," he replied in French. "I'd marry her in a heartbeat."

Ollie shook his head. "Don't be ridiculous. You'll never get married, and she won't ever move. She has a career here, and she would never leave Matt. I know this."

"I would marry *her*. And what do you mean she would never leave Matt? They're not together. They'll never be together."

"They're not *together*, but they're bonded for life. I don't get it, so don't ask me, but I just know."

"That's fucked up. How do you put up with it?"

"She introduced us and has done everything for him." Ollie shrugged, even as he wondered the same thing occasionally. "You said it yourself; she is something else. I love her, and she is directly responsible for my happiness, so she and Matt can be as bonded as they want. Not to mention that they were a pair long before I came along, and there's no way I would step between that. I recommend that you don't either. Don't complain a bit, or she will cut you out of her life like a tumor. I promise."

Guy looked out the window at the passing cars and took a deep breath. "Good advice, cousin. It's so early anyway. I just want to focus on the next time I get to see her." He grinned.

WEED

24

No Such Thing
as Bygones

MATT KICKED HIS BOAT SEARCH into high gear after shelving his search the previous summer. He found a fifty-foot Sunseeker Predator that fit his specifications in late April and secured a mooring adjacent to the local yacht club in Truro. He was antsy to get it in the water once the mechanic made the modifications he requested.

"Looks beautiful, Matt," Ollie said, looking over Matt's shoulder at the computer screen. "It's got a kitchen, two showers, a washer, dryer, and two bedrooms? Are we going to live on it?" Ollie ran his hand through his hair as he thought of the humidity.

Matt shook his head with a grin. "No, Ollie. But we could go to the Caribbean if we wanted, or Key West. Sleep on the boat. Fuck on the boat."

"Ah, now that got my interest." Ollie grinned and put his hand on Matt's shoulder. Matt turned his face up for a kiss and put his hand between Ollie's thighs. Ollie touched his tongue to Matt's, tracing his finger over the outside of Matt's ear. "I love you."

Matt's desk phone buzzed and they parted as though they were caught naked.

"Mr. Hawthorn is here to see Oliver. Is he in there with you?" Stacey asked. "Kerry said there was no answer."

Matt pressed the speaker button. "Yes, send him in." He stood and walked around his desk as Bill came through the door dressed in a blue cashmere sweater and charcoal grey pants.

"Bill," Matt said with a smile. "Great to see you, sir." He greeted him with a firm handshake and a one-armed hug.

"Matt. Good to see you too. I thought you were traveling."

"I was supposed to, but sent one of my developers instead. He could handle the client better than I could."

Bill looked at Ollie with a happy smile and stepped in for a hug. "Hey, Ollie. I hope you didn't forget about our squash date."

"Or course not, Bill. I'll just go get my bag. Back in a flash." Ollie left through the connecting door, hidden slightly by the built-in bookcase that jutted into the room (just as Naomi had intended).

Bill watched him leave and then looked around the office before looking at Matt. "I never noticed that door in all the other times I've been here."

Matt slid his glance away, looking briefly at Ollie as he disappeared from view. "Saves a lot time. You know I can't sneeze without asking him if it's legal for me to."

Bill grinned and shrugged. "Sure."

Ollie came back through the door carrying a bag with a squash racquet handle sticking out of the side compartment. "Ready when you are."

"Uh oh. You have a special bag?" Bill said dramatically. "I hope you didn't play pro back in the UK."

Ollie laughed. "No. But I did play enough." He looked at Matt. "I'll see you at you home."

"After dinner though," Bill interrupted. "What do you feel like, Ollie. Seafood or French?"

"Both sound great, you decide."

"You guys should do French, save the seafood for me," Matt said with a smile.

"Then let's have seafood and you join us," Bill suggested.

Matt nodded his head side to side. "If I can. Persephone's then?"

"Perfect. I have a reservation for six thirty."

"I'll try to join you. Ollie, I'll text you if I can't. Have fun." Matt shook Bill's hand again before going back around his desk.

"This place is fantastic," Ollie marveled as they walked into the Tennis and Racquet Club on Boylston. "Quite grand."

"I'm glad you like it." Bill beamed happily. "I've been a member forever, here and at B&T. I can't believe we've never played squash before today."

Ollie followed him to the locker room. "I know. I didn't think it was popular here. People are all about tennis or pickle ball."

"It's coming back around I think." Bill smiled as they unzipped their bags and changed.

Ollie unbuttoned his shirt and saw the hickeys on his chest from the night before. He quickly turned and kept his back to Bill as he doffed his button down and pulled on a t-shirt. He shed his pants, pulled on his shorts and turned to find Bill lacing his sneakers.

"Let's hit the court, see if you're as good at squash as you are at tennis." Bill grinned as he led Ollie to their reserved court.

"Best of three or five?" Bill bounced the ball.

Ollie twirled his racquet. "Depends on how good you are, Bill, and how late you want to play."

"Best of three then," Bill said with a confident grin, executing a backhand serve.

"You're quite good, Bill." Ollie praised and wiped the sweat from his brow. "Though I shouldn't be surprised. I think we're going to have to call it a draw if we're to make our dinner reservation." He looked at his Rolex.

Bill wiped his forehead. "Great game, Ollie." He slapped Ollie's shoulder gently. "I look forward to breaking this tie soon."

"Absolutely."

"Let's hit the showers and go to dinner. I'm starving." Bill led the way out of the court and back to the locker room.

Ollie showered, putting his sweaty clothes in his bag and took out fresh socks and boxer briefs. He skipped his usual short trunks because of Matt's comment about them, though Bill had already seen him in them (and less) at the polo club. He put his grey Tom Ford suit back on but left off the tie and kept the top button of his white shirt unbuttoned. Bill watched with a small smile as Ollie put product in his hair and slicked it back.

"I know it must seem ridiculous to you, I'm sorry," Ollie said putting everything in his bag and zipping it. He skipped using the hair dryer as he felt as though he was taking forever to get ready while Bill sat and waited.

Bill frowned. "Don't apologize. You have great hair."

Bill parked his silver Jaguar at the curb and gave the key to the valet with a folded bill. "Leave it out front, please."

"Mr. Hawthorn," the host greeted them. "I have your table waiting."

Ollie followed Bill and the host to a table with four chairs in the middle of the dining room. They sat across from each other and looked at their menus.

"Hello, I'm Andrew, and I'll be your server . . ." the waiter trailed off as he met Ollie's eye. "Well, well, well. Look what the cat dragged in."

Ollie's stomach plummeted as he swallowed his gasp and looked between Bill and Andy. "Hello, Andy," he said calmly and ran his hand through the unruly waves of his still damp hair.

Ollie felt Bill's eyes on him and struggled to maintain his composure. *This isn't happening. Please be a nightmare.*

Andy scanned his eyes over Bill appraisingly and looked back at Ollie and his wet hair with a knowing smile. "Interesting turn of events. Can I get you something from the bar? Perhaps an Old Fashioned?" Andy asked with a quirked brow.

Oh, fuck you, Andy.

"Please, do the right thing and switch our table with another server," Ollie gritted out.

"Oh, no, Ollie. I'll take excellent care of you and your *friend*," Andy said with an edge.

"Andy. Please," Ollie said meaningfully.

Ollie was so focused on Andy and keeping him from revealing anything, that he'd almost missed Bill's beckoning finger to the host who appeared in a flash.

"Yes, Mr. Hawthorn?"

"We'd like a table by the window," Bill stated with a clenched jaw as he stood.

Ollie stood reflexively at Bill's commanding glance.

Fuck, that's hot. And so like Matt.

"Of course, Mr. Hawthorn. Is everything alright?" The host looked sharply at Andy.

Bill ignored Andy as though he was spam in his inbox. "Yes, Ethan. We just want a quieter spot." He turned expectantly as Ethan straightened and led them to another table.

Ollie smiled to himself with relief as Bill gestured for him to follow the host to the new table. "How do they know you here, Bill?" he asked once they were seated, hoping to deflect any inquiry.

"I know Rich, the chef-owner, and I'm an investor in his restaurant group." He paused. "Ollie, what was that all about?"

Ollie sighed, feeling himself blush. "Bill, please. It's awkward."

Bill twisted his mouth and scanned his eyes over Andy across the room. "Ah. He's an ex."

Ollie closed his eyes as he felt himself blush an even deeper red and touched two fingers between his brow to smooth the frown lines. "I'm so sorry. What an embarrassment."

Bill shook his head and waved his hand dismissively. "Don't be embarrassed. I've lived too long to be bothered by much. We all have skeletons in our closets, and embarrassing exes. And, Ollie, you're with me. You have nothing to worry about," he said firmly. "Let's look at the menu."

"Thank you." Ollie smiled and pulled his phone out. He looked at the blank screen and his stomach tightened with worry.

Bill looked up and caught Ollie's frown. "What?"

"Matt hasn't texted to say he can't make it." Ollie looked back up at Bill and cleared his throat. "And . . . there's a particular tension between Matt and Andy."

Bill put down his menu and looked at Ollie with concern. "What do you mean?"

"I mean, perhaps we should meet Matt somewhere else."

"Okay. I can get us a table at The Furies," Bill said casually as he made to stand and then stopped suddenly. "Oh, too late, Ollie."

Ollie turned his head to see Matt striding into the restaurant, a smile on his face as he made eye contact with them. He was so impossibly handsome, he was like an apparition, and heads turned as he made his way toward them in his perfectly tailored suit.

Bill stood and shook Matt's hand warmly as Ollie did the same with a stomach full of butterflies. Ollie locked eyes briefly with Matt before Matt sat in the seat between Ollie and Bill facing the dining room.

"How was squash? Who won?" Matt asked as he put his napkin in his lap.

"It was a tie, that we will be meeting soon to break," Bill said with a grin. "Ollie's quite the squash player, though I can't say I'm surprised."

Ollie smiled lightly but his eyes felt tight. "Bill is the one who's a great player. I don't feel hopeful about winning the rematch," Ollie said with a chuckle, trying to hide his nervousness, and not succeeding. He knew he had to tell Matt, who was bound to notice Andy eventually.

Matt frowned. He looked at Bill and then around the restaurant. "Bill, everything alright?" He slid a glance at Ollie.

"Of course, son. It's all good. What do you want to drink? We haven't ordered yet."

Ollie cleared his throat. "Matt, just for your information," he said carefully. "It appears that Andy works here."

Matt's entire body went still as he met Ollie's gaze. He looked down at the table and then slid his glance at Bill, who was watching him carefully. He began nodding slowly. "Is that right? He talk to you?" He held Ollie's gaze.

Ollie shook his head once. "No." He flicked his eyes to Bill at the lie.

Matt looked at Bill questioningly.

Bill shrugged. "Who?"

Matt relaxed visibly. "Good. I'd love a Hendricks martini, dry, with a twist," he said to the waiter who appeared beside Ollie.

Matt suffered through the small talk that Bill and Ollie insisted on while waiting for their drinks and reviewed their menus. He had thought it was unusual that Bill and Ollie were at a table by the window (when Bill always sat in the middle of any dining room he was in), until Ollie's confession. Matt noticed Andy waiting on Bill's usual table and watched briefly, his anger simmering. He knew Ollie and Bill had relocated to a table along the wall because of something Andy had done or said.

Matt smiled to himself at the flash of fear on Andy's face when their eyes met. He suspected that Andy had planned on intimidating Ollie during dinner, but when he saw Matt sitting at the table, he had pulled up short and turned white, just like a schoolyard bully in the presence of authority.

Matt had two martinis with the oysters and calamari, and had wanted to order a third, but Ollie looked at him with a frown.

"You aren't Don Draper, Matthew."

"Fine, I'll have water with dinner."

"Ollie tells me you bought a boat," Bill said with a smile after the server had deposited their meals. "You'll have to come visit me on Nantucket. Of course, flying is easier, but you'll have to make the journey by boat at least once. I have a mooring out front as you know."

"Definitely. Ollie and I will bring Chuck and Jayne."

"Great." Bill turned his attention to Ollie. "Your folks coming in August? You should bring them out to the island. You know I have plenty of room, and I'd love to see them again and play tennis with your dad."

"They'd love that, but not by boat. My mother gets seasick. She can only handle the harbor or the bay." Ollie smiled and took a small bite of his branzino. He felt Andy's eyes on him periodically and forced himself to eat. He had been starving when they arrived after two hours of squash, but promptly lost his appetite. He watched Matt keeping an eye on Andy and hoped he wasn't plotting anything.

Bill was studiously ignoring Andy, and kept Matt's attention as best he could through dinner and dessert, talking about work, and the stock market, and travel. They discussed a few potential ventures and made a plan to meet after the upcoming board meeting to review a list of companies. Bill flagged their waiter for the check after dessert and put several hundred-dollar bills on the table.

"Thank you for dinner, Bill," Matt said with a smile.

"Thank you, Bill," Ollie added.

"Thank you both for the company, and thank you again, Ollie, for a great game today. Best I've had in years," Bill added with a smile that Ollie returned.

They stood and filed out of the restaurant with Bill leading the way and Matt behind Ollie. Andy watched them from the other side of the restaurant with a blank expression on his face. He saw Andy flinch and looked over his shoulder at Matt who was staring at Andy with a dark look on his face.

Shit, Ollie thought as he remembered Matt's threats to Andy that day in his office.

The night was dark and cold, spring not yet strong enough to exert her authority over winter as they walked to the curb. The valet brought their keys and moved the cones from around their cars. Ollie retrieved his bag and then hugged Bill goodnight.

"Squash next week I hope, Ollie," Bill said with a smile.

"I can't wait." Ollie nodded and glanced at the restaurant as Bill turned away.

Andy was in the window watching them speculatively, and judging from his expression, he had been standing there for a while.

Ollie looked in the rear window of the Maserati and saw Matt's eyes locked on Andy.

Fuck.

Ollie opened the passenger door and buckled his seatbelt without looking at Matt. It was a short drive down Charles Street to Beacon and back to the townhouse on Marlborough.

Matt was silent, and stiff, and unreadable. "Dinner was delicious," Ollie said to break the silence, not wanting another angry night.

"It always is." Matt nodded as he pulled into Ollie's spot next to his car. He got Ollie's bag out of the back and unlocked the back door.

"I have a little bit of work. I'll be up shortly. Wait for me in bed," Matt said with a quick glance at Ollie before getting off the elevator on the third floor.

"Okay," Ollie breathed with a nod and rode to the top floor.

Well, at least Matt didn't say the shower, so he couldn't be too upset about the evening. He looked at the copper ceiling tiles and then around the tiny space as the elevator hummed its way up.

Matt appeared nearly forty minutes later, undressed in the walk-in closet, and made a brief trip to the bathroom. Ollie put his phone on the side table with a flutter in his stomach as Matt turned off the light and climbed into bed.

"Come here," Matt commanded softly, his voice sounding far away in the dark.

Ollie slid across the bed into Matt's tense arms, his body coiled but not angry. Ollie's brain hummed cautiously, but not worriedly as Matt kissed him slowly. Matt's minty tongue swept into Ollie's mouth possessively as he rolled Ollie onto his back with a small sigh and buried his fingers in the waves of Ollie's hair.

"*Perfetto, amore mio.*"

Matt kissed his neck, his lips finding the hollow behind his collarbone with ease as Ollie ran his hands down Matt's back, Ollie's fingertips reading every ridge of muscle like a memory. Matt's five o'clock shadow scraped against Ollie's sensitive skin as he placed open-mouthed kisses all along Ollie's neck and shoulders.

Matt brought his lips back to Ollie's and they kissed unhurriedly as the passion built between them. Matt didn't make any move to stop, or progress, just rolled his hips slowly, rubbing his hard length against Ollie's.

Ollie opened his eyes to find Matt watching him with smoky eyes and an inscrutable expression.

"What are you thinking?" Ollie whispered against Matt's lips with a belly full of uncertainty.

Matt's mood was somewhere between passion and low-level anger, and Ollie wondered if he would need his safe word.

Matt made a low sound and kissed his way down Ollie's chest, biting his nipples as he eased Ollie's underwear off. Matt rolled his tongue around each raised bud before skimming lower. He nipped the flesh around Ollie's bellybutton and met Ollie's gaze before dipping between his legs.

"Oh, god. Fuck that feels good," Ollie moaned as Matt sucked the tip of his cock into his mouth and pressed his tongue into the slit.

Matt took him deep and Ollie's eyes rolled back into his head, distracted from worrying about Matt's mood by the feeling of his cock hitting the back of Matt's throat. Ollie slid one hand into the short waves of Matt's hair and bent his other arm behind his head as he thrust deeper into Matt's throat.

Matt's mouth was warm and wet, and his tongue was like velvet as he swirled it sensuously under Ollie's foreskin and then up and down the vein along the front of his shaft. He flicked a glance up at Ollie, his eyes glinting in the dark, and slipped a lubed finger into Ollie's asshole. Ollie had been so focused on Matt mouth he hadn't heard the pop of the lid.

Matt kissed the sensitive crease of Ollie's groin and then rolled his tongue around Ollie's smooth balls. He thrust his finger slowly in and out as Ollie panted with pleasure. Matt knew just how to light him up, and make his extremities tingle.

"Oh, right there," he sighed, as Matt rubbed his prostate, and then groaned emphatically when Matt pressed on it from the outside with his thumb, effectively squeezing the gland between his fingers.

Pre-cum pumped out of the tip of Ollie's cock and dripped onto his abdomen. Matt lapped it up and murmured something in Italian, and then repeated it in a firmer voice, but Ollie couldn't make out the words. Not that he'd be able to understand much of them. A second finger joined the first inside Ollie as Matt took off his underwear with his free hand and dribbled some lube onto his cock.

Matt sat up on his knees and coated himself, the sight and sound of his slick hand moving over his hard length made Ollie's mouth water. He tugged Ollie forward onto his lap and entered him slowly, a guttural moan ripping from his throat as his eyes fluttered. Ollie held his intense gaze before closing his eyes and losing himself in the glorious sensation of Matt's rhythm, the small circles he was making before driving his point home.

Over and over.

Matt leaned down for a lingering kiss, licking Ollie's lip before pulling away and propping himself up on one elbow. He buried his face in Ollie's armpit, his nose tickling the hair, and breathed deeply. Ollie felt Matt's cock jump and swell inside him and tightened his legs around Matt's waist in response.

"You smell so good," Matt groaned and rested his forehead on Ollie's bent arm.

He snapped his hips and thrust harder, pounding into Ollie like a man possessed. Ollie tucked his knees to his chest with a moan as Matt sunk even deeper. He felt so impossibly full of Matt's cock and everything he was doing with it: from the burn, to the pace, to the sounds Matt was making.

Matt reached between them and gripped Ollie's cock with his slippery hand and stroked him tightly, twisting his wrist over the tip in that way that drove Ollie mad.

"I'm so close," Ollie panted as the pleasure built in his groin.

Matt pulled back and began slamming into Ollie, the angle just right for them both. His eyes focused on Ollie with dark intensity and Ollie couldn't look away.

"Christ, I'm gonna come." Ollie cried out, thick ropes of cum shooting all over his chest and spilling over Matt's fist as he worked him through it, never slowing his pace.

"*Ti amo, il amore mio*," Matt said as he gripped Ollie's shoulder in his other hand. "*Tu sei mio*," Matt added firmly in a deep voice before pulling out and groaning his release loudly as he came all over Ollie's chest. He very deliberately seemed to be aiming to cover all of Ollie's torso, like he was marking him.

"*Je t'aime*." Ollie cried as he bent his knees and flexed his feet.

Matt lowered himself and kissed the soft dip of Ollie's neck where it met his shoulder. "You are mine," he growled low against Ollie's ear, his lips raising goosebumps on Ollie's skin.

"I am," Ollie agreed and wrapped his arms tightly around Matt's neck.

"Every bit of you. And I take care of what's mine." Matt gave him a quick kiss before reaching for the towel on the side table.

25

Every Breath You Take

OLLIE WOKE TO A NOTE on the pillow.

Gone for a run. Back by 8—M

Ollie looked at his watch and then at the ceiling, and calculated that Matt was in the gym down the hall. He showered hurriedly for work and took care dressing before heading to the kitchen on legs that were slightly sore from playing squash.

He made a batch of oatmeal and cut some fruit as Matt came down the stairs, dressed in a black Brioni suit, a crisp white shirt, and a bright blue Armani tie, with the silver trident collar bar shining under his throat.

"God, you're gorgeous," Ollie said with a deep breath while the memory of their lovemaking heated his blood. "I could never get enough of looking at you."

"You look spectacular yourself, Ollie. I love that suit on you." He swept his eyes up and down Ollie's body in that way of his before kissing him softly on the mouth. "Thanks for breakfast."

They ate in silence as Matt scanned through his phone, prepping for the day. He took Ollie's empty dish and put it in the dishwasher along with his while Ollie put the leftover fruit in the fridge.

Ollie followed Matt to work, letting a red light slow him down as usual so they didn't arrive at the same time. He didn't see Matt until the last meeting of the day where Matt said he had a dinner meeting with a client in Cambridge, and wouldn't be home until late. Ollie went back to his office and reviewed his calendar for the following week with Kerry before leaving her to lock up his office.

He worked out in the home gym and ate at the kitchen island, leaving his dishes next to the sink before showering and bringing work to bed. Matt appeared in the bedroom doorway just before eleven, dressed in black track pants and a black zip hoodie, and smiled at Ollie sitting up in bed.

"Hey, babe," Matt said as he walked past him into the bathroom and Ollie heard the shower turn on.

Matt reappeared ten minutes later; the low-light and shadows highlighted every muscle in his torso. He stopped at the side of the bed, plugged his phone in and put it on the side table. He climbed under the covers and raised his eyebrows with a small smile.

Ollie exhaled softly and put his work down. He crossed the expanse of the bed and pressed himself against Matt's naked body, breathing in his fresh clean scent with a happy sigh as Matt's lips covered his nipple.

* * *

As soon as the weather warmed, Ollie resumed his regular running route after work. He used the exercise to clear his head of contracts and mergers and employment law. He looped his way through the city and then along the Charles for several weeks, until foot traffic picked up as the weather improved. Then he just ran along the Charles as Matt would, up one side and down the other, but never going nearly as far as Matt did.

Weekends were busy with football, where Naomi would occasionally turn up to watch. Her presence on the sideline was like a ray of light in a beach chair. After the games she'd usually join him and his teammates for a drink.

"Hey, gorgeous." He kissed her one Saturday in May. "Sorry I'm a sweaty mess," he apologized with a happy smile.

"Ollie, you look gorgeous when you're all sweaty. Don't apologize." Naomi beamed. "Great game. You were amazing as always, and you look like Beckham with that hairband." She nodded at his hair pushed back off his face and hugged his waist.

He smiled humbly, pleased with the praise. "We're going to some pub in Somerville. Jezebel's, I believe it's called. Join us?"

"Of course. I love going for drinks after a big win." She grinned.

Ollie put his arm low around her hip as he walked past his teammates to his car.

Half the team showed up at the bar to celebrate their win, rowdily taking over one whole section of the restaurant next to the bar. Ollie bought the first round and was slapped on the back in thanks. He clinked his glass to Naomi's with a smile and drank a big swallow as they made small talk with his teammates.

Ollie finished his pint and gave Naomi a kiss on the cheek. "I'll be right back, love."

He fist-bumped the team goalie as they passed each other on his way into the men's room. Ollie flushed the urinal and washed his hands before splashing water on his sweaty face. He pulled his hairband off and took a picture of himself in the mirror. He sent it to Matt without comment, knowing Matt loved seeing his hair wavy and wild.

Ollie pocketed his phone with a smile and made his way back to Naomi, who was no longer with his mates but chatting with a dark-haired man who had his back to Ollie. There was a fresh beer next to her glass of wine and he picked up as he turned to face her companion.

His stomach dropped as he met the man's eyes. "Andy. What are you doing here?"

Naomi's eyes went wide. "You two know each other?"

Andy ignored her and looked at Ollie with a cold smile. "Oh, Ollie. You and your teammates are in my stomping grounds. This is my pub. I should be asking you what the fuck you're doing here."

Ollie slid his glance at Naomi. "Watch your mouth."

"Oh. Is this your girlfriend then?" Andy asked with a smirk. "Does she know about your boyfriend? Or rather, I mean your boss," Andy said pointedly, raising his eyebrows with a smug expression and took a swig of his beer.

Ollie frowned his stomach suddenly filled with lead. "What are you on about?" He felt Naomi's worried eyes.

"Your place isn't far from the restaurant. I happened to see you go into your fancy row house on my way in one day. All hot and sweaty from a run," Andy began. "I stopped to marvel. You looked glorious, and it's quite the location. Then I continued on, turning up my collar to the wind, and imagine my surprise as I saw your boss going up the front stairs and in through the same door. I wondered at first, but since your house is on my route, I noticed a lot of things over many weeks. First, you drive the Maserati mostly. Nice fucking car by the way. And he's got a fancy Range Rover; so why does your boss drive your car as if it were his own? Then I started thinking about all the things that maybe get ignored by the average person who doesn't pay attention. But to any-one who might care, all the pieces suddenly fell into place." He paused dramatically. "Your Mr. Dion wasn't an angry boss; he was a protective lover." Andy made an appreciative sound. "He was quite the silverback gorilla when I came to your office. It was actually kind of hot, until he took my phone that is," Andy added angrily.

Ollie's mouth went dry as he fought to keep the emotion off his face and silently cursed to himself at his carelessness of not going in the entrance to his flat under the stairs as he used to.

"You're imagining things. I have a condo in his building. I knew nothing about real estate in Boston and he hooked me up. We don't live together," Ollie scoffed, thinking quickly. "I presume there are other people who live in your building. Are they all your boyfriends?"

"No. Just my flatmate. like you and your boss."

"I have a girlfriend. You've just been harassing her," he added pointedly as he glanced at Naomi.

Andy pulled a face. "I was a perfect gentleman, unlike your boyfriend."

"Shut up, Andy."

"Ollie is my boyfriend, and Matt has a girlfriend. She's one of my best friends," Naomi interjected and put her arm around Ollie's waist.

Andy raised his eyebrows. "Do you know your boyfriend is gay?" He glanced at Ollie. "I know firsthand. He's *very* gay." He widened his eyes dramatically with a small laugh.

Naomi frowned. "The term is 'bi,' and of course I know. We've been dating for two years. In fact, he mentioned he dated a complete douche back in England. From the stories, I had hoped to never meet you." She looked at Ollie. "Let's go home."

Ollie put his arm around her and turned away from Andy. They said a quick goodbye to his teammates and made their way to his car. He opened the door for her and walked around the car while his mind reeled.

He pushed the start button, willing his heart to stop racing, and looked at Naomi. "Sorry about that. Thank you. You were brilliant." He gave her a small smile.

"I meant what I said. What a douche." She looked at him with soft eyes. "What was that all about? What happened between him and Matt?"

Ollie explained about Andy's visit to the office, the videos, and Matt's reaction, leaving out everything that happened back at the townhouse.

"Jesus Christ!" Naomi exclaimed with wide eyes. "What an asshole. I'm glad Matt was ruthless." She shook her head. "I'm so sorry."

Ollie twisted his mouth. "You're right. In fact, that's what my friends and I called him at uni. Andy-the-Asshole. I was young and stupid. He cheated on me left and right." Ollie swallowed and drove carefully through the streets as he made his way to Storrow Drive. "Matt was very angry. He demanded that I tell him if Andy ever spoke to me again." He slid a glance at Naomi. "Can you please not say anything. I will tell him, but I don't want him to hear it from anyone but me."

"Do you have to tell him?" Naomi put her hand on his thigh. "I swear I will never breathe a word."

"Of course I do. He has like a weird spidey-sense, or maybe I'm terrible at keeping things from him."

"Well, he can't be mad. Andy ambushed you, and I will absolutely corroborate that."

Ollie covered her hand with his. "I love you. Thank you."

"I love you too." She kissed his cheek.

He dropped her off in front of her apartment in Coolidge Corner and said goodbye with a brief hug and kiss. He pulled away from the curb after watching her go in the door and headed back into town. Telling Naomi that he had to tell Matt was one thing, the thought of *actually* telling Matt was another. He pulled over further up Beacon Street and opened his door to throw up. He took a water bottle out of the center console and rinsed his mouth before popping in a piece of gum.

Ollie closed his eyes as adrenaline and anxiety coursed through his veins and tried to catch his breath. He checked his phone and saw the heart-eye emojis Matt had sent in response to his bathroom selfie and felt another wave of nausea.

"Fucking Andy," he cursed loudly as he put his car into first gear and pulled away from the curb.

Ollie got off the elevator on the second floor, looking to get a glass of water from the kitchen and pulled up at the sight of Matt at the kitchen island with a box of pizza open in front of him.

"I thought you'd still be working." Ollie nodded in the direction of Matt's home office.

"I was hungry." Matt smiled. "Did you guys win?" He ran his eyes up and down Ollie's bare legs. "You leave any mud on the field?"

Ollie smiled and pushed his anxiety away. "Of course we won. And I hardly have any mud on me, thank you very much."

Matt folded his slice of pizza and took a big bite. "I love the mud streaks. I can picture you running, your legs are so spectacular as you chase that ball so earnestly. God, you're so good at it, so sexy. I honestly don't know which sport I prefer watching you play. Sexy bare legs, or tight white pants and leather boots on a horse," he said around the bulge in his cheek.

Ollie smiled. "I should shower."

"Yes, please. I draw the line at mud in the bed." Matt stood to put the pizza box in the fridge and paused. "Did you eat?"

"Yeah. We grabbed a bite at the pub," Ollie lied. "Naomi came. She sends her love."

"Oh great. I'm glad you had a cheering section," Matt said with a brief kiss, before walking down the hall to his office.

Ollie showered and wondered and worried whether he should tell Matt or wait until morning. He toweled off and put on his pajamas before heading down a flight of stairs to the home theater, where he turned on the TV and half-watched a movie, his mind still unable to focus. Two hours later he caught movement in his periphery and turned to see Matt standing in the doorway with his sexy grin. Ollie's stomach flipped in response, both from desire and worry.

"You coming to bed, or am I fucking you in here?" He raised his eyebrows.

Ollie turned off the TV and kissed Matt in the doorway. He ran his hands down Matt's back, before turning to the stairs with Matt in tow.

Matt groaned in Ollie's ear as he came, his hips jerking and his grip forceful. "God, Ollie."

Ollie sighed with relief and kept his knee up, mostly to block Matt from touching him because his worrying affected his ability to get hard.

Matt made a happy sound and kissed Ollie's neck. He ran his hand down Ollie's body and slowed over his thigh before attempting to roll him onto his back.

"Tonight was just about you, Lieutenant," Ollie whispered with a kiss.

Matt frowned and pulled up. "You don't want me to go down on you?"

"No, I have a bit of a headache. I think I'm dehydrated."

Matt looked down at Ollie's arm, and then nodded. "I knew you didn't enjoy that."

Matt got out of bed and went into the bathroom. Ollie got up when he came back and brushed Matt's knuckles with his own as they passed each other, mostly to test whether he'd pull away or not.

He didn't.

Ollie felt a flash of relief and cleaned himself quickly with the bidet.

Ollie turned off the bathroom light and faltered in the doorway at the darkened bedroom before making his way carefully to the bed. He climbed under the covers and laid on his back. Matt was barely breathing.

Oh *shit.*

"What's going on, Ollie?" Matt asked after a moment in a quiet voice.

"Nothing. I just have a bit of a headache, as I said."

"You're acting strange, like you're not even here."

Ollie exhaled unhappily and squeezed his eyes tight. If he didn't tell Matt immediately, Matt would be furious. If he told Matt right now, Matt will be furious.

He swallowed roughly. "I saw Andy."

He felt Matt's body tense. He was silent for several beats. "What do you mean *saw* Andy?"

"After the game in Somerville, Naomi and I went to a pub with a few teammates, as I said. I went to the bathroom and came back to find Andy speaking with her." Ollie heard Matt exhale angrily. "He knows where we live. He said he watched us for weeks," Ollie whispered.

Matt threw back the covers with a growl, got out of bed and strode to the closet.

"Matthew." Ollie leapt out of bed to follow him. "I told him about my flat, and that we don't live together. Naomi corroborated; she said I was her boyfriend. She called him a douche," Ollie added lightly. "Please come back to bed. I'll handle it. Don't worry about it."

"Oh, don't worry about it? Says the man so riddled with worry his dick won't get hard," Matt scoffed. "I'm going for a run." He dressed quickly, put on his reflective shirt and took his shoes with him as he left the room.

"Matt. Please stay," Ollie called futilely.

Matt came back well after midnight and glanced at Ollie as he passed the bed on his way to shower. Ollie waited to hear the shower turn on before getting out of bed to join him, unsure of Matt's mood but willing to do whatever he wanted just to ease the tension. Ease Matt's anger. He opened the shower door and admired Matt briefly before stepping in. Matt turned to look at him with a brooding expression before giving Ollie a small smile.

"I'll wash your back," Ollie said quietly.

"And then I'll do yours." Matt slid a glance at the bottle of lube on the shower shelf.

Ollie nearly sagged with relief as took the washcloth from Matt.

"I love you," Ollie said as he washed the lube and cum from his ass for the second time that evening.

Matt smiled at his beautiful boyfriend and turned off the water when Ollie was done. "I love you too."

Matt studied him as they toweled off in silence. Ollie was his everything, and he felt like he'd failed to protect him. He brushed his teeth next to Ollie and then followed him to bed. Matt wrapped his body around Ollie's and kissed his neck gently.

"That man will never come between us or bother us ever again. I'm gonna get him deported. He's clearly overstayed his visa."

Ollie nodded. "Good."

Matt listened to Ollie's breathing turn even and smooth, and rolled onto his back. He stared up at the ceiling and thought about the big plans he had for Andy.

26

Houseguests

OLLIE MOVED A SECTION of his closet downstairs to his condo, as well as personal effects, for appearances, in anticipation of Cassie and Genny's arrival on July second. The cousins were going to share the king-sized bed in the guestroom and Ollie was going to fake-sleep in the primary suite.

"When you come through customs, find the free shuttle bus to the Boston Logan dock, like we did when you were here with Mum and Dad," Ollie had said to Cassie over the phone. "When you get to the dock you can tell the people there you want to go to the Charlestown Navy Yard, and they'll summon a boat for you. I'll meet you there, I have to get Matt and Chuck too."

"I remember how, don't worry," Cassie replied. "Am I gonna get to meet your boyfriend this time?"

Shit.

"Uh, no. We broke up. Too much travel." Ollie lied.

"Oh, no. Sorry to hear that," Cassie crooned.

"It's alright. Well, gotta run. See you on the second." Ollie pressed end.

Thirty minutes later his phone buzzed.

"Hi, Dad."

"Oliver. What's this I hear from Cassie? Did you and Matt break up again?" his father asked in a panicked sounding voice.

"Shite. No, Dad. Sorry for the scare." Ollie shook his head with a wince. "Cassie was asking to meet my boyfriend, and I can't always keep saying he's out of town like some imaginary partner."

Ollie heard his dad exhale a sigh of relief. "Can't you just tell her it's Matt? It's been nearly four years."

"I know. But Matt is adamant, and I can't go against him. If this were all happening in London, it would have surely come out by now."

"Yes, well, I suppose for Matt's sake it's all well and good, but we do miss you. Make sure he doesn't isolate you," David cautioned.

"Oh, Dad. Stop worrying. It's all good, I'm not isolated, you've seen." Ollie looked at his watch and saw he was ten minutes late for a sales meeting. "Gotta run. Call you soon."

* * *

Ollie watched the ferry from Logan glide into the pier at the Charlestown Navy Yard and greeted Cassie and Genny with hugs and kisses.

"This city is beautiful," Genny remarked in French, her brown eyes wide as she looked around.

"I told you." Cassie laughed.

"Hey, Cass." Ollie caught her attention. "Check out Matt's new boat." He pointed at the large, sleek yacht parked in one of the slips along the pier. "He's taking us out in the harbor for the fourth. Apparently, they have a big celebration and an old ship from the Revolutionary War gets paraded about."

"Cool!" Cassie's eyes lit up. "Cor, that's quite a fucking boat." She looked at Genny. "Remember, I called dibs."

"Finn is coming." Ollie raised his eyebrows and led them to his car. "And so is her friend, my best girl here in the states, Naomi. You're going to love her, she's fantastic. She designed their beach houses and my condo."

"Well, he said they were just friends." Cassie flipped her hair from her shoulder and grinned as Ollie pulled the car into traffic. "He'll come to realize there are other fish in the sea."

Ollie's phone buzzed on the counter next to the sink as he was getting out of the shower.

What time you
coming upstairs?

Ollie smiled at the text from Matt.

ASAP, but we haven't left
for dinner yet and I just
got out of the shower

Send a pic

You'll have to use your
imagination and wait
until after dark, Lt

It's been so long I forget
what you look like naked

Ollie laughed.

U saw me naked this morning!

I might forget what you look
like naked, but I certainly
can't forget what your shrill
indignation sounds like, in
that adorable accent of yours

Ollie's mouth dropped open.

Shrill, Lt? I'm sorry, were u "
asking me for something?
BC now I'm certain that
I'm not going to send u
anything

Ollie rolled his eyes and began styling his hair. His phone buzzed again. Ollie opened the messages and saw a photo of Matt's erection.

Plz accept this as my most
sincere apology for calling u
shrill. You're HARDLY ever
 shrill. But you're always
gorgeous, and on my mind.
See above photo as proof

Ollie laughed and looked at the photo with a sigh. *Magnificent,* he thought, and made himself hard looking at it. He snapped a full body shot in the mirror, one hand behind his head, and was careful to include his legs and armpit while omitting most of his face before pressing send.

Oh my . . . plz hurry
home after dinner

Ollie took Genny and Cassie to the Beehive in the South End for dinner, which was busy for a Monday night, but they managed to get a table on the patio. They didn't stay long because jetlag hit Cassie and Genny hard after food and a couple of drinks. The girls collapsed in bed, and Ollie waited to be sure they were asleep before sneaking upstairs, though he wasn't planning on staying the night.

"Genny thinks you're a dreamboat, but of course you knew that from last summer," Ollie teased and then licked Matt's nipple. "I hope she doesn't swoon overboard when she sees how sexy you look in your swim trunks." He waggled his eyebrows.

"I think you're a dreamboat, and I hope I don't swoon overboard when you bend over the drink cooler in your swim trunks. Love this ass." Matt grinned and squeezed Ollie's bottom.

"I'm gonna sleep downstairs. Cass was weird at the Cape last year, and here I have no excuse. I think we should just let her know you live up here."

Matt pulled a face. "I don't know. That seems a little hard to explain, your boss living upstairs. Let me think about it, especially if you're trying to tell me that you don't plan on sleeping with me at all while she's here." He shook his head. "That's not happening."

Ollie felt a little thrill. "It'll be like when you're traveling, and then when we see each other again we won't be able to keep our hands off each other. Very sexy," Ollie said softly.

"I already can't keep my hands off you." He rolled on top of Ollie and kissed him. "You telling me you need more?"

"I do. I really do," Ollie sighed against Matt's mouth.

* * *

Matt finished his last set of push-ups and stood. He grabbed a towel and headed out of his home gym thinking about the coffee he was going to make for himself and wishing he was bringing a mug to a naked Brit in his bed. He was wiping the sweat from his bare chest when he caught movement in the corner of his eye. He turned his head sharply to find Cassie and Genny staring at him with wide eyes.

The were holding coffee mugs and looked to be on their way to the roof stairs.

Fuck, Matt thought as his mind raced for an excuse.

"Oh crap!" Cassie exclaimed. "I'm so sorry we weren't expecting anyone to be awake. Wait, you live here?"

"Morning, Cassandra, Genevieve." He turned and decided to say nothing as he made his way down the hall away from them. He was going to have to have a word with Ollie.

Ollie went to the kitchen after a shower and saw Cassie and Genny sitting in the front living room. He poured himself coffee and rummaged for things to make breakfast.

Cassie sauntered in. "So, you never said. Who lives upstairs?"

Ollie looked her over, suspicious at her casual tone. "Why do you ask?"

Cassie fought a smile and shrugged. "No reason. Just curious as to why you have access to the roof and all. You must know them *pretty* well."

Ollie groaned inwardly and then cringed. "Matt lives upstairs. Did you disturb him or something?"

"No. He must've been working out." Cassie got a swoony look on her face. "He was all sweaty and shirtless."

He turned with relief that she hadn't been snooping and began pulling pans out. "You want eggs? Scrambled or over easy?"

Cassie snorted. "Why didn't you just say so from the beginning? Why were you so cagey last year?"

Ollie scoffed. "Because you're a nosey pain in the arse, and I knew you'd be weird about it. I knew fuck all about Boston real estate, still don't to be honest, and he offered me a really good deal." Ollie shrugged and began cracking eggs.

"Oh, well I suppose it is convenient, but Christ, I wouldn't want to live and work with my boss," Cassie pulled a face, and then looked at the ceiling. "Yours on the other hand. I could definitely live with. Especially if I caught him coming out of the gym every morning," she chuckled salaciously. "I've never seen a body like his."

27

Gilligan's Island

The weather on the harbor for the Fourth of July was idyllic. Cassie and Genny gawked at Matt in his navy-blue swim trunks just like Ollie suspected they would, while Matt ignored them. The USS Constitution made her first turnaround in the inner harbor since going into drydock in 2015 and the crowds lined the piers and boats crowded in the harbor. Matt followed the ship from a distance to Castle Island where she did her twenty-one-gun salute, before heading back to port.

Genny and Cassie took a million pictures while Matt explained the history. When the smoke cleared, Matt pulled away from the ship and drove the Sunseeker out to Spectacle Island. He had his small American and Navy SEAL flags flying, one above the other, from their flagpole on the back of the boat, and they fluttered proudly in the breeze.

Matt dropped anchor close to the island with one eye on the depth gauge and one on his watch for the tide. He dove off the gunwale in a smooth, splash-less dive, ecstatic to be in the water and reluctant to get back on the boat. He swam to shore and then back again.

Ollie watched with a smile from the boat in the swim trunks that he wore with no intention of swimming. He put his arm around Naomi with a squeeze as they watched Matt glisten under the waves like a fish. Matt was a marvel in the water, and to Genny and Cassie's delight, he caught a fish with his hands and brought it up to show them.

"Guy said you did that in Lyon and I didn't believe him!" Genny exclaimed.

Matt smiled as Ollie wondered just how Matt had actually done that.

"You should see him swim with dolphins; they love him," Finn called to them on her way back to the boat, and then stopped suddenly as she looked at Matt. "What the fuck is that behind you?"

Ollie gasped at the sight of a large harbor seal bobbing in the waves behind Matt, who turned entirely too slowly for Ollie's liking with the fish still in his hands. His heart leapt into his throat and was about to scream as he heard Matt say, calmly as could be:

"Hey, buddy. You want this?"

Ollie watched Matt hold out the fish. The seal opened its mouth and took it gently before gulping it down and disappearing under the surf with what Ollie swore later was a wink.

Cassie gasped and fled for the boat with a loud shriek. Genny was already well ahead of her and pulling herself onto the diving platform by the time Cassie reached the boat.

Ollie looked at Naomi, who was wide-eyed. "That did not just happen," he said incredulously and looked back at Matt who disappeared under the surface just like the seal.

The swimmers took turns rinsing off in the showers below deck, talking excitedly about the encounter, while Matt was nonchalant.

"That thing was massive, and to think it was swimming all around us. It could have attacked me," Cassie exclaimed.

Matt shook his head with a chuckle. "They're very gentle, and it's definitely more scared of you than you are of it. Besides, they don't attack humans. Not usually," he added with what Ollie hoped was a teasing grin.

Cassie shook her head and scoffed. "I'm done swimming here."

Finn and Naomi sunbathed on the bow of the boat while Cassie and Genny sat in the back with Matt and Ollie, listening to Ollie's playlist of pop music coming through the speakers.

"You spend a lot of time in the water as a Navy SEAL?" Cassie asked Matt. "What is it that you would do all day? Besides apparently hand-feeding *actual* seals," she teased with a laugh.

"No. I mean, I did my fair share of assignments that required me to be in or on the water, behind the wheel of a boat, but most of it was inland. In an armored vehicle. I always drove." He gave Ollie a lopsided grin with the admission. Ollie loved nothing more than teasing him about his need to always be the one to drive.

Ollie looked at the sky and laughed as he got up. "Of course you did."

Matt watched Ollie go to the cooler and then bend at the waist as he contemplated the selection. When Cassie and Genny got up to get one as well, and all three of them had their backs to Matt, Ollie wiggled his ass. Matt choked back a laugh as he stared at the most perfect vision he'd ever seen and silently thanked the swimsuit gods for their design.

Ollie glanced back at him over his shoulder with a smirk. "You want a beer, Admiral?"

Matt raised his eyebrows behind his Ray Bans. "Yes, but one from underneath. I want it *ice* cold. Really dig for it, Ollie."

Matt saw Ollie's shoulders shake as he stifled a laugh and passed two beers to his sister before getting one from the bottom of the cooler for Matt.

"Did you see any action? Like combat?" Cassie continued her interrogation as she and Genny sat back down.

Matt took a swallow of beer and looked out at the water. Why did she have to ruin the mood with questions about his service. "Of course."

"Christ!" Cassie's eyes went wide. "Really? Like was shot at? And shot at people?"

"Cass, it's not like the movies." Ollie frowned. "It's not exciting."

"Yes, Cass." Matt met her gaze. "I was actually shot."

"You're joking!" Her mouth fell open while Genny sat up and scanned her eyes over him.

Matt shook his head and pointed at the two-inch puckered scar above his right hip. He remembered Ollie's stunned reaction to the story of how he got that scar and hoped Cassie wouldn't prod for more details.

"Bloody hell," she breathed, staring at the scar. "Did it hurt?"

Matt closed his eyes with a sigh. "Of course it fucking hurt."

He opened his eyes and looked at her as he stood.

This conversation is over.

He grabbed two more cans of beer and walked to the front of the boat to see Finn and Naomi.

Cassie looked at Genny and then Ollie. "Do you think he's killed anyone?" she asked softly.

Ollie twisted his mouth, thinking of the story Matt told him, and the likely countless others he didn't. "America has been at war for nearly two decades in Afghanistan, and run missions in places they would never admit. He was a Navy SEAL. They send them to the most horrific and dangerous places on earth. What do you think, Cass?"

Ollie stood and went inside to use the bathroom. He hoped Matt's mood wasn't ruined for the rest of the day.

"Mind if I join you?" Matt said as he appeared silently next to Finn and handed each of them a beer.

"Please do, and thanks," Finn and Naomi replied nearly in unison as they took the beers.

Matt sat and leaned against the railing and turned his face up to the sun. "Gorgeous day."

"The most perfect day. Christ this boat is phenomenal," Naomi said admiringly.

"Thanks. It's so fun to drive. Chuck and I took turns on the way here from Truro."

"So fun." Chuck nodded in agreement. "What brings you to the bow?"

Matt sighed. "Cassie is playing twenty questions back there, asking me about being a SEAL, my time in the service, and she's just a little too nosy for her own good." He shook his head with a grimace. "She was traipsing through my townhouse in the wee hours this morning with Genny. Caught me coming out of the gym."

"What? Oh shit. What the hell were they doing?"

"Headed to the roof. Ollie and I were going to tell her that I lived up there, so I guess it saves us the trouble. . . ."

Matt wished again that Cassie had never come for a visit. She was far too nosy and the thought of her finding out about him and Ollie filled him with a sense of dread. She could never keep her mouth shut and his whole life would be laid bare.

"Wouldn't it just be easier to tell her about you two? She's his sister. She wouldn't care."

Matt saw Finn frown at Naomi who then looked at Matt with a worried expression.

"She's a child without a filter." Matt shook his head firmly. "No. She can't know."

"Right, sorry. I totally get it," Naomi placated with a smile.

Matt looked out over the water, feeling out of sorts. Finn sat up and took his hand. "Why don't you take us back to the inner harbor so we can drop anchor, eat the feast I brought, and watch the fireworks."

"Okay." Matt kissed her forehead and stood, helping Finn and Naomi to their feet.

Finn always had a calming effect on him, and he was especially appreciative of it in the company of Ollie's family. He walked past Ollie and the girls, flashed a small smile and pushed the button to pull up the anchor.

"Chuck, come be my first mate," he called to her as he started the engine.

Matt stepped aside to make room for Finn and watched out the front and side windows as she piloted the boat toward the inner harbor.

"Slow it, Chuck. Is that someone flagging us down?" He pointed over her shoulder. "Let me take over." He put his hand on her hip as she stepped aside and drove toward the boat in distress, using the joystick next to the throttle to get in close. He shook his head. "Looks like they didn't pay attention to the tides and got themselves stuck."

"Why are we slowing, Admiral?" Ollie called from the back of the boat where he was sitting next to Naomi.

Matt slowed about fifty yards from the beached boat and checked the depth sensor. He dropped anchor and took his shirt off. "We've got a beached boat, Ollie. Open the deck box and get me the rope." He refrained from adding 'really dig for it,' and hid a smile at the thought.

Ollie found the rope and handed it to Matt with a serious expression on his handsome face. Matt put the coil over his neck and under his arm and dove off the back platform.

Ollie watched Matt swim away and then as he climbed the short ladder on the other boat, lifted the rope off his neck and then stopped short before boarding. Ollie frowned at the hesitation and wished they were closer so he could see what it was that caused Matt to pause. There were six people, three men and three women, on the nineteen-foot speedboat and none looked particularly dangerous.

He watched as Matt shook hands with the men, chatted briefly and then walked to steering wheel, followed by one of the men. They had a brief exchange where Matt pointed at the gauges and pushed some buttons, before he walked back to the rope and tied one end to the cleat on the back. He shallow dove into the water with the other end of the rope and swam back toward his boat.

"This would have been a great deal easier if any of those idiots had a swimsuit on and could jump in to help me dislodge the hull," he muttered irritatedly as he pulled himself onto the platform and tied the rope to the cleat on the back.

Ollie knew Matt was just grumbling and not looking for a response. His eyes followed Matt into the cabin where Matt slowly eased the throttle forward and then eased it back. Matt opened the side window and gestured for the people on the other boat to move toward the front, and then repeated the back and forth of the throttle until the other boat was tugged free of the sandbar.

Matt put the boat back into neutral and went to the back of the boat to reel the rope in. Ollie admired how Matt's muscles flexed with the effort, and then caught himself before Cassie noticed. Ollie heard him muttering under his breath in Italian and wondered if he was bitching about the fact that no one on the other boat made any effort to untie his rope from their boat.

Once the boats were side by side, the bumpers on Matt's boat hanging down to prevent scratching, Matt jumped across the gap and undid his knot.

"That brunette looks familiar. Is she a celebrity?" Cassie mused with a frown, interrupting Ollie's admiration of Matt-the-hero.

Ollie searched the faces of the other boat passengers and his stomach clenched. It was Sam, Matt's ex-girlfriend. The one he was dating when he and Matt met, and then dated again after breaking up with Ollie. The one he got pregnant, before she miscarried. Ollie winced and shook his head with a stomach full of lead.

Finn came and stood by his shoulder. "Jesus Christ. Of all people," she said under her breath.

Yeah, no shit.

Naomi came to his other side and put her arms around Ollie's waist, knowing the history between Sam and Matt. He put his arm across her shoulder and leaned in for comfort.

"Hi, Sam," Finn called across the water in a friendly voice.

Sam was wearing a white one-piece bathing suit that looked like a bikini with a strip of fabric up the middle of her torso connecting the top and bottoms, and a cat's cradle's worth of skinny straps over her back. Sam looked softer around the edges and Ollie thought she looked prettier than she had before when she was rail thin and muscular. Ollie waved hello and gave a small smile that felt fake. He could've happily gone the rest of his life never having had to lay eyes on that woman ever again.

"Hi, Oliver," Sam said, ignoring Finn. "Thanks again for pulling us free, Matt," she said with a flirty smile to Matt's back.

Matt straightened and looked at her. "No problem. Happy to help." He looked at the rest of the group. "Who's driving?"

Ollie was pleased Matt had barely given her a passing glance, but still wished he was back on their boat.

A dark-haired man with a five o'clock shadow raised his hand. "I am."

"Keep an eye on that depth gauge, and remember, red right return going into the harbor." Matt glanced at Ollie and then looked back after a pause. "Or you can just follow me back."

"I will, thanks. Nice boat, by the way," the dark-haired guy said appreciatively as Matt turned to climb on the gunwale. Ollie noticed Sam watching Matt with hot eyes and wanted to shout, 'he's mine.'

"Thanks," Matt said. He took the rope and jumped across to the back platform of his boat. He pushed the other boat away with his foot.

Matt walked past Ollie without saying anything and got behind the wheel. He pressed the throttle forward slowly until they were clear of the other boat and then opened it up. Ollie's mind was racing, but probably not nearly as much as Matt's was.

"Who was that, Ollie? I mean it, she looked familiar." Cassie appeared at his shoulder.

"That was Matt's ex-girlfriend from the photos you showed me a few years ago. That's why she looks familiar." Ollie walked to the cooler and got a beer.

"Oh right. Awkward." Cassie nodded and looked back at the boat following them. "Looks like she finally ate a sandwich."

Ollie joined Matt at the helm. Matt looked at him without turning his head and sighed.

"Fucking amateurs." He shook his head. "Not one of the guys had a bathing suit on, or any knowledge of the tides, or buoys, or fucking boating in general. Said they didn't know you could swim here."

Ollie wanted to put his arms around Matt, partly to soothe him and partly to soothe himself. "Well, you were quite heroic." He looked over his shoulder to be sure Cass wasn't in ear shot. "I can't wait to give you your commendations later."

Matt looked at him and smiled, the tension leaving his brow. "Oh, will there be a ceremony as well?"

"Of course," Ollie replied nonchalantly.

Matt made a thoughtful sound. "What's the dress code?"

"It's quite strict, actually," Ollie answered quietly, pulling a dramatic face. "But for you, it will be no problem. You have the most beautiful birthday suit, and you look magnificent in it."

Matt chuckled low in his throat and skimmed his eyes discreetly down Ollie's body before turning his attention back to the window. "I expect that dress code to extend to the Master of Ceremonies."

"It does, but he'll be fully dressed." Ollie shrugged and bit his cheek to keep a straight face. "Enforcing the dress code is actually part of the ceremony."

Matt laughed and shook his head. "Go away, Oliver, or I'm gonna throw your sister and your cousin overboard and start the ceremony early."

Ollie bit his lip and left the cabin, pleased with changing the mood for them both.

Matt dropped anchor in the harbor where they would be perfectly positioned to see the fireworks. Finn had packed two coolers of food, some of which she cooked in the kitchen below with Ollie's help. They gathered around the table in the main cabin, which was big enough to fit everyone. Finn and Naomi had changed into maxi dresses and Cassie and Genny in shorts and crop tops. Matt put on his usual après-boating attire of track pants and a white zip hoodie with no shirt underneath. Ollie had on gym shorts that came to his knees, and a grey Oxford hoodie.

"You look like a college student, Oliver. No one would ever know that you're actually a big shot GC for one of the most successful cybersecurity companies in America." Matt grinned.

"Well, I learned not too long ago, to never judge a book by its cover," Ollie countered raising his eyebrows.

Matt gave Ollie a quelling look and turned when Genny spoke.

"That boat you rescued is anchored quite close to us, like a stray following you home." She gestured with her chin.

Matt craned his head and sighed. He ran his hand distractedly through his hair. When he'd said for them to follow him back to the harbor, he hadn't meant for them to follow them to anchor.

Finn rubbed his thigh. "Let me get you another drink. Anyone else want something?"

"There's scotch in the cabinet," Matt said.

Finn went to pour him two fingers of scotch over ice and got beers for everyone else.

Matt took the glass from Finn and looked over at the boat next to them to find Sam staring back at him. She had put on a cover-up over her suit and was sitting next to a dark-haired guy with a man bun. Sam gave Matt a small smile, full of meaning. He nodded his head slightly in return and stood with his glass of scotch to head inside, suddenly uncomfortable with her scrutiny and the memories she roused.

"Thanks again, Matt, for freeing us," the man with the five o'clock called across the water, and raised his beer in toast. "It's not every day that one gets rescued by an actual Navy SEAL. I owe you one."

Matt paused and scoffed quietly behind his friendly smile. "Like I said, no problem. Enjoy the fireworks."

He disappeared inside and hoped Ollie wouldn't let the encounter get to him. It was just the kind of reminder that Matt didn't want or need, for either of them.

Ollie snuck upstairs after Genny and Cassie went to bed. He caught his reflection in the giant mirror opposite their bed and smirked before continuing to the bathroom where he found Matt undressing for the shower with a disgruntled expression on his face.

"Everything alright, Lieutenant?" Ollie asked softly. "You've been quiet since the fireworks."

Matt looked over his shoulder at Ollie and shrugged. "I'm fine. Just running over my acceptance speech in my head." He quirked his eyebrow at Ollie and closed the bathroom door between them.

Ollie looked at the door pensively. He wasn't going to push it; it was clear Matt was upset over seeing Sam. He didn't blame him; he too had been upset. At least now, after their years together and Matt's conviction about his feelings, Ollie knew he had nothing to worry about when it came to Sam. He straightened his shoulders and got into bed, fully focused on the plans he had for Matt.

"Christ, Lieutenant. I love you in that suit," Ollie said as Matt came out of the bathroom naked and freshly showered.

Matt climbed into bed next to Ollie with a broad smile. "I'm ready to receive my awards, and then enforce the dress code." He scanned his eyes over Ollie's hoodie and pajama bottoms.

"Oh good. Because there are several I am going to bestow upon you," Ollie said kissing him soundly, happy with Matt's change of mood. "And I can't wait to hear your thank yous, preferably at the top of your lungs."

28

Reckless Abandon

"WHO'S THAT FROM?" Ollie asked two days later as he came through the connecting door at work, gesturing to the bottle of McCallan scotch on Matt's desk.

"Gilligan," Matt answered, looking up briefly.

Ollie frowned as he ran through the names of people they knew. "Who?"

"*Gilligan's Island?*" Matt said questioningly. "It's a TV show from the sixties about seven people who get stranded on an island after a three-hour boat tour. My dad loved that show. You never heard of it?"

"Again, with the sixties? No, definitely not," Ollie scoffed. "But I take it this Gilligan is like Mr. Bean or something?"

"Okay, Ollie. I still don't know who that is, but if you mean inept and somewhat bumbling, then yes. It's from the guy on the harbor."

"Ah. Well, here are the policy reviews you requested and some changes we need to make to the new marketing materials. I thought maybe you'd like to see them before I send them over to Sydney in marketing."

"Thanks."

He paused at the glass door and turned back. "We're watching Mr. *Bean* tonight." He stepped into his office without waiting for a response.

Matt stared at the TV in the home theater, and then back at Ollie who was laughing so hard he couldn't breathe. Matt raised his eyebrows and shook his head. "Are you high?" he asked calmly, while resisting the urge to tackle Ollie and capture his laughs until they filled his soul.

"Jesus, Matt. This is hilarious!" Ollie wiped his eyes.

"I love you. And I love that you find this funny. But it's awful, I'm sorry."

"What do you find funny then?" Ollie scoffed.

Matt thought for a moment. "Well, if I actually had the time to watch TV, between work and fucking you, I'd have to say, *Arrested Development* or *The Office*."

"I've never seen that first one. We could put it on."

Matt shrugged. "If you want to do that, rather than this." He pulled the front of his lounge pants down to reveal his hard on and felt his dick pulse under Ollie's appreciative eyes. "You're adorable when you laugh. *Such* a turn on."

Ollie raised his eyebrows. "Christ, that thing is beautiful."

Matt met Ollie's lips with a desperate kiss and let Ollie take his shirt off. He ran his hands up Ollie's smooth back as Ollie stroked Matt's dick. With one last kiss Ollie got down on his knees between Matt's thighs and sucked just the tip into his mouth.

Matt groaned and watched him with hot eyes. "Fuck, you're gorgeous with my dick in your mouth."

Ollie hummed with pleasure and stripped off his shirt before diving back on Matt's cock. He pushed Matt's foreskin down with his hand and ran his tongue around the wide head.

Matt groaned with pleasure and after a few minutes of watching Olie work his magic he gripped Ollie's hair in his hand.

"Take off your pants. I wanna fuck you," Matt said as he reached for the lid of the small wooden box on the side table with his free hand.

Ollie pulled off Matt's cock with a sassy pop and pushed his pants down. He was just rising up off his knees when they heard a voice.

"Ollie?" Cassie called from down the hall.

Matt and Ollie froze. "What the fuck is she doing up here?!" Matt exclaimed as he immediately began pulling up his pants.

Jesus, fucking Christ, this girl, Matt thought angrily as his heart raced.

Ollie stood and pulled his pants up hurriedly while Matt zipped up and then pulled on his shirt as Ollie did the same.

Ollie sat at the opposite end of the sectional and wiped his mouth as his heart pounded nearly out of his chest. He watched Matt pull a throw pillow into his lap just as Cassie appeared in the doorway a moment later.

She looked at them both and then at the TV. "Oh, you're watching *Mr. Bean,*" she said happily.

"What are you doing up here, Cass?" Ollie scowled as his erection deflated. "This is Matt's house. You can't just let yourself in."

She frowned, chastised. "Oh, sorry. I didn't realize. You weren't downstairs."

"What do you want? I thought you guys were going to be out all evening," Ollie continued calmly though his heart was still racing.

She glanced at Matt and then back at Ollie. "We came back because I forgot something, and then I wanted to ask you for your key, because I don't know how late we'll be out."

Ollie stood and ran his fingers through his hair. "Fine, let's go. I'll get it for you." He looked at Matt who had gone white. "Thanks for at least trying to watch *Mr. Bean.* Sorry he's not your cuppa. I'll see you at work tomorrow."

Fuck, Ollie thought. Matt was shitting three tons of bricks, and Ollie wished he could stay and calm him down.

"Good night." Matt picked up the remote and changed the show without looking at them.

Ollie knew what Matt was thinking and hoped his sister wouldn't pick up on the vibe as he followed her to the lift.

"You're acting weird," Cassie remarked as they rode the elevator down.

"No, I'm not," Ollie scoffed. "I'm just irritated that you think you can swan around my boss' house. I might not even have been up there and he could've been with Chuck. He's a very private person. I don't even go up there uninvited."

"Okay. I said sorry," Cassie said defensively and paused. "Your shirt's inside out," she remarked, looking closely at him.

Ollie looked down. "Oh, I must have washed inside out and never noticed."

Cassie made a face and a suspicious sound. "If I didn't know any better, I'd think the two of you were up to something. He looked a little green around the gills." She narrowed her eyes.

"Don't be ridiculous," Ollie scoffed. "I wish," he added in a dramatic voice for effect.

"Right, you do," Cassie agreed and punched his arm.

The elevator doors opened, and they stepped through the entry into the kitchen. "Did he really hate *Mr. Bean?*"

Ollie chuckled, partly with relief that she believed his lie. "Yeah, totally. It was awkward." He looked at Genny in the doorway and handed Cassie a spare key from the hook on the wall. "Be safe tonight. Don't talk to any weirdos or leave your drinks unattended."

He walked them to the door and then returned to the kitchen to search the junk drawer for the elevator keys. Ollie then went back to the elevator and turned every floor to lock, something they'd never had to do before. He got off on the fifth floor and found Matt on the treadmill in the gym.

"Christ, that was close," Ollie remarked as he crossed the room to stand in front of Matt. "She noticed my shirt is inside out," he added with a breathless laugh.

Matt looked at him with a guarded expression. "Yeah. Too fucking close." He shook his head breathing heavy. "I thought I was going to have a heart attack."

"So, you decided to come in here and force one?" Ollie frowned. "How fast are you running?"

Matt twisted his mouth, and slowed his speed. "We can't have sex when we have company. Jesus, if she hadn't called out, or if she had come up a minute later when I had my dick in your ass."

Matt closed his eyes and ended his run, the machine slowing to a stop. He stepped down, grabbed his water and watched Ollie as he drained the bottle.

"I know. It was reckless, but we thought she was out for the evening." Ollie followed Matt out of the gym and down the hall to their bedroom. "We don't have to worry anymore. I locked all the floors in the elevator, and the door to the stairs in my condo is locked too. You'll just have to remember your keys while they're here and then I'll unlock the floors when they leave."

"Wish we'd thought of that before they came," Matt scoffed.

"I know. I should've locked them after they wandered up to the roof." Ollie sighed. "But I told her she can't come up any more anyway, so she won't try again." He closed the bedroom door behind them. "I'm not finished with you," Ollie said softly, his eyes darkening.

Matt stopped and looked at him, running his eyes slowly over Ollie's body. "You gonna suck my sweaty dick?"

"No," Ollie scoffed with a laugh. "But you can fuck me in the shower." He stripped off his shirt and dropped it on the ground before stepping out of his lounge pants and left them in a puddle in his wake.

29

Bait and Bleed

"I'VE GOT A QUICK TRIP to Manhattan this week, I should only be gone a night at most, maybe two," Matt said when Ollie came through the connecting door into his office the week after Cassie and Genny left and everything was back to normal at home.

"Oh. Who's the meeting with?"

It wasn't unusual that Matt would have last minute travel on the eastern seaboard, but Ollie was usually privy to the necessity in advance.

"That company we signed a contract with last year; they're interested in more." Matt glanced at Ollie and looked back at his computer.

"That's great news." Ollie put the contracts he reviewed on Matt's desk. "My parents come next week. I'm going to pick them up, and get changed and take them to dinner with Naomi. Then I was hoping we could go to Nantucket, take the plane and spend a couple of days with Bill."

"Sure. That sounds great. I might even be able to join you."

Ollie frowned. "Oh. When I said we, I meant we." He gestured with his finger between them.

"It all depends on how New York goes," Matt answered, not looking up.

"Okay. Well then, I hope it goes according to plan."

"Me too, Ollie." Matt smiled and looked at him before turning his attention back to his computer.

* * *

Matt drove to Manhattan on Wednesday instead of flying, declaring both New York City airports abysmal. Ollie kissed him goodbye and went to the office where he was buried under a mountain of work. He worked late into the evening to stave off the quiet before collapsing into bed that night and nearly sleeping through his alarm the next morning.

Ollie showered and dressed, then stopped at a bakery for coffee and a breakfast sandwich before losing himself in work again. He thought about Matt and wondered if he'd be back in time for dinner. They hadn't spoken since he left for the city, just a few texts back and forth, and nothing that morning. Matt often used his travel time to hyper-focus and immerse himself in work. Matt found that it stimulated his creativity (and several new product ideas had been birthed by such methods). Similarly, Ollie used Matt's travel to get caught up with his own work, which felt as ceaseless and unending as the ocean tide.

Ollie was nearly to the bottom of his current stack of contracts and policy reviews on his desk when he saw movement in Matt's office after lunch. He stood and went to the door.

"Hello, handsome," Ollie said with a smile and brushed a soft kiss over Matt's waiting mouth. "How was New York?"

"Hot as fuck and smelly. I hate that place." Matt shook his head as he sat down.

Ollie wrinkled his nose in commiseration. "How did the meeting go?"

"Successful. Didn't get a new contract yet, but I was able to accomplish what I set out to." He smiled at Ollie and turned his computer on. "I want to plow through some work here Ollie, and then take you home and plow you." He waggled his eyebrows.

Ollie laughed with a frown. "Please never refer to sex as plowing. It's disgusting."

Matt stood, took Ollie in his arms and kissed his neck and paused as he seemingly mulled something over. "Okay. I'm going to take you home, strip off your clothes piece by piece, bite my way down your perfect, sexy stomach, give you *The Italian Job*, and then hold your ankles in my hands and fuck you so hard, you lose your voice screaming in ecstasy," he whispered against Ollie's neck.

Goosebumps raised all over his body and all the blood rushed to Ollie's cock as he moaned at the image.

"Then I'll fill you with my cum and stuff that trident missile into your ass so it can't drip out."

"Okay, Lieutenant," he breathed. "See what happens when you put it that way?" He looked down at his tented trousers and then cupped the bulge in Matt's pants. "So much better. Now, hurry up and get your work done. I do so hate to be kept waiting."

30

Gone Baby Gone

OLLIE, NAOMI, AND HIS PARENTS boarded the SharkFinn Gulfstream, bound for Nantucket, the second morning after David and Maggie's arrival in the States. Ollie's parents sat on one side of the plane, while Naomi and Ollie sat on the other, facing them. The flight was so short, Ollie didn't bother with a flight attendant and got everyone waters from the galley once the plane was in the air.

"Do you have siblings?" Maggie was asking Naomi when he sat back down. "And are they in Southern California with your parents?"

"I have an older sister who works for a non-profit in L.A. and a younger brother who's doing his residency in Chicago."

"Oh, lovely. What brought you to the east coast?"

"I studied design at the University of Pennsylvania, where I met Finn. Then I followed a boyfriend to Manhattan, which was hectic and competitive for design, and miserable for romance. When he and I broke up, I came to Boston." Naomi gestured outside the window. "I loved it from the visits with Finn, and the design world here is more my speed." She looked at Ollie with a smile. "It was the best decision I ever made. In the past three months I've moved to a bigger showroom and hired three designers and a CAD specialist to share the workload. It's exciting and overwhelming at the same time."

"Wow. That's wonderful. Congratulations!" Maggie exclaimed.

"Ollie's helped me every step of the way, with the business paperwork, the personnel paperwork, and all the corporation stuff. I'd be lost without him." Naomi squeezed Ollie's hand. "Your son is the smartest person I've ever met."

Ollie brought her hand to his mouth and kissed her knuckles. "It's been my pleasure. You've done so much for me."

Maggie beamed with pride. "He was always such a precocious child, curious about everything. When he wasn't on the pitch chasing a football or on the back of a horse, he had his nose buried in a book or a far-off look on his face as he daydreamed."

"Mum. I didn't daydream," Ollie laughed.

"Oh, yes you did. All the time," Maggie insisted. "Don't you remember? You would lay in the garden for hours, alternating between reading and just staring at the sky or the flowers or the bees."

Ollie blushed, thinking he still did that. "You make me sound like *Ferdinand* the bull. Was I also swanning around in a tutu?"

Naomi laughed at Ollie. "I think it's adorable. You must have been the cutest little kid. And I loved that book."

"I'm just glad Matt's not here to hear this. I would never hear the end of it from him. He'd probably start calling me Ferdie just to torment me." Ollie picked up his bottle of water and took a swig.

"Speaking of Matt, when will he be joining us on Nantucket?" David asked.

"Hopefully after work. He's just got a big deal he's working on with Fred, our CFO. He'll meet the plane in Hyannis and leave the car so we can drive to Truro after our visit."

"Wonderful. I've barely seen him since we got here." David nodded.

"You might not see much of him on the island either. I hope you brought your trainers. There's a tennis court and Bill's dying to play."

"Oh, wonderful. Your mother and I both did. I can't wait."

Naomi pulled out a design magazine and moved to the couch mid-cabin when Ollie's phone started pinging with a few work-related texts from Matt. Ollie's parents scrolled through Nantucket sights they wanted to visit on David's phone and then looked up as the pilot began their descent.

"Oh, did you hear about that missing Englishman?" Maggie asked Ollie, changing the subject as she started putting things back in her purse.

"No. Why do you ask?"

"Well, he disappeared from Boston, for one thing, and he's your age and went to Oxford. Maybe you knew him?"

Ollie felt his stomach sink as his throat went dry.

No. It can't be.

He glanced at Naomi, who looked up from her magazine and met his gaze. "Oxford's quite large, Mum. Millions of colleges, as is Boston, you know. What is his name?"

"Andrew Taylor. It was all over the news at home as we were leaving, and we caught it on the telly here last night. He's been missing for over a week."

Ollie felt the cabin spinning. "Uh, never heard of him," he answered shakily, afraid to look at Naomi. He swallowed roughly. "What did the news say? I mean, perhaps he's just on a bender or traveling the States and doesn't have cell reception."

"He was a waiter and never showed up for his shift or something. And his roommate said he never came home. His keys and phone and personal stuff were left behind. The roommate did say they had been broken into a few months ago, but the police think that was unrelated." Maggie shrugged. "They're not ruling out the possibility of his disappearance being related to the fact that he was gay. The roommate is his boyfriend. He seemed quite upset, and said Andrew would never have left without his phone." Maggie looked at Ollie. "You alright? You've gone white."

"I'm fine. That's just frightening is all. I hope there's not some killer loose in Boston preying on gay Englishmen," Ollie chuckled nervously. He looked at Naomi who was watching him worriedly.

$$31$$

Limbo

OLLIE AVOIDED EYE CONTACT and being alone with Naomi when they landed. The dread and uncertainty in every cell of his body sent him rushing to the bathroom as the contents of his stomach demanded release. He rinsed his mouth, took a mint from his bag, and rejoined the group at the curb. Bill greeted them exuberantly and then helped put their luggage in the back of his Explorer.

Ollie stared out the window, lost in thought, with Naomi's fingers intertwined with his, as Bill pointed out sights to Maggie and David on the way back to his house. The driveway to Bill's compound was long and winding and lined with trees and a salt marsh off to the left. Maggie and David both gasped quietly when they saw the house, a massive, grey, cedar-shingled house with a wrap-around porch, a pool, and two matching guest cottages off to the right side of the main house. Beyond the house was the ocean. Bill pulled up next to the stairs in the circular drive and honked twice.

Finn came to the screen door with a big smile and Jayne and Kodi, Bill's black lab, came bounding out like black shadows to greet them with furiously wagging tails. Bill showed Ollie's parents to their suite in the main house overlooking the water while Finn showed Naomi to the room next to hers.

Ollie made his way to the guest cottage closest to the house, where he had stayed with Matt the previous summer. He put his bag on the dresser in the bedroom with the queen-sized bed and fished out his tennis clothes. He was eager to have a distraction from thinking about Andy and Matt. He left his clothes in a heap and laced his sneakers before grabbing his racquet and meeting his parents and Bill on the court.

Bill and Ollie won the tennis match with a challenge made from David for the following morning. They shook hands and went their separate ways to shower before having cocktails on the deck. Ollie closed the door to the silent cottage, made his way upstairs and stripped off his sweaty clothes as he walked. He left his underwear and socks in a puddle on the floor of the bedroom before turning on the shower.

He let the warm water course over his sweaty body and closed his eyes as he turned to rinse his hair. He mindlessly shampooed and then lathered his body as he ran over the things Matt said after each encounter with Andy. His threats and his promises all echoed loudly in Ollie's head as the soap suds traveled down his body.

He wondered about Matt's recent trip to Manhattan, and the night back in June when Matt came home dressed in all black. Ollie felt a burning in his chest knowing what Matt was capable of, and that Andy was missing filled him with dread. He was torn and confused and felt like throwing up again.

Ollie thought back to the first term of his first year at Oxford, when he met Andy. He had noticed him immediately at a meeting of the Socratic Society, even before Andy had commanded the attention of the group. Andy's eyes had landed frequently on Ollie as he spoke from across the large wooden table in one of the meeting rooms on campus. He had been so taken with Andy's dark looks, the way his longish hair curled over his collar, that one front tooth that crossed slightly over the other, and his ever-present, confident smirk. Andy had watched Ollie with an intensity that made him feel as though they were the only two people in the room.

Ollie had nearly quivered when Andy approached him after and asked him out. Andy had pursued Ollie aggressively, and was the kind of person whose goal was to claim and conquer. Ollie had been so naïve, so eager to please him, doing whatever Andy wanted, that the first time he caught wind of Andy cheating, he looked the other way. His friends had berated him for it, and they were right, of course.

Ollie cringed under the stream of hot water as he remembered how he put up with Andy's cheating for months. So embarrassed with himself he never mentioned Andy to his parents, knowing they would have hated him on sight. It wasn't until he caught Andy in the act, on the sheets Ollie had bought him, that Ollie could no longer deny the facts. Ollie broke up with him immediately, and Andy let him go without a backwards glance.

Nearly everything Andy had said during their relationship turned out to be a lie or an exaggeration. He was a classic player and Ollie was only able to see it with distance. Ollie treated that disastrous relationship as a learning experience, and was stronger because of it. Everything he had learned had guided him to Matt. Ollie knew Matt was the one from the moment he laid eyes on him, despite the fact that, at the time, he'd been certain that Matt was straight.

Ollie turned the water off and stepped out of the small shower stall still lost in thought. He dried himself off and left the towel on the counter as he moved on autopilot toward his suitcase in the bedroom. He laid his clothes on the bed and pulled on his briefs before going back into the bathroom with his styling cream and hair dryer. He pushed the towel into the corner of the counter to make room for his products and hair dryer and stared at himself in the mirror. Ollie had to continue to trust in Matt and believe that he would never risk losing Ollie or his freedom for someone like Andy.

But, Ollie thought as he slicked his styling cream through his hair and turned on his hair dryer, *if Matt had something to do with Andy's disappearance, I will never say a word.*

Ollie went to the main house, dressed in beige linen pants and a soft, white linen shirt so sheer, his nipples showed through the fabric when the breeze blew it against his skin. His sleeves were cuffed to the elbow and exposed his tanned forearms and his Rolex. He had the top two buttons undone and the tiny trident tines on his necklace glinted in the early evening sun as he followed the sounds of conversation to the porch overlooking the ocean.

Matt was standing with David, looking gorgeous in a white Tom Ford linen suit. He had a light blue shirt underneath with the top two buttons open and his matching silver necklace with the tiny moon shone against his dark skin. His short, dark hair was stylishly messy as usual and his teeth shone white against his tanned skin. Matt turned toward the stairs before Ollie even stepped onto the porch, as if he smelled him or sensed him before he appeared.

Matt smiled as his eyes swept over Ollie appreciatively and lingered on his shirt as the wind blew gently. "There he is," Matt said happily in his gravelly voice.

Ollie walked forward, helpless against Matt's gravitational pull. He shook Matt's hand and felt a nervous tingle pulse through him at the contact. He wanted Matt's kiss as reassurance, but Matt pulled away as he always did when Bill, or even Ollie's dad, was around.

"I hear you and Bill won today." Matt smiled. "Well done."

"Well, he and I have been practicing. It wasn't a fair fight," Ollie said, suppressing the image of how easily Matt had subdued Andy in his office.

Matt shrugged. "I hear there's a rematch tomorrow. I'm looking forward to watching." He shook the ice in his glass. "I need a refill, and I brought your beer."

Ollie took the glass from Matt, their fingers brushing in the exchange. "You need a refill, Dad?" Ollie looked at his father.

"No, but thank you."

Ollie stepped through the French doors and saw Naomi and Finn sitting with their heads together in the front room. The giant, round glass window overlooking the ocean was framed behind them. He crossed the expansive room to the bar and made Matt another gin and tonic and opened a bottle of beer for himself.

"Ollie, wait. Come here for a minute," Finn called as Ollie turned to go back outside.

"I should give Matt his drink," Ollie replied, a falter in his step. He knew they'd been discussing the news and wasn't sure he was up for discussing it with either of them.

"Just a for a second," Finn said more firmly.

Ollie walked over and sat on the arm of the couch next to Naomi. He gave her a small smile as he balanced the glass and his beer bottle on his thighs. He raised his eyebrows at Finn warily.

"Matt didn't have anything to do with Andy's disappearance," Finn stated quietly. "I hope you know that."

Ollie glanced at Naomi who was nodding.

"What do you know about Andy?" Ollie asked softly.

"Naomi told me. But Matt would have too. He doesn't keep anything from me," Finn answered.

Ollie stifled a scoff, thinking of the many things he knew Matt would *never* tell her.

"Andy was a blackmailer who probably tried to blackmail someone he shouldn't have. I'm sorry he's missing, but Matt didn't do it." Finn shook her head.

Ollie appreciated Finn's vehement defense of Matt, but resented her doubt of his belief in Matt.

He's my lover, not yours.

"I know," Ollie replied in a harsh tone, and then reined himself in at her wince. "Andy had so many videos on his phone. He likely made more and done just what you said." Ollie sighed and stood with a slight head nod. "Matt's waiting for his drink."

Ollie went back outside and handed Matt his drink with a smile.

"Something smells delicious, Bill." Matt clinked his glass to Ollie's beer bottle and then held it up to Bill.

Bill raised his glass in return. "Just a little Nantucket clambake for our first-timers." He nodded to David and Maggie and then waved to Finn and Naomi inside. "Let's go eat."

Ollie followed his parents to the table at the other end of the deck, ever aware of Matt just behind him. He wondered if the brush of fingers on the small of his back was imagined or real.

The caterers brought out fresh shucked oysters, cups of chowder, and plate after plate of food to the table, then cleared away the dishes as they went. Ollie had a perfect view of the sun setting over the protected harbor with the ocean beyond that Bill's house faced. It was as though the sun was lighting the water on fire and Ollie found his eye drawn to it repeatedly.

He tuned out the conversation around him and focused on the sound of the waves, a music so irresistible to him because of Matt, but dragged his eyes away when he felt Matt's gaze. Matt was watching Ollie pensively, with heat behind his eyes. Ollie returned the gaze before looking down at his mostly untouched plate of food, and forced himself to take a bite.

After dinner they played lawn games until finally David, Maggie, and Bill called it a night.

Matt looked at Finn. "We can't go to bed without playing spoons; it's our Nantucket tradition."

"We'll play in the living room." Finn jumped up to grab three spoons and a deck of cards. They taught Ollie the rules and played several rounds. Ollie drank a beer with nearly each round while ignoring Matt's side eye.

"How was your trip to France?" Naomi asked Finn with a wink.

"*Tres bien*," Finn replied with a smile and looked at Ollie. "Your cousin is something else, and I mean that in the best of ways. I just don't see a future with him living there and me living here." She glanced at Matt and then back at Ollie. "And he felt the same. I hope our fling doesn't make anything awkward, you know, going forward. It's why I avoided his advances when we first met."

"Don't worry about it," Ollie placated with an uncoordinated wave of his hand. "Guy will maybe cry at a bar somewhere for half a second, and then fall into bed with someone. No offense," he added hurriedly. "That's just how he is."

Matt laid his cards down. "We're going to bed. Goodnight, ladies." He stood and held his hand out to Ollie.

Ollie blinked, feeling the full effect of his buzz, and looked at Matt's impatient fingertips. "Goodnight, everyone." He stood on his own and made a half bow to Finn and Naomi before striding to the deck door.

Ollie felt Matt behind him but couldn't hear his footsteps on the lawn and his heart skipped a beat when Matt's shoe scuffed on the steps of the cottage porch. Matt reached over Ollie's shoulder to hold the screen door, enveloping Ollie in a heady mixture of Matt's heated skin and cologne.

Matt locked the door behind them with a loud click that made Ollie jump. Ollie cleared his throat, wishing his nerves weren't so frayed and straightened his shoulders as he crossed the open living space to the small fridge for water. He turned to see Matt staring at him with an inscrutable expression.

"Are you drunk?" Matt asked.

Ollie slid his glance away and went up the stairs. "No, not entirely."

Ollie undressed inside the bedroom, leaving his clothes on the floor with the ones from earlier and went to brush his teeth in his underwear at the sink. Matt came in similarly dressed a moment later and met Ollie's eyes in the mirror. Matt picked up Ollie's towel from the corner of the counter and hung it up with a small shake of his head as Ollie spat in the sink and wiped his mouth.

Matt held his gaze while brushing his teeth then rinsed his toothbrush. "What's up?" Matt asked with a slight frown. "You've been in and out all night."

"Nothing. Everything's fine."

Ollie focused on getting into bed, his limbs stiff and uncooperative. He plugged his phone in, chugged half the water bottle and rolled on his side, facing the windows that overlooked the pool.

Matt followed him. "Oh, is that right?" he asked with an edge as he got into bed next to Ollie. "Then take off your underwear. I wanna make you come."

Ollie closed his eyes and waited, feeling short of oxygen. His buzz had undone all his prior certainty in Matt's innocence. He stayed on his side and willed himself to breathe.

"What did you do to Andy?" he whispered.

"Nothing, yet. I'm trying to get him deported, I told you," Matt answered in a calm voice.

"He's missing, Matt. Don't play dumb," Ollie said harshly.

"I don't know what you're talking about. Look at me, Ollie," Matt commanded.

Ollie slowly rolled onto his back to find Matt on his elbow looking down at him. His face was half in the shadows and his body was rigid.

"If Andy is missing, I had nothing to do with it. Doesn't mean I don't wish that I did. That man threatened you, and then us, more than once. If he got his comeuppance, I don't feel one ounce of sorrow for him." Matt thinned his lips and held Ollie's gaze. "He filmed you without your consent, attempted to blackmail you, and then stalked us at our home. I refuse to feel bad about whatever happened to him, and you shouldn't either." He ran his fingertip from Ollie's shoulder to his wrist. "Kiss me."

Ollie quivered under Matt's caress. Every fiber of his being wanted to believe, like Finn, that Matt was not responsible. He rolled on his side and turned his face up for a kiss.

Matt made a low sound like a hum, and ran his hand down Ollie's side, slowing over his thigh and bringing Ollie's knee up to rest on his hip. He kissed Ollie unhurriedly, his tongue sliding alongside Ollie's in a slow dance. Matt ran his fingers up the back of Ollie's thigh and into Ollie's underwear. Ollie closed his eyes on a sigh as Matt's fingertip slid into his crease and circled around his hole.

"I love you," Matt murmured against Ollie's lips.

"I love you too. I hope that if you marry me someday, it isn't to keep me from talking about this in a courtroom." Ollie sighed and then stilled when Matt stopped stroking with his finger.

Matt pulled his head back and searched Ollie's face with his smoky eyes before flashing his sexy grin and pressing his tongue back into Ollie's mouth. His finger pressed just as gently into Ollie, and Ollie couldn't help but moan. He couldn't ever help his body's response to Matt.

"You're gonna spread for me." Matt sucked on Ollie's bottom lip and growled low in his throat as Ollie complied without hesitation. "And I'm gonna fuck you so hard, fill you so deep, I never have to hear that asshole's name out of your mouth. Ever. Again."

Ollie's cock twitched excitedly in his underwear. Matt ran his thumb over the wet spot with a pleased sound before easing Ollie's briefs off. Just as Ollie began wondering how hard Matt meant, Matt rolled him onto his stomach and smacked Ollie's ass sharply.

"Who does this belong to?" Matt slid down Ollie's body. Ollie felt Matt's breath ghosting over his tingling ass cheek.

"You," Ollie's voice trembled with need.

"Who's the only one who knows exactly what your body needs without being told?" Matt spread Ollie's cheeks and nuzzled with a deep breath.

"You," Ollie moaned and shifted his hips on the bed, seeking friction and Matt's warm tongue.

Matt chuckled on his exhale. "Well, seems as though my questions were merely a formality."

Ollie craned his head over his shoulder. "What do you mean?" he asked breathlessly.

"Mint and cloves." Matt nipped Ollie's ass with his teeth. "You were expecting my tongue in your ass despite being worried that I might be a murderer."

Ollie felt his cheeks redden. "No. It's habit. Your tongue is always in my ass."

"No, it's because you're fine knowing that I would absolutely be fifty shades of morally grey in order to keep you safe. I protect what's mine." Matt smacked Ollie's ass again, the sharp sound echoing in the small room, and then buried his face in Ollie's crease.

Ollie closed his eyes and sank into the bed, feeling himself come apart with every shared moan, every whispered word, and every thrust of Matt's tongue and fingers. He spread his legs wider and lifted up, the buzz of alcohol and lust in his body guiding his movements.

"That's it. Fuck yourself on my fingers," Matt growled. "Beg for my cock." Matt licked a stripe around Ollie's hole and added a third finger, stretching Ollie open as he ground his erection on Ollie's bent lower leg.

Ollie moaned and swiveled his hips, gasping every time Matt's fingers grazed his prostate. "Please. Give me that magnificent thing, you fucking tease." Ollie reached back and slid his fingers into Matt's hair, gripping insistently.

"Someone needs to teach you some patience." Matt bit Ollie's ass and sucked a bruising spot on the white flesh. "But tonight, that someone isn't me. In fact. . . ." Matt withdrew his fingers and his body, leaving wet spot on the back of Ollie's calf, "I don't even have time for lube."

Ollie felt the tip of Matt's cock like a whisper to a scream as he thrust inside without hesitation which stole Ollie's breath. Matt paused with a groan. His lips brushed Ollie's ear, and then he began moving, circling his hips every three thrusts.

"You feel incredible," Matt panted in Ollie's ear. "I love the way you take my cock, the way you never tell me no."

Ollie moaned and bit his lip as Matt pounded into him. Dirty Matt was his favorite Matt, and Ollie never thought he'd like, no, *love* that kind of thing.

"I could never tell you no. My ass is yours," Ollie forced out on an exhale. "Fuck me harder, Lieutenant," Ollie cried out. The burn of Matt's cock stretching his ass turned into pleasure as Matt rolled his hips and hit that sweet spot inside, over, and over.

Matt bit Ollie's shoulder with moan. The Italian he was muttering began to sound like one long word. He pressed his hand onto Ollie's lower back as he slammed into Ollie with focused intent.

"*Il tuo culo è mio*," Matt grunted and pulled Ollie to his knees.

Ollie felt Matt's fingers dig into his ass cheeks. He thought of all the finger-sized bruises that would be left behind and moaned.

"I'm so close," Matt panted, shifting his weight to rest on his haunches and pulling Ollie with him. "Come for me, Ollie. Come with me."

Matt spit in his palm and took Ollie's cock in his hand. He guided Ollie's pace with a strong grip on his hip. Ollie turned his face to Matt's for a sloppy kiss then rested his head on Matt's muscled shoulder and buried his fingers in Matt's wavy hair.

"Oh, god," Ollie cried. "Just like that. Don't stop." He looked down at Matt's hand stroking his cock in sync with his thrusts and felt himself come apart, bit by glorious bit. Matt's moans and grunts and shallow breaths tipping him over the edge.

"Oh yeah, Ollie. God you're so beautiful when you come for me. I'm gonna fill your ass. You ready?" Matt let go of Ollie's cock and wrapped his arm around Ollie's waist as his hips jerked involuntarily. "Fuuuuck. Christ."

The rest of Matt's expletives were in Italian and matched the fervor of Ollie's French.

Matt wrapped his body around Ollie's when he came back to bed and kissed his neck as he tucked Ollie against him. "You don't actually think we're gonna get married, do you?"

Ollie thinned his lips as his blissful post-orgasm mood was ruined by Matt's scoffed out question. "No, Matt. I didn't mean it like that. I don't expect it."

"Okay good, because that's never going to happen. We can't. But I love you more than anything, and I want to spend the rest of my life with you. You know that." Matt nuzzled Ollie's neck and tightened his arms.

"I know. I love you too." Ollie closed his eyes with disappointment.

Maybe someday he'll change his mind, Ollie thought wistfully before drifting off.

Ollie woke early, seeing just the fingertips of the sun in the distance through the window. He winced at the flash of pain behind his eyes when he turned his head to look at the note on Matt's pillow. With a groan he rolled onto his back and rubbed his temples, then smiled when he saw a big glass of water and two painkillers on his nightstand.

He swallowed the pills and laid back to stare up at the ceiling. Andy's disappearance worried him again in the cold light of day. It was absolutely something Matt was not only capable of, but something he threatened to do. If Matt had gone after Andy, that asshole would never have stood a chance.

Matt would never take such a risk though. Ollie assured himself before falling back to sleep.

Ollie woke again two hours later to the smell of coffee and stretched languorously.

"Morning, sleeping beauty." Matt grinned. "How's your head?"

Ollie reached for the coffee and sat up on his elbow to take a sip. He ran his eyes over naked Matt. His hair was still damp, though his face was unshaven, and Ollie suppressed a shiver at the thought that scruff rubbing over his sensitive skin. He gave Matt's semi the side-eye before responding.

"Fine. Thank you for the Excedrin. Really does the trick."

"You know what else does the trick, Mr. Sexy?" Matt closed his laptop and put it on the side table.

Ollie put his coffee down with a smile. "No. But I bet involves ten inches of Italian sausage."

Matt made a pleased sound and rolled on top of Ollie with a laugh. "You and I both know it's more than ten inches."

32

Hallelujah

OLLIE'S PARENTS' VISIT was over in the blink of an eye, and he and Matt were back in the Seaport for a full day of staff meetings. Ollie's head was spinning by midafternoon, and he went back to the executive suite for a brief break.

"Matt back?" Ollie paused in front of Stacey's desk. There was a question burning in his mind and he didn't want Matt around to hear it.

"No. He's still in the conference room."

"Okay, thanks." He paused and turned back as though he just had a thought. "Where did Matt stay in New York?"

"The Four Seasons." Stacey reached for a folder on her desk and pulled out a paper-clipped batch of papers. She flipped through until she came to a hotel bill. "Did you need the receipt?"

"No, thank you. I wasn't sure if he'd found himself a new hotel to try. There are so many in the city." He shrugged nonchalantly.

"He always stays at the Four Seasons wherever he travels because of the lap pool," Stacey added.

"Right." Ollie nodded. He knew that Matt preferred the Four Seasons for just that reason, and then smiled to himself with relief.

* * *

Ollie was sitting on the roof in the late afternoon sun two weeks later surrounded by paperwork and lamenting to himself that summer was officially over. Matt was still at work, but Ollie had wanted to enjoy the outdoors while the weather still permitted. He had a contract in his lap when his phone buzzed with Naomi's name.

"Hello, gorgeous."

"Hi. Are you sitting down?" Naomi asked somewhat breathlessly.

"Yes. I'm on the roof; it's beautiful. You should be here, and my view would be complete." He smiled.

"They arrested somebody in connection with Andy's disappearance," she blurted.

Ollie sat up, the papers slipping off his lap. "What?! Who?"

"The news didn't say much because the police are being closed lipped, but it sounds like a guy Andy was having an affair with who happened to be married. *To a woman.*"

"Bloody hell," Ollie breathed. The relief washed over him like a wave. "I'm going to look it up. Thank you so much for calling."

"I know it's a big relief," Naomi said. "I never thought he did it," she added quietly. "You know that, right?"

"Of course. And it would be okay if you had a bit of doubt. I did when I first heard. He's military. Trained to protect," Ollie soothed.

"Right," she agreed. "I'm gonna call Finn now. Have a great night. I love you."

"I love you too. Thank you so much for calling. You really made my day; my year."

Ollie ended the call, and after a brief hallelujah, gathered everything up and left the roof deck on a mission.

"Jesus, Ollie. Something smells phenomenal," Matt said as he walked into the kitchen and put down his folio and phone on the kitchen island. "What's for dinner?"

Ollie turned from the stove and went to the fridge. He pulled out the cocktail shaker that contained gin and a splash of Lillet and added ice. Then pulled out the chilled martini glass that had two jalapeño-stuffed olives on a metal cocktail skewer. He shook vigorously and poured, handing it to Matt with a smile.

Matt looked at him with a bemused expression. "What's going on, Oliver? You pregnant?" he asked with a grin.

Ollie snorted and clinked his whisky glass to Matt's. "Dinner is fresh pasta from that place in the North End you love, tossed with a creamy roasted butternut squash sauce, baked fennel with parmesan, and Chilean sea bass with a basil chimichurri. There's also a kale salad to start and oysters I need you to shuck," Ollie beamed. "Oh, and this." He pushed a platter with wonton chips surrounding a perfect circle of minced and seasoned tuna tartare atop mashed avocado flecked with cilantro.

"Okay, Ollie. Do I only have a day to live?" Matt shook his head and scooped a chip through the thick layers. "What's going on for real?" He made a sound of pleasure as he chewed.

"They arrested someone in connection with Andy," Ollie said quietly.

Matt raised his eyebrows and finished chewing. "Did they? That's great news. But why are we celebrating? You said you believed me. Was that a lie?" he asked calmly.

Ollie frowned, wary of Matt's tone and gaze. "No, of course not. I'm just glad they found the person who did it. It's peace of mind. I'm glad there's not some maniac out there who has it in for gay British men."

"You'd have nothing to worry about if there were, because I won't ever let anything happen to you."

"Okay, when you say things like that, you can't question me, or be angry at me for momentarily doubting you, Lieutenant. Or feeling relief at being proven right," Ollie said softly, putting his arms around Matt's neck. "I know what you're capable of, and I trust you implicitly. I love you," he whispered against Matt's throat. His stubble was enticingly prickly against his lips.

Matt put his glass down and palmed Ollie's bottom, pulling him in tight as he squeezed. "I love you. And I know it's cause for celebration.

I really don't fault you for doubting me and being relieved. Because I absolutely would have killed him, without a second thought. I did it in my mind a hundred different ways," Matt said in a clear voice. "That I didn't, was only for your sake."

After dinner, Matt cleared the dishes and cleaned the kitchen while Ollie sat at the island with his wine. He watched Matt's body move fluidly around the kitchen with cuffed sleeves and wet arms.

"You got a little drool on your chin again," Matt said without looking at him.

"I told you. I don't drool. But you are magnificent to watch. I can't wait to continue the celebration upstairs. So, hurry up."

Matt closed the dishwasher and washed his hands then dried them on the kitchen towel. "Why does it have to be upstairs? I could bend you over the desk in my office or yours. Fuck you on the couch, maybe in the elevator." Matt raised his eyebrows.

"Oh, how very nineties-hair-band of you." Ollie chuckled.

Matt spun Ollie's barstool around to face him and placed his hands on the island on either side of him. Ollie slid arms around Matt's waist as they kissed. He untucked Matt's shirt and ran his hands over Matt's smooth warm skin, feeling the goosebumps rising under his fingertips.

Matt sighed at the contact. "Or, we could do it here on the floor, you on top," he murmured against Ollie's lips. "Or you bent over the counter, my tongue in your ass, then your dick down my throat."

Ollie watched Matt adjust his rapidly swelling cock. "Or maybe you just get on your knees now. All this talk is making little Matt very eager to come out and celebrate."

Ollie chuckled and unbuttoned Matt's shirt, all while placing open-mouthed kisses along Matt's jaw and neck. He licked both nipples before lowering to his knees. Matt exhaled a sigh as Ollie deftly undid his belt and then pants and kissed the outline of Matt's erection through his boxer briefs.

"Such a tease," Matt growled and ran his fingers through Ollie's hair. "Take it out."

Ollie smiled and held Matt's dark gaze as he peeled Matt's boxers down. He nuzzled his face into Matt's trim bush and breathed deeply, savoring Matt's musky scent. He licked and sucked up and down the thick vein that pulsed along Matt's hard length as Matt moaned and tightened his grip in Ollie's hair. Ollie grasped the base of Matt's cock and guided the tip into his mouth. He closed his eyes and savored the heavenly flavor of Matt's cock and pre-cum.

Once his cock became slippery with saliva Matt began thrusting his hips, forcing his cock deeper into Ollie's throat.

"Ahhh, Christ. That feels so good," Matt whispered huskily and ran one hand from Ollie's hair over his ear and along his jaw. He caressed Ollie's bottom lip with his fingertip as he continued to roll his hips unhurriedly.

Ollie tugged gently on Matt's balls and rolled them between his fingers and tasted another burst of pre-cum on his tongue. His eyes watered and saliva dripped from his chin, but he wouldn't stop until he had a throatful of cum or unless Matt told him to. After a moment Matt did just that, by pulling Ollie off his cock and tilting his head back to meet his gaze. Matt's eyes were dark with lust and the intense look on his face drove a hot bolt of desire straight to Ollie's cock.

Ollie wiped his chin as he caught his breath. "What next, Lieutenant?"

Matt helped him to his feet and kissed him with a whole lot of tongue. He produced a small bottle of lube from the counter behind him and Ollie grinned.

"You sure do know how to multitask. Where and when the fuck did you find that?"

"The back of the junk drawer, while I was distracting you with my cock down your throat." Matt smirked and dug his fingers into the waistband of Ollie's grey sweatpants and eased them down.

Matt stepped back and admired Ollie's hard cock straining against his black mesh underwear. "Fuck, these are sexy. They new?"

Ollie nodded. "Got them a few weeks ago. Was saving them for a special occasion." He turned. "They lace up the back."

Matt exhaled a soft moan as he ran his eyes over the red silk stitching up Ollie's ass crack and the tiny bow on the elastic of the waistband. "Oh, I'm gonna undo that with my teeth."

Matt knelt and Ollie felt his warm breath on the small of his back. Matt kissed first one divot and then the other on either side of Ollie's spine just above his underwear. He nipped Ollie's ass cheek through the sheer material and ran his tongue up the woven laces. Ollie shivered with pleasure and watched over his shoulder as Matt undid the red bow with his front teeth.

Matt ran his hands up the outer sides of Ollie's legs and then took a cheek in each palm and gripped tightly. Using his fingers he peeled open the underwear without pulling the laces from their holes.

"Man, your ass is so fucking hot in these. I think I'm just gonna make a hole in here," Matt loosened the red ribbon over Ollie's asshole with his thumbs, "and fuck you with them on. I wanna see which is softer, your tight ass or this silk ribbon."

Ollie stroked his aching cock and moaned as Matt replaced his thumbs with his tongue. Matt smacked Ollie's ass cheek and ordered him to stick his ass out so Ollie quickly shuffled his feet and arched his back. Ollie dropped his head forward and gripped the counter as Matt's tongue licked and probed in earnest. It wasn't long before Matt added a finger and then another as he continued to make Ollie dizzy with need.

Ollie heard the snap of a lid and looked back over his hip to see that Matt had somehow shed his pants and was sitting back on his haunches, admiring the view as he stroked himself. His shirt was open and his cock was rock hard and dark red.

"You gonna do something with that?" Ollie asked, his voice husky from panting and moaning.

Matt rose to his feet in one fluid motion. He dribbled some lube on his fingers and pressed them back inside Ollie. "Yes, Oliver. I'm gonna destroy that pretty little hole of yours, and probably the underwear too."

Matt lined his cock up, adjusted the opening in the laces again to accommodate his cock and slid inside Ollie with one slow thrust. He reached under Ollie's arm and gripped his chest, pulling himself flush with Ollie's back as he rocked his hips. He waited for Ollie's nod and then began moving as he kissed Ollie's neck.

"You feel incredible. You're definitely silkier than that ribbon, but fuck, does it ever turn me on." Matt slid his hand lower and groped Ollie's cock through the material. "Shit, you're soaked," Matt breathed. "So wet for me, you probably don't even need any lube."

Ollie let out a long moan that ended on a whine when Matt slipped his hand inside Ollie's underwear and stroked him. "I'm so close, Matt," Ollie said and then swore in French when Matt pulled his hand away with a teasing sound.

Matt gripped Ollie's hips and drove into him over and over before sliding one hand down Ollie's thigh and lifting his knee onto the bar-stool next to them. Ollie gasped and then moaned at the new angle. He was definitely close to having one of his rare, hands-free orgasms but craved friction on his cock. He palmed himself over the mesh and immediately cried out.

"Just like that. Oh, god."

Matt leaned forward with a loud groan and clamped down with his teeth on Ollie's shoulder as he came. It wasn't a painful bite, but it was one that would leave a mark because of the suction. Ollie felt Matt fill his ass as he filled the front of his underwear. Ollie's cum was seeping through the material and pooling in his hand and he scanned the island for a towel as he caught his breath.

Matt skimmed his hands up Ollie's sides and then wrapped around his front tightly. "God, I love fucking you. So perfect," he panted in Ollie's ear.

"That was incredible. I'm gonna be feeling that for days." Ollie smiled and turned his head to kiss Matt.

"I love you, Ollie."

"I love you, Lieutenant."

EPILOGUE

STACEY BUZZED MATT'S DESK PHONE the following day. "Mr. Hawthorn is here to see you, sir."

Matt frowned briefly, knowing there was nothing on his or Ollie's calendar, and the next board meeting wasn't for another six weeks.

"Send him in."

Matt stood, buttoned his suit coat, and walked around his desk as Bill came striding through the door in his commanding way.

He shook Matt's hand and hugged him tightly.

"Bill. An unexpected pleasure." Matt smiled.

"Good to see you, son." Bill returned the smile. "I won't keep you, but I didn't want to call." He paused. "I saw the news."

Matt's mind raced as he tried to catch Bill's meaning, before realization washed over him. He nodded stiffly. "Right."

"You know, I kept my mouth shut when I first heard the name and the news about his disappearance this summer. I would have always kept my mouth shut." Bill held his gaze. "I'm glad they caught the guy, and that it wasn't you. But, if it had been, I would have protected you. That waiter. . . ." Bill paused and shook his head. "He wouldn't take no for an answer, and wouldn't leave Ollie alone. I wanted to punch him for making Ollie squirm." He looked out the window behind Matt.

Matt nodded with a smile. "I agree, sir. One hundred percent. Though I wanted to do quite a bit more than just punch him. It gives me great peace of mind to know you are by my side."

"Solidly, Matthew." Bill smiled and hugged him again. "Ollie's a gem, and I love him as much as I love you. I have really enjoyed getting to know him, and his family. You're a lucky man. Now, I will let you get back to work. That's all I wanted to say. Tell Ollie I'll see him at the barn, and I want to see you boys for dinner soon."

"I will, sir. Thank you." Matt smiled and watched Bill leave. He exhaled, sat in his chair and stared at the seagulls swooping over the harbor.

Ollie found Matt like that a short while later. "You meditating, Lieutenant?"

Matt smiled and took his feet off his desk. "Sort of. Bill was here. He said he'll see you at the barn."

"Bill? Did you have meeting scheduled?"

"No. He came to see me about Andy." Matt widened his eyes dramatically. "On the one hand I'm glad everyone thinks I'm this ruthless killer, because I don't want anyone to fuck with me or you. But on the other hand, I don't want my loved ones to think that of me."

"Matthew," Ollie soothed, "we don't, and those who don't know you, do. So, you have the best of both worlds, so to speak."

Matt looked out the window again. "Well, I killed for my country, I most certainly would kill for the man I love." Matt shrugged and held Ollie's gaze. "I guess I really can't blame them."

Ollie exhaled, not knowing how to respond. It was unnerving that the man he loved (with all his being) had ever killed anyone. He looked at the floor and then back at Matt.

"Right." Ollie nodded. "Well, I hate to be the bearer of bad news, but Bryan needs to see you immediately, not for murder," Ollie added quickly with a small grin. "But one of the sales team made some promises we can't keep."

Matt stood and took a deep breath. "Maybe murder," he teased, one side of his mouth lifting before kissing Ollie and leaving with a chuckle.

ACKNOWLEDGMENTS

THANK YOU to Duney Roberts, my former work husband (until he left for a better job) turned walk/run/cocktail bestie. He went through this book with "The Elements of Style" in one hand, and a fine-tooth comb in the other. This book is so much better because of it! His comedic commentary in the margins was an added bonus.

Thank you again to Sigrid Silberman for another brilliant and beautiful book cover! Her ability to take a description and make it a reality, combined with her meticulous attention to detail is astonishing and I'm so lucky to know and love her.

Thank you again to Julie Gallagher, who makes my manuscript into a book, and the image that Sigrid designs into a book cover. She is a fountain of knowledge and expertise and I thank the gods for putting her in my life.

Thank you to my faithful reader John Stella, who knows Matt and Ollie almost as well as I do. His critiques and early support were essential in the character development and series evolution. As were our lunches and cocktails at the Colonial Inn 😊.

Thank you to Kevin Groppe, someone I've known since high school, who told me the book was "loooong" (he was right). His support and willingness to emcee my events when needed has been invaluable.

Thank you to my ARC readers Bernice, James, and Doll, influential Book Tok peeps on TikTok who have amplified my books and brought beaming smiles to my face. Thanks to everyone who has left a review for my books, good or bad. Art is subjective and there's no wrong opinion!

Thank you to my besties Hally Mix, Kristin Brothers, Edie Perkins, Sara Morrison, and Kim Bertrand, for their steadfast support of me and my writing. Showing up at my events, listening to me talk about my characters, sending me marketing opportunities and ideas, and spreading the word about my books—you're amazing human beings and I'm so grateful for you.

Thanks also to Kim for the beautiful picture of the Boston skyline, a picture she took from the ferry she used to commute to work on when she lived in Charlestown.

Thank you to Erin McEwan, intern extraordinaire. She created my website, turned Sigrid's fountain into a rainbow, and sourced and photoshopped the polo player on the cover. If you look closely, you can see the tiny shark fin on his shirt. Because of course Ollie's polo team is sponsored by Sharkfinn.

And finally, thank you to my husband, the saint. He has been the most patient and supportive human being on the planet. He deserves a medal or something.